"Problem?"

Ellis's eyebrows knit [...]
after we left the compound. It's suspicious."

"Do you think they're from the compound?"
Dakota inquired.

"Could be."

"Why would they tail us?"

"Deakins might not have been as forthcoming with those documents as he'd like to appear."

"Are they planning to chase us and retrieve them? Seems foolhardy."

Just then, the sedan closed in, tailgating aggressively.

Ellis kept his cool, noting, "They're really testing my patience."

"Can you see the driver?"

"All I see is sunglasses and a hoodie."

"Tap the brakes," Dakota said.

"And brace for impact? No, thanks."

Before they could decide on a course of action, the sedan suddenly rammed into the bumper of their car, the impact causing the back end to get squirrelly. Ellis fought to gain control of the vehicle.

The car skidded onto the shoulder, narrowly missing a thick oak tree. Their aggressor sped past, leaving them in the dust.

Dakota coughed, waving away the dust cloud.
"You okay?"

Dear Reader,

Cold case stories are my secret love. There's something about stories that involve solving painful or violent mysteries that will always engage my muse.

While my story is fictional, there are far too many real-life stories without resolution—and crimes against Indigenous women have been happening without consequence for too long.

The time is now to end the cycle of violence.

As always, "see something, say something" and you might just save a life.

Hearing from readers is a special joy. Please feel free to find me on social media or email me at authorkvanmeter@gmail.com.

Kimberly Van Meter

COLD CASE KIDNAPPING

KIMBERLY VAN METER

ROMANTIC SUSPENSE

Harlequin®
ROMANTIC SUSPENSE™

Recycling programs
for this product may
not exist in your area.

ISBN-13: 978-1-335-50258-2

Cold Case Kidnapping

Copyright © 2024 by Kimberly Sheetz

 Harlequin Enterprises ULC
22 Adelaide St. West, 41st Floor
Toronto, Ontario M5H 4E3, Canada
www.Harlequin.com

Printed in Lithuania

MIX
Paper | Supporting
responsible forestry
FSC® C021394

Kimberly Van Meter wrote her first book at sixteen and finally achieved publication in December 2006. She has written for the Harlequin Superromance, Blaze and Romantic Suspense lines. She and her husband of thirty years have three children, two cats, and always a houseful of friends, family and fun.

Books by Kimberly Van Meter

Harlequin Romantic Suspense

Big Sky Justice

Danger in Big Sky Country
Her K-9 Protector
Cold Case Secrets
Cold Case Kidnapping

The Coltons of Owl Creek

Colton's Secret Stalker

The Coltons of Kansas

Colton's Amnesia Target

Military Precision Heroes

Soldier for Hire
Soldier Protector

Visit the Author Profile page
at Harlequin.com for more titles.

Chapter 1

The hallway at the Bureau of Indian Affairs office was filled with the faint hum of fluorescent lights overhead as agent Dakota Foster mentally steeled herself for the meeting she'd been dreading since her superior, Isaac Berrigan, dropped the file on her desk last week for review.

Unlike her first case, which involved a drunken cheater who got whacked by his wife one night when she'd had enough of his bullshit, this case had a real chance to make a difference—and she was hungry for a personal victory.

She didn't even mind that it was a co-op with the FBI, until she read who the FBI agent assigned to the case was and her heart sank like it was tied to a bucket of cement and tossed into Flathead Lake.

Of all the FBI agents who could've been assigned, why Ellis Vaughn? The last time she saw that train wreck was two years ago and the memory still had the power to make her wince.

Sometimes, late at night, when her brain refused to shut down, her thoughts wandered into forbidden territory— opening that tightly sealed locked box where she'd stuffed memories of Ellis—and it still hurt when she thought about what could've been.

But doing so felt like weakness and she couldn't abide such a slip in her self-control.

Her drive had pushed her to become the first in her family to graduate from college—a hard-won accomplishment for an Indigenous woman who grew up on a Montana reservation—which then propelled her into the world of law enforcement, before transitioning to the BIA. There, she quickly gained a reputation for her unwavering commitment to chasing justice for the Indigenous people even when it meant going head-to-head against bureaucratic red tape and relentless opposition. She was ambitious and efficient, and she prided herself on being organized and no-nonsense.

Which left little room for self-indulgent pity parties.

Besides, Ellis was her polar opposite and a relationship with someone she had little in common with was an exercise in futility. Something she should've known better years ago.

It wasn't that Ellis was lazy or lacked ambition, but he operated in a state of chaos that made her head spin and Ellis never found a rule he didn't mind bending or breaking.

But some rules had serious consequences for breaking— a tough lesson he learned the hard way.

Whatever, the past is the past, she told herself, drawing a deep breath before pushing the door open to the debrief room. She was early but her colleague Shilah Parker was already there. She looked up as Dakota entered. "I just finished going over the file… The original vic, Nayeli Swiftwater, was from the Flathead Reservation. That's your neck of the woods, right?" she recalled.

Dakota nodded and slid into the seat beside her. She and Shilah had worked the drunk case—and in doing so, had become tight friends. She recalled the Swiftwater case with a subtle wince. "Yeah, I remember when that hit the news. I was sixteen at the time, but it'd only been three years since my older sister, Mikaya, was killed so I was following the case as much as a kid could."

"Ouch, that had to have been rough," Shilah commiserated. "That would've hit too close to home for me."

Dakota remembered being hyperfocused on Nayeli's case for that very reason. "Each time the case came up in the news, it was like swallowing razor blades, but I couldn't stop watching or reading anything that popped up. I think I was clinging to the hope that if Nayeli's case got solved, maybe that would mean there was hope for Mikaya's case. Naive of me, I know, but I couldn't help myself. I needed something to make the pain manageable."

"The pain of hope," Shilah murmured, understanding, returning to the case. "Well, it's been a long time coming but I'm happy to see a cold case like this getting some attention. Maybe with some luck, eventually there will be answers for Mikaya's case, too."

Dakota had long since abandoned hope for answers in her sister's case but the resurgence of Nayeli's case renewed her sense of purpose—the reason why her job was so important—even if the memory dredged up the inevitable pain of losing her sister.

"Maybe," Dakota agreed, blinking away the tears that were never far whenever Mikaya's name was brought up. She gestured to the case files. "This case was so brutal. Nayeli was nineteen and a single mother when she was killed, but her baby was never found. Cases like these never fail to punch you in the gut. I'd always held out hope that the baby would turn up."

"If you don't find an infant within the first forty-eight hours…" Shilah trailed, shaking her head.

It was a heartbreaking statistic that they wished wasn't true but even if the kidnapped child wasn't harmed, their faces changed so much in the first year, even with age pro-gression software, they were difficult to recognize without an identifying mark or feature.

Unless a twist of fate intervened and seventeen years later that infant reappeared out of nowhere, creating an all-hands-on-deck frenzy to reopen the case.

Isaac Berrigan, the task force leader, walked into the room, along with Sayeh Griffin and Levi Wyatt, and not more than two minutes later, Ellis Vaughn, catching the door with a flash of that charming grin that made most women weak in the knees, followed.

"Looks like I just made it," he said, shaking hands with Isaac and Levi, nodding to Sayeh, before swiveling his gaze to Dakota.

The moment their eyes locked, the tension between them was immediate and palpable—and hard to smother.

When Isaac had broached the subject of putting her on the case with the FBI agent, she hadn't disclosed that she and Ellis had history and she wasn't about to do that now, either, which meant she had to stove her natural reaction to seeing him again.

Dakota studied him for a moment, taking in the dark circles under his eyes and the faint lines etched into his features—signs that the years that'd passed since their breakup two years ago hadn't been a cakewalk. Despite the lingering tension between them, she couldn't deny that Ellis was brilliant at his job, and his troubled past only seemed to fuel his determination to bring criminals to jus-tice, something she'd always admired.

It'd taken a long time to get over Ellis and seeing him again wasn't doing her any favors, but this case was big-ger than her feelings.

Isaac, a man who hated politicking and posturing, made

short work of the introductions in a gruff voice before taking his seat at the head of the table.

"Agent Vaughn," Dakota said, managing a tight smile as she extended her hand, ignoring the flutter in her stomach the second their palms met.

"Agent Foster," Ellis replied, shaking her hand firmly before finding his seat opposite her. There was a time when his hand in hers had been the calm in the storm, no matter what life had thrown their way. Now they were strangers and that's the way it would stay because the past needed to stay in the past. The sudden prick at her heart only focused her resolve that much more.

"I assume you've all read the brief," Isaac started, opening the file. "The gravity of the situation is only outmatched by the sense of urgency to find out how a six-week-old infant that's been missing for seventeen years just showed up as a coma patient in a Butte hospital."

Seventeen-year-old Cheyenne Swiftwater was admitted into Saint James Hospital after a solo rollover car accident, suffering a major head injury. According to the police report, the teen overcorrected on a turn and flipped the car. She was ejected from the vehicle and was put into a medically induced coma to bring down the swelling in her brain.

"It's a miracle she survived the wreck," Sayeh murmured, surveying the crash scene pictures. "It's not often that getting thrown from a vehicle actually saves your life. If the seat belt hadn't failed, she would've been crushed."

"Situations like these make idiots say that seat belts don't save lives," Isaac grumbled, but added, "Luck was riding shotgun with this girl, that's for sure."

"No ID found at the time of the accident," Shilah said, reading over the report. "How'd they get an identification?"

"They had her listed as Jane Doe until her fingerprints

were put into the system, tripping the FBI database for Missing and Exploited Children," Ellis answered, adding, "Imagine our surprise when Cheyenne Swiftwater popped up."

Nayeli's baby. The sixteen-year-old Dakota wanted to sob with relief that the child was alive, but the adult BIA agent had to stay focused and detached. She wouldn't dare do anything that would cause Isaac to side-eye her involvement with the case. "Did Cheyenne say where she was headed?" Dakota asked.

"She's awake but she doesn't know who she is or where she was going," Ellis said. "Doctors are saying it's short-term memory loss due to the head injury and there's no telling how long it might last but we need to find out where Cheyenne's been all this time."

"There's also no guarantee she's been in Montana. For all we know she could've been anywhere. Who's the car registered to?" Levi asked.

"An eighty-year-old Stevensville man who's been dead for at least five years. No surviving kin," Ellis answered, shaking his head. "If he was the one who abducted Cheyenne, he took the truth to his grave."

"We can put the media to work—area newspapers, news outlets, even social media—to see if anyone recognizes her," Dakota suggested. "Someone out there is bound to know something."

Isaac nodded with approval. "Good call. Dakota, you and Agent Vaughn will go to Saint James Hospital and speak with the girl first thing tomorrow. Talk to her doctors, see what you can find out. Levi and Sayeh, you'll handle the press, get the word out. Shilah, run background on the girl's mother. See if there's anything from the past that might've been missed."

The debrief room's fluorescent lights hummed overhead, casting a harsh glare on the case files spread across the table, a visual reminder that emotions didn't matter in this situation. The import of this case was huge but Dakota fought a well of complicated thoughts and feelings at the reopening of Nayeli's case. Solving what happened to the stolen infant of a murdered Native mother was the kind of case that would make all of her sacrifices worth it, but it didn't change the fact that Nayeli's case was located too close in her heart to Mikaya's for her to remain completely unbiased.

And Ellis had to know this, but he hadn't raised the alarm, so she'd give him that.

Perhaps Ellis's silence was a sign that he was willing to keep the past buried if she was—and Dakota was determined to prove that she could.

If she had to work side by side with Ellis, she'd do it as a professional should.

"We can drive together," Ellis offered but Dakota shut that down real quick.

Oh, hell no. Just because she was ready to show that she could keep the past in its place didn't mean she wanted to ride shotgun with the man like they were buddies. "I'd prefer separate cars. We can meet at the destination."

Ellis accepted her counter with a nod. "I'll call ahead, let the hospital know that we're coming. Let's meet at the hospital at eleven hundred. Does that work for you?"

Dakota put the time into her schedule with a short, "It does," and quickly added her own checklist into her notes for tomorrow.

Berrigan nodded. "Good. All right, you have your assignments. Let's bring home another win—and it goes without saying, stay safe." The last case nearly cost them Sayeh and Levi but a win was a win and their case had given the task force the added weight they'd needed to go harder on more complicated cases.

Such as this one.

The team started to disperse but Ellis hung back, which made Dakota want to run from the room, but they were officially on the same team for the time being so being professional was her emotional armor.

"It's been a while," Ellis said in an attempt at small talk, which she didn't want or need.

Since they were alone, Dakota dropped the act that they were strangers meeting for the first time. She turned to Ellis, addressing him in a low tone. "Look, I'll only say this once—our past doesn't matter. What matters is this case. We're adults. I can handle being civil and professional but don't try to charm me into anything more. Whatever we once had is now dust and ash with zero hope of resurrecting. Got it?"

"Geesh, Dakota, all I said was *It's been a while*. I wasn't trying to resurrect anything," he assured her, shaking his head as if she were overreacting, but there was the tiniest flicker of something else behind his eyes even as he added, "I was just being polite. That's a thing, you know."

"Don't do that," she warned, hating how he was trying to turn this into a problem on her end. "I know how you operate and I'm not interested in playing your games. Focus on the case, keep the past where it belongs and we'll do just fine."

Ellis looked away, accepting her terms with a stiff nod, but as she started to leave, he added, "Well, it's still good to see you, even if you don't share the sentiment."

She'd eat her shoe before admitting that she missed Ellis, but damn him for even saying such a thing to her. The time for sharing such thoughts was long gone. She ignored the heat flushing through her body and blurted, "I'm seeing someone." Which was a complete lie but she needed him to know that she wasn't pining for his stupid ass. "And it's pretty serious."

That subtle arch of surprise in his brow as well as the micro-expression of hurt before he smiled with a congratulatory, "That's great. I'm really happy for you, Dakota," made her instantly angry. He wasn't supposed to be nice about learning that she'd replaced him in her heart but how else was he supposed to react? What did she want, for him to fall to his knees and publicly humiliate himself with an overt display of a broken heart? That might soothe her bruised ego but would create major turmoil affecting their case, so no.

"Thanks," she returned stiffly, clutching her files to her chest. "So, tomorrow, then. Eleven hundred hours. I'll see you at Saint James."

"Don't get the wrong idea but we should probably exchange numbers…" he suggested as Dakota started to walk out the door, adding, "Unless, your number is the same, because mine hasn't changed."

She swallowed, hating that she hadn't changed her number. At the time, when her heart was still weeping, she'd desperately hoped that her phone would ring in the middle of the night and it would be Ellis begging for another chance. That call never happened but she also couldn't bring herself to change numbers. She lifted her chin. "I never got around to changing mine," she said, hoping to convey that he hadn't been important enough to warrant top priority.

If her statement hurt him, his brief smile and short nod didn't show it. "Great. Eleven hundred, then."

Dakota didn't trust herself to stay in that room a moment

longer. She left without another word. Ordinarily, working with a new partner—especially interagency co-ops—she would've been more accommodating, maybe even offering to take them to lunch to get better acquainted, talk shop, the usual, but she already knew all she needed to know about Ellis Vaughn.

He'd grown up with a sadistic "one-percenter" outlaw biker father who'd kicked the crap out of him whenever Ellis had even sneezed wrong, and who'd eaten a bullet from a rival gang when Ellis was a teenager, which was the best thing that could've happened.

Ellis, determined to be different from his old man, went into law enforcement, taking great pleasure in taking down violent dirtbags with similar MOs as his father but his maverick style had rubbed his superior the wrong way. After the last assignment had barely gone the right way, Ellis was unceremoniously kicked out of the narcotics unit and sent to the missing persons division.

She remembered that day all too well.

"They demoted me!" Ellis had roared, slamming into the kitchen with all of the rage of a man wronged. "That son of a bitch Carleton demoted me to the goddamn missing persons division!"

Dakota, alarmed at seeing this side of Ellis, tried to call him down. "It's not exactly a demotion. Missing Persons is an important division with a lot of opportunity for growth… You might even say that Carleton did you a favor."

"It's a paperwork division with no action," Ellis had shot back, his narrowed gaze hot with scathing mockery. "He did it on purpose because he knows I need to be where the action's at. This is punishment, Dakota. Don't insult me by trying to make me think it's not."

She'd tried to empathize with Ellis's situation but she'd

warned him that he had to stop playing fast and loose with the rules or else it was going to backfire on him. It was the lowest-hanging fruit of an "I told you so" but facts were facts.

"I'm not trying to do anything but point out a perspective that you might've missed," she retorted, stung. "And if you didn't want to leave the narcotics division, you shouldn't have pressed your luck when Carleton told you to cool it. A dead agent is the last thing anyone wants and that's exactly what was going to happen if someone didn't put you in check. I'm sorry, Ellis, but I agree with Carleton's decision."

It might've been true but it'd been the wrong thing to say at that moment.

Ellis was a powder keg of rage, guilt and self-recrimination that only needed the slightest spark to ignite—and Dakota had just lit the match.

Ellis had grabbed the first thing his hand could grasp and the crystal cookie jar shattered into a million pieces against the wall.

In her life and career, Dakota had seen too many red flags go ignored only to grow monstrous with time and she couldn't let the incident slide. It would've been easy to chalk up the situation as a moment of anger that got out of hand and might never happen again but Dakota didn't play with those kinds of odds.

The memory of the shattering glass echoed in her mind— as did her decision to leave. At the time, Dakota had been grateful that Ellis neither tried to make excuses for his actions nor did he try to stop her from leaving. Did Ellis ever think of that night? Or did he walk away from everything they'd shared without a backward glance? It wasn't her business to know or ask but the questions poked at her during quiet moments.

Or not-so-quiet moments—like now.

After the breakup, she'd rationalized they'd been kidding themselves from the start. Their relationship had never stood a chance. Compartmentalizing the reason for their breakup had helped manage her grief but it didn't stop the sting when he was standing in front of her.

Dakota knew that Isaac had picked her to work with Ellis because of her connection to the Flathead Reservation. She appreciated that he cared even when he acted like he was insensitive to anything but the outcome of a case, but working side by side with Ellis was going to take its toll.

She might put up a good front, but privately, seeing Ellis again had just taken a sledgehammer to that carefully sealed box. The thing was, they never had any closure over what'd happened and why they broke up.

It'd been more than the crystal cookie jar—it was the explosion of unfettered rage that'd scared her.

Even if they'd both agreed it was for the best, neither had actually had that conversation, which, in hindsight, was probably necessary to process the pain, but Dakota couldn't handle seeing him again for fear of slipping in her decision to end things. So, when she walked away, she hadn't looked back—and he hadn't come looking, either.

In her mind, that was further confirmation that he'd agreed.

But seeing him again was going to put the strength of that mental box to the test. What might happen if it finally sprang open after all these years of being tightly shut?

Don't go there, Dakota. Focus, focus, focus—all that matters is the case.

It would have to be the mantra that got her through this.

Chapter 2

Ellis knew seeing Dakota again would be like a punch to the solar plexus but two years' absence should've been enough time to get over the woman.

The immediate heat flushing through his body at first sight was proof that a hundred years might not be enough.

Dakota had an energy that vibrated with intensity; that inner passion for justice vibrated from her core in a way that drew him straight to her. He'd always admired her tenacity and stubborn will but her rigid sense of fair play had ultimately cleaved their love in two.

Well, that and his stupid temper. The last year of anger management classes had taught him a lot about his triggers and why he'd erupted that night at the one person who'd been the straightest shooter in his life. It hadn't been her fault that his actions had cost him but he'd taken his rage out on her—and an unsuspecting crystal cookie jar that'd been a gift from her grandmother.

Even with two years between him and that excruciatingly embarrassing moment, the memory still had the power to make him want to fall through the floor and disappear. He'd made it his life's mission to be different from his shit-bag father and yet, in a flash, he'd channeled his violent spirit, erupting with vicious rage at someone who didn't deserve it.

And it'd scared him. That's what he hadn't been able to admit. So, instead, when Dakota had walked—and with good reason—he'd let her.

That was then. This is now. It was time to move on.

Which was all well and good, except they had the kind of chemistry that couldn't be ignored, which should make working side by side interesting.

Similar to working with a hungry lion—death by snapping jaws could be imminent but at least it would never be boring.

Was he worried? Hard to answer. Dakota was a consummate professional and damn good at her job. She wouldn't let anything stand in her way of solving a case—especially one like this. But there was something between them still, he could feel it—and she did, too.

For both their sakes, he'd do his best to smother it. Neither could afford a messy break in their focus when each had something big riding on the outcome of this case.

Just as he knew she would be, Dakota was already in the parking lot, waiting. She didn't waste time on pleasantries, or even a half-hearted, perfunctory smile. God, his memory hadn't embellished the woman's beauty. Even in conservative street clothes, hair pulled in a tight ponytail, she was still stunning. He remembered with sharp clarity how it felt to let those long dark, silky strands slide through his fingertips. There wasn't a thing he *didn't* remember about Dakota Foster, but her hard-as-nails, zero-bend attitude was something he didn't miss.

They walked into Saint James Hospital, signed in with their credentials and made their way to the ICU department to meet with Dr. Patel before going into Cheyenne's room.

Dr. Patel, a man with a slight build and sharp, intelligent brown eyes, said with a subtle South Asian inflection,

"I understand you're here to question my patient," he said, eyeing Ellis and Dakota warily. "But I must insist that you proceed with extreme caution. She's still very fragile. She's stable and her memory is improving but she struggles with details. She also tires easily so please keep your questioning to only what is necessary. Also, she doesn't respond to the name Cheyenne. She says her name is Zoey."

Ellis appreciated the information, asking, "Last name?"

"Grojan."

Ellis shared a look with Dakota, both thinking the same. Time to run background on the name Zoey Grojan. If she attended public school, went to the doctor or otherwise used public aid in anyway, that would give them a place to start looking for her whereabouts the past seventeen years.

"Thank you, Doctor," Dakota murmured. "We'll be mindful of her injury. Can you give us any guidance on how best to approach this?"

"Of course," Dr. Patel replied, softening slightly. "Try to avoid causing her too much stress or asking her to recall anything traumatic. Her brain is still healing, and we need to give it time."

That was like asking the sun not to rise. Everything surrounding the girl's existence was traumatic but Ellis would try. "Understood," Ellis said, his focus unwavering as he confirmed with Dakota. "We'll do our best to keep this as painless as possible."

Dr. Patel nodded and led them into the sterile room.

The seventeen-year-old girl looked small in the bed. She was petite with light brown hair, the bruising on her face standing out in a garish purple, black and blue across her cheekbones. The swelling had gone down, leaving behind a mess as the injuries continued to heal, but he supposed it was a small price to pay for being alive. The crash photos were pretty gnarly.

"Miss Zoey? These are the agents I told you were coming today. Are you up to talking to them?"

"Yes." The girl regarded them with wary apprehension, but in the same gaze, Ellis saw a flicker of resilience. The girl was a fighter. Ellis recognized the innate strength despite her battered body. She gingerly sat upright, wincing at the motion. A large bandage covered half her forehead and the steady beep of the machines monitoring her vitals punctuated the silence.

While some people purposefully angled for a position within the missing persons division, it was too far removed from the action he craved. In the two years since being unceremoniously dumped in the division, his opinion hadn't changed—there was too much desk work when he preferred to be in the field.

The narcotics division had been constant action—the threat of danger around every corner had fueled his need for adrenaline in a way that Missing Persons never could. Not that it wasn't important work, but he was working his ass off to prove to Carleton he was ready to return to the action.

To prove that he'd changed in the ways that mattered.

Carleton seemed receptive to the idea, hinting that a win with this case might go a long way. So, he was going to throw everything he had at solving this case—through any means necessary.

The doc warned about pushing too hard, but the urgency of the situation made it impossible to tread too lightly. They needed answers—where had Zoey/Cheyenne been for the past seventeen years?

Might as well start at the obvious. "Hey, Zoey," he started in a soft, soothing tone, "my name is Ellis Vaughn and this is my partner, Dakota Foster. We're here to talk to you about your accident."

Zoey cast a nervous glance at Dr. Patel. "I don't remember much. Everything is kinda murky in my head."

"That's okay, we'll just see what we can get. Don't worry if you can't remember, okay?" Ellis said, purposefully hiding his impatience with a smile. "Just tell us whatever you can remember, no matter how small."

Zoey nodded, nervously fidgeting.

"You're not in trouble," Dakota assured the girl. "We just need to ask you a few questions about what happened and try to put together some missing information. Think of it like a puzzle and each piece has a place. Let us figure out where the pieces go."

"I'll try," she said.

"Anything you can tell us will help," Ellis said.

"Okay," she murmured, her voice barely audible.

"Zoey," Dakota began again, gently taking her hand. "Can you tell us anything about where you were going? Any details at all?"

The room seemed to hold its breath as Zoey considered the question, her brow furrowing in concentration. Finally, she said in a halting tone, "I don't remember where I was going but I...remember a farm of some kind? The sound of cows, chickens and maybe goats? I'm not sure... I remember firewood stacked on the side of the house."

"Did you live there?"

"I think so?"

"And your parents... Do you remember them?"

Zoey frowned, confusion creeping up on her expression. "Sort of? But I can't see their faces."

"That's okay," Ellis said, encouraging her. "What else?"

"I wanted to get away," she continued, slowly recalling,

"I felt...closed up, like stuck in a bubble or something. That doesn't make sense, though, does it?"

"We're not sure yet, but you're doing great," Dakota assured her. "The doctor says your name is Zoey Grojan... But we know you as a different name."

"What do you mean?"

"Does the name Cheyenne Swiftwater mean anything to you?"

Zoey's expression crinkled into a baffled uncertainty. "Should it?"

They had to be careful how quickly they presented the facts of her case. She might not be ready to hear that she'd been kidnapped as an infant. "We'll get back to that," Dakota said quickly, moving on. "Do you remember the names of your parents?"

Zoey shook her head, her eyes welling with tears. "What if I never remember who I am?"

Dr. Patel intervened, shooting them a warning look for agitating his patient. "Don't worry, Miss Zoey, your memory will return. Your brain is still healing. Give it time."

"I'm sorry, I'm trying to remember," Zoey said to Ellis and Dakota as if needing their approval. "I'm not trying to be difficult."

Beneath the resilience there was a sweetness to Zoey that reminded Ellis of kids that were homeschooled. No shade against public school systems but homeschooled kids were just different, somehow softer than those exposed to a wide range of personality types and social situations, both good and bad.

"You're doing great," Ellis reassured her with a smile. "Rest now. We'll be back to talk more tomorrow. You focus on getting better."

Dr. Patel followed them out and away from Zoey's doorway. "Every day she gets stronger but brain injuries are unpredictable. I'll permit you to see her tomorrow but I need your assurances that you won't push harder than she's ready."

Both Ellis and Dakota agreed, even if they were both guilty of wanting to push a little harder.

They left the hospital and returned to their cars.

"Looks like we'll need to get a hotel because we'll be here for a few days at least," Ellis said, checking his watch.

Dakota agreed but added unnecessarily, "Separate rooms, of course."

"Of course," Ellis confirmed, slightly annoyed that she felt compelled to make that point. She'd made it pretty damn clear that she'd rather give a feral cat a bath than be anything more than passingly civil with him.

Fine by me. He wasn't going to chase someone who didn't want to be caught. Like he didn't have a phone full of women who wouldn't mind some private time with him. He didn't need the emotional scraps from an ice queen. *Whoa, was that called for? She left for a good reason, remember that, buddy.* The downside to going to therapy? Your therapist's voice was always in your head. "Closest hotel to the hospital is the Wayfair Inn," he said.

"I don't need anything fancy. Just a decent bed and a shower. I packed a suitcase just in case we ended up needing to stay."

Of course she did, Little Miss Always Prepared. He'd actually always appreciated that about her. Glad to see some things hadn't changed.

"Yeah, same," he lied. He'd have to run over to the mall and grab a few things.

"Great," she said, moving to unlock her car. "Let's get checked in, then."

Dakota climbed into her sedan and punched the address into GPS, then, she was gone.

Damn—it's like that, then.

Ellis sighed and climbed into his own car. This case, and working with Dakota, was going to be like serving penance before transferring straight to hell.

Dakota couldn't get away from Ellis fast enough. Maintaining a professional distance hadn't prevented her from getting a whiff of his cologne—a signature scent that complimented his personality in a way that was intoxicating—and it brought back a slew of memories best forgotten.

Memories with the power to burn.

Put it away, Dakota growled to herself, irritated that she was even thinking of those things. Refocusing with fierce purpose, she navigated to the Wayfair Inn, which, as Ellis said, wasn't far from the hospital.

Ellis was only five minutes behind her. He entered the lobby just as she was finishing with her registration. She received the key, saying, only for safety and professional purposes, "I'm in room 218, second floor. Debrief tomorrow at 0700?"

"Only if it involves a copious amount of coffee and a doughnut," Ellis returned, reminding her that he wasn't an early riser.

She supposed they couldn't get to the hospital too early and grudgingly changed the time to 0800, which would put them back with Zoey by ten hundred, a more reasonable time.

Ellis agreed and she left him at the registration desk to sign in.

Once in her room, door firmly locked, she did a quick safety check of the room, making sure there weren't any two-way mirrors or loose locks on the windows, and that the door didn't have a gap between the frames. Being in law enforcement had completely corrupted the way she saw people. The complete depravity of humankind was too much to leave to chance. Although, if someone was stupid enough to try anything with her, they'd find themselves in a world of hurt. In her spare time, she volunteered at the women's shelter teaching self-defense. Maybe if her sister had known how to defend herself, she would still be here.

Removing her gun from its holster, she set it on her nightstand, always within grabbing distance when she traveled.

Grabbing her cell, she called Shilah to let her know she was checked in and what she'd learned from talking to the girl.

"She's pretty banged up," Dakota said, pulling her shoes off and wiggling her toes in relief. She hated wearing shoes. As a kid growing up on the reservation, she'd rarely worn shoes during the summer and into late fall, even. The bottoms of her feet had grown so calloused she could withstand almost anything without wincing, but she had "city feet" now.

Even so, she loved being free of the restrictive shoes. "Her face is bruised and her brain is still healing but I think a few more days of rest and she'll be ready for harder questions. Refresh my memory about the details on her biological mother."

"Not a whole lot beyond what was originally printed when she was killed," Shilah shared. "Let's see, the basics—Nayeli Swiftwater, nineteen, formerly of the Flathead Reservation, was found dead in her Whitefish apartment April 8, but there was no sign of her six-week-old infant, Cheyenne. Nayeli was working for one of the bigger chain hotels as a housekeeper and sending as much as she could to her disabled mother back at the reservation. Her mother has since been moved into a subsidized, long-term care facility in Missoula. Nayeli had a younger sister, Nakita, who got into trouble with drugs but has since cleaned herself up and lives in Missoula as well, presumably to be close to her mother."

"No other family?"

"Nakita has two kids but they're pretty young, only ten and six."

"Okay, thanks. Can you email me all of that information?"

"Sure." There was a beat, then Shilah asked, "Am I imagining things or was there tension between you and the FBI agent? Do you know each other?"

Dakota mentally cursed her inability to hide her emotions better. She'd always been accused of wearing her feelings on her sleeve and anyone wanting to know how she felt could just look at her face. She didn't want to lie to Shilah but she also wasn't ready to share. Still, it was hard to get the words out. "Uh, yeah, we have some history, nothing serious, but I don't really care for the guy."

"How'd you meet?"

A bar of all places. She hadn't known he was FBI, and he hadn't known she was BIA. They'd just been two people blowing off steam who happened to click one night over too many beers. And possibly a few shots of tequila. "It was casual. Like I said, nothing serious." The white lie tasted bitter but she and Ellis weren't planning a reunion tour of their relationship so it wouldn't matter. "But we're both professional so it shouldn't be a problem."

But then Shilah said, "Well, he's damn fine," and Dakota wanted to howl at the moon for the immediate insecurity that crawled up her throat. Of course Ellis was fine, that was his superpower. Women flocked to him like geese looking for something tasty to nibble. Shilah added, "I know you're too straitlaced to play like that but, girl, I wouldn't fault you none."

Dakota forced a chuckle she didn't feel, saying, "Well, if you knew his true personality, you'd understand. Ellis Vaughn is a hot mess."

A thread of concern replaced Shilah's playful interest. "Is he going to be a problem? Isaac could probably have him replaced if he's going to be a detriment to the case."

"No, Ellis is actually a really good investigator," Dakota said, "I can handle his personality. It'll be fine. If I thought he was a threat to the integrity of the case, I'd say something immediately."

That much was true. Dakota wouldn't let anything derail this case—and that included her personal feelings, one way or another.

Shilah relaxed, saying, "All right, so you're heading back to the hospital tomorrow?"

"Yes, hopefully, we can push a little harder."

"Sayeh and Levi sent out press releases to all the news outlets. You should start seeing the bulletins on the evening news in the area."

"Good. I don't think it'll take long before we start getting traction once the media does its thing," Dakota said, hoping that was true. The faster they got answers, the faster they could close this case.

She didn't want to spend a moment longer with Ellis than she had to.

For a number of reasons—not all of which were professional.

Chapter 3

Ellis arrived at the hospital a few minutes early, just as Dakota pulled into the parking lot. Was he trying to prove to Dakota that he'd changed since they'd broken up? No, but he also didn't want to hear her gripe at him for showing up a few minutes late. Some things weren't worth the hassle.

Whomever she was dating now, he wished them luck if they weren't cut from the same rigid piece of wood because Dakota didn't bend for anyone.

Dakota noted his bakery bag with a frown. "What's that?"

"Chocolate doughnut," he answered, adding, "For Zoey. Hospital food is the worst."

"How do you know she can have a doughnut?" Dakota asked. "Did you clear it with Dr. Patel?"

"It's a doughnut, Dakota, not drugs."

Dakota wouldn't budge. "She could have a food allergy. You're not giving her that doughnut," Dakota said with a stern shake of her head. "Absolutely not. It's unprofessional."

"The kid just went through something terrible. Something sweet might go a long way toward getting her to feel more comfortable around us. Did it ever occur to you that she's been conditioned to distrust strangers? She needs to trust us enough for her subconscious to open up to talking."

"And you think a doughnut is going to do that? You're putting a lot of faith in the power of a pastry."

"The power of chocolate," he corrected with a wink. "But if it puts your mind at ease, I'll ask her doc if it's okay before offering it to her. Does that meet with your approval?"

Dakota grudgingly agreed but he could tell she didn't like it. Of course she didn't like it. His methods weren't detailed in the manual in some obscure subsection of code that could be studied and analyzed. Sometimes you had to listen to your gut—and the kid felt lost and alone. Chocolate hit the center of the brain that controlled endorphins. Endorphins were the feel-good hormone. The kid needed something to make her feel safe.

Hence, chocolate.

"Let's keep the off-roading to a minimum," Dakota said stiffly before they walked into the hospital, going through the same motions as the day before. He ignored that bit of advice as unnecessary. She didn't need to school him like a rookie. He cut her a short look but otherwise kept his mouth shut.

As they walked to Zoey's room, Dakota debriefed him. "Shilah didn't find much more about the birth mother aside from what was already known but I forwarded the information to your email. Also, last night I caught a news report from the local stations with Zoey's information and photo. We should be wary of any crackpots showing up claiming to be Zoey's parents. This situation is ripe for human traffickers looking for an easy target."

Ellis nodded in agreement. "Hopefully, Zoey remembers a bit more today."

"Here's hoping," Dakota said, crossing her fingers.

They knocked softly on the doorframe before entering

Zoey's room. Same as yesterday, Dr. Patel hovered like an overprotective helicopter parent, reminding them to be conservative in their questioning.

"Good morning, Zoey," Dakota said with a warm and engaging smile. "How are you feeling today?"

"A little better," she admitted, casting a glance at Dr. Patel, assuring him that she was okay. They must've had a private conversation prior to Ellis and Dakota arriving, establishing some kind of code. She saw the bag in Ellis's hand, suddenly curious. "What's that?"

Ellis smiled, holding the bag up. "This is a chocolate doughnut from the mom-and-pop doughnut shop I found near my hotel, and if it's okay with your doc, it's got your name all over it. That is…if you like chocolate."

Zoey's eyes widened with excitement as she looked to Dr. Patel. "Please?"

Dr. Patel was uncertain. "We have no way of knowing if you have any food allergies," he said, to which Ellis knew in his bones Dakota was smugly saying in her head, "That's what I said," but in light of Zoey's hopeful expression, he relented, saying, "I suppose you're in the safest place if it turns out you're allergic. Go ahead."

Ellis handed Zoey the bag and she gleefully pulled the doughnut out, taking a deep sniff of the pastry with complete delight before sinking her teeth in for a huge bite. Her squeal was worth any pushback from either the doctor or Dakota, although he had to admit, even Dakota smiled at the simple happiness the doughnut created for the girl.

"I *never* get to eat chocolate," Zoey admitted, savoring the bite. Then her eyes widened at the admission, realizing she'd remembered something. "Oh! That's right, chocolate was a big treat in my house. I remembered something!" She quickly took another bite as if it had magical powers.

"My mom was real strict about sugar because 'sugar rots your teeth,' she said. We used honey or agave to sweeten things but nothing compares to this. Oh, this is sooo good! Thank you!"

Strict parents who didn't believe in letting their kids have sugar could be a clue.

Even the doctor smiled, losing some of his watchful stance. When it became apparent no allergic reaction was imminent, he said, "You seem to be tolerating the pastry without any ill effects. If you think you'll be okay, I'll leave you with the agents but if at any point you feel taxed, don't feel bad about ending this little visit."

Zoey smiled and nodded. Ellis waited for the doctor to leave the room before whispering out of the side of his mouth to Zoey, "I don't think the good doctor likes us very much. Maybe I ought to bring two doughnuts next time."

Zoey's small, tremulous smile was a win he'd take. Operation: Win Zoey's Trust seemed to be working. He dragged a chair to her bedside, saying, "I don't blame him, I blame the media. FBI agents get a bad rap. We're either the bad guys running over the little guys or we're the larger-than-life badasses that no one can relate to. I promise you, I'm no badass. The real badass," he shared in a conspiratorial whisper as he cast a glance in Dakota's direction, "is my partner. She can probably twist my spine into a pretzel without breaking a sweat but no one's going to think that because at first glance, she doesn't look strong enough to break a breadstick in half. Looks are deceiving, though."

Dakota chuckled in spite of herself—probably killed her to crack a smile at his joke—but he secretly enjoyed getting her to smile. Old habits died hard, he supposed.

Zoey's grin widened, until she winced from the pain and she sobered again, reminded of why they were there in the first place. "I think I remembered something new last night after you left," she shared.

Both Dakota and Ellis were all ears. "Yeah? What was that?" Ellis asked.

"Well, you asked me about my parents and I can't remember their names yet but I do remember my bedroom."

"Can you share what you remember?" Dakota prompted, pulling out her notebook.

"I remember my bedspread has a patchwork quilt and there are pencil sketches on the walls that I think I drew. The window overlooks a farm with all sorts of animals, but people, too. That's the part that's confusing to me."

"Maybe they're working the farm?" Dakota suggested.

But Zoey shook her head as if that didn't quite fit what she felt as true. "No, there's a lot of people...like entire families? Does that make sense?"

The wheels in Ellis's head started to turn faster. Was it possible Zoey lived in a commune? That would explain why there was no record of Zoey in the public school system and why she gave off a sheltered vibe. It also connected with the newfound information about her parents' strict stance on sugars. Many communes shied away from foods known to create dental issues as they had limited access to dental health. "Is it possible you lived with a bunch of families?" Ellis asked.

Zoey frowned as she tested that theory in her head. She winced but nodded even though she couldn't really be sure. "I think that might be right."

"Do you remember going to school at any point?" Dakota asked.

Zoey nodded, adding, "Yes, there was a room with a bunch of kids, different ages though, and we all did our own thing... I guess I was homeschooled?"

Bingo. Ellis nodded. "It would seem so. Nothing wrong with that, though," he assured her when her expression dipped into embarrassment. "Lots of kids are homeschooled these days."

"Yeah?"

Dakota chimed in, "Oh sure, with the internet, almost anyone can open a charter school these days. It's nothing to be ashamed of."

"But is it weird? Seems weird. Why wouldn't my parents want me to go to public school?"

Probably because you were kidnapped at six weeks old. But she wasn't ready to hear that just yet. "I'm sure they had your best interests at heart," he said with a disarming smile. "But let's celebrate the fact that you're starting to remember things. That's a great sign."

"You think so?"

Dakota immediately agreed. "Oh yes, absolutely. Your brain is healing quickly. Before you know it, you'll be back to normal."

But that caused her expression to falter, as if she wasn't sure she wanted to go back to what she'd known and that was another important key.

Ellis had a feeling the girl had been running for good reason.

Dakota hated that Ellis had been right to bring the doughnut, but also hated that she couldn't seem to let him have the win without feeling uncharitable. Maybe it was because she knew how slippery a slope it could be when Ellis started breaking rules. Not every means to an end was worth the risk. What if Zoey had been allergic to chocolate and started going into anaphylactic shock?

Then her doc would've sprung into action, logic reasoned, refusing to let her cling to a bullshit argument for the sake of her ego. The fact was, Ellis's instincts had been spot-on and she needed to let him have the win.

And it was something she wouldn't have thought of.

Ellis had once accused her of being too stiff to bend with the wind, which ultimately kept her rooted in one spot without hope of any growth.

She'd found his comment ridiculously unsupported by fact.

But maybe there was something to being able to bend a little.

She swallowed, forcing a bright smile for Zoey's benefit. They needed her to trust them. She grabbed a chair and pulled it closer, sharing, "If you like chocolate, I'll have to introduce you to my absolute favorite dessert—chocolate cheesecake. Now, I'll be honest, it's so rich, you can only eat a few bites before you tap out, but ohhh, those bites are worth it."

"I would love to try it," Zoey said, her eyes shining, admitting, "I think I have a sweet tooth."

"That's okay, there are worse things to have," Ellis said. "And I have to agree with Dakota, chocolate cheesecake is the best. We'll bring you some tomorrow."

Dakota ignored the flutter of memory that popped unwelcome in her head of the night Ellis had surprised her with a mini chocolate cheesecake and they'd shared it, feeding it to one another between kisses during a rain-soaked night, sitting beside a cozy fire while the storm raged outside the apartment.

Shaking off the feelings that rose up to choke her, Dakota said, "So, is it possible you lived in a commune?"

"What's a commune?" Zoey asked, confused.

"It's a small, tight-knit community that share like-minded

belief structures, living on one property," Dakota explained, trying to lessen any stigma. "In this economy, we're seeing more people returning to that kind of community living."

"Um, yeah, I guess so," Zoey said, chewing on the side of her cheek. "Seems like that might be right."

Dakota tried to keep her excitement hidden. They were on the right track. All signs pointed to Zoey being raised off-grid somewhere, which would explain why the girl just disappeared after being abducted.

"Is there anything else you can remember? Any detail, no matter how small, might help," Ellis said.

Zoey stilled, pausing to wipe at her face with the small napkin, her gaze darting as if fighting the urge to share yet understanding the need to divulge certain information. Dakota wondered if Zoey's memory was better than she wanted to let on. If the girl was running from something bad, it made sense that she didn't want to be found.

Yet, there was a softness about Zoey that didn't lend itself to the suspicion that she was being purposefully deceitful. Dakota sensed Zoey was a sweet girl at her heart but there was definitely something she didn't want to share.

"Zoey...we're here to help you," Dakota assured her in a gentle voice. "I promise you, we can protect you if you're in some kind of trouble."

Zoey held Dakota's stare before flitting to Ellis's and Dakota could feel her wavering. The tension in the air was palpable. *C'mon Zoey, you can do it...* Dakota held her breath, sensing Zoey was close to revealing something important.

But then an anguished voice at the door caused them all to swivel their attention to a man and woman staring at Zoey with tears in their eyes. Both Dakota and Ellis rose to their feet in a protective stance, halting their rush toward Zoey's bed. Ellis immediately demanded, "Stop right there. Who are you?" with his hand resting on his holster, beating Dakota to it.

The woman, dressed in a simple cotton dress, her graying hair pulled into a severe bun, skidded to a shocked stop, drawing herself up as if offended by their mistrust, her chin lifting as she answered, "We're Zoey's parents and we're here to bring her home."

The hell you are—but you might just be the ones who killed her actual mother.

Chapter 4

"I beg your pardon?" The woman's confused expression mingled with the shock of being denied access to Zoey. The reaction seemed genuine enough but Ellis knew people to be very good actors when it suited them. The woman looked to her husband for backup, urging him to take control of the situation. "Ned, do something!"

The man, small-framed with a balding pate, tried to settle his wife. "Now, now, Barbara-Jean, they're just looking out for Zoey," he said. Introducing himself to Ellis, he said, "My name's Ned Grojan and this here's my wife, Barbara-Jean. We've been looking for Zoey since she run away and we came as soon as we saw her picture on the news."

"We're going to need to see identification," Dakota said firmly.

Ned pulled an old driver's license from his wallet and handed it to Ellis. Ellis didn't need to see the expiration date to know that it'd expired a long time ago. He narrowed his gaze. "This expired ten years ago. Do you have current ID?"

"We don't drive and we live off the grid," the woman replied stiffly as if it were none of their business how they lived and wouldn't stand for any judgment.

"How'd you get here if you don't drive?" he asked, returning the useless ID to the man.

"We have friends who brought us," Ned answered. "They're waiting in the lobby while we sort this all out."

"I hate to be the bearer of bad news but you're not leaving with Zoey anytime soon," Dakota said. "It will take time to process your identification seeing as you don't have current ID."

"This is preposterous," the woman sputtered indignantly. "Zoey is our daughter and you have no right to keep her from us."

Ellis turned to Zoey and saw the anguish and fear in her eyes. She definitely knew the couple but had she been running from them? Wordlessly, Dakota picked up the same vibe and stepped into action. "Why don't you come with me? We'll talk about this in private," she said, ushering them from the room, despite the woman's protests.

Ellis turned to Zoey. "Do you recognize that couple as your parents?" he asked.

Zoey hesitated, tears filling her eyes, her mouth working as if she didn't want to answer but felt compelled to. "I think so," she finally admitted in a small voice. "They look real mad."

"Have they hurt you?" Ellis asked quietly. "I can't help you if you're not honest. Tell me why you're afraid right now."

"I don't know," she said, shaking her head. "I'm so confused. I ran away for a reason but I can't remember why. Why would I run from my own parents unless they did something bad?"

It was solid logic. Ellis appreciated her attempt at reasoning things out under extreme circumstances. "I don't know but we'll help you find out," he said. "I promise you, you're not going anywhere with anyone until you are ready and able."

Zoey sagged with relief, her shoulders dropping from

around her ears. "Thank you," she said. "I'm sorry if I'm being too much trouble."

"No need to apologize, Zoey. We're here to protect you and to find out what happened." *Such as how a six-week-old infant was kidnapped from her murdered mother.* That was at the top of his list. "I'll be back. Try not to worry."

Ellis left Zoey, found Dr. Patel, informed him of the situation, and everyone was taken to a private conference room for questioning.

"This is a travesty," Barbara-Jean exclaimed, pacing like a trapped cat. "My daughter suffered a major head trauma and I'm stuck in this room with you instead of by her bedside. I want to talk to your supervisor," she said, stabbing a finger in Ellis's direction. To Dr. Patel she said, "And shame on you for keeping a mother from her child. You should know better."

But Dr. Patel took the woman's judgment with barely a blink, saying, "Madam, my concern is for my patient, not your feelings. I will tell you the same thing I told the agents—if you stress my patient, you will be escorted from the premises."

Ellis was starting to appreciate the doctor's blunt manner. He gestured to the empty chairs around the conference table. "Let's all have a seat and talk," he said.

"I don't want—"

"Barbara-Jean!" the man cut in tersely. "Sit down. You're making things worse. Zoey is safe, that's what matters. The agents are just trying to make sure we're not deviants or something."

"Deviants?" Barbara-Jean gasped, sinking into the chair. "That's an obscene thought. We're her parents. And since when do FBI agents get involved with a runaway girl involved in a car accident? Something isn't right and if I don't start getting answers real soon..."

Might as well get to the meat of things. Ellis swiveled his gaze straight to the indignant woman. "Great. I'd also like answers. Where were you on the night of April 8, 2006?"

The woman balked with confusion. "What? What kind of question is that?" She looked to her husband, who was equally baffled by the sudden shift in direction. "What does that have to do with our daughter's accident? What's going on?"

"That's the night Zoey's *biological* mother was murdered in her Whitefish apartment and her infant daughter—the one you claim is your daughter—was kidnapped," Dakota provided flatly, watching for their reaction just as he was. "So you can imagine how we're not so keen to just let you waltz in and take custody of Zoey."

Neither reacted in a way that betrayed guilt, only deep, horrified bewilderment.

Ned spoke first, reaching over to clutch his wife's hand in support. "I'm sorry but I think you've got us turned around a bit. What do you mean?"

"My partner was pretty clear," Ellis said. "Before Zoey was Zoey Grojan, she was born Cheyenne Swiftwater. Did you know her mother, Nayeli Swiftwater?"

"I'm her mother," Barbara-Jean shot back in a watery tone as she tried to hold herself together. "She's my daughter. You can't take her from me."

"Did you know Nayeli Swiftwater?" Ellis asked again, ignoring the woman's declaration.

Barbara-Jean's lip quivered as she looked to her husband but she shook her head in answer. "I've never heard of that name before in my life."

Dakota looked to Ned. "And you?"

He also shook his head. "We adopted Zoey in a closed adoption. We never knew her birth parents and preferred it that way. We thought it best to raise Zoey without the burden of knowledge that she was adopted."

"Do you have paperwork supporting the adoption process?" Dakota asked.

"Of course," Barbara-Jean answered, but her lip continued to quiver as if she were barely holding herself together. "Back at home."

"We're going to need to see that documentation," Ellis said. "What was the name of the adoption agency?"

"It wasn't an agency," Ned admitted, looking uncomfortable, as if just now realizing that there might be some truth to the horrific story they were investigating. "It was private. We didn't ask a lot of questions because we were so happy to finally have a child to complete our family."

"Did you think a baby just dropped out of the sky?" Dakota asked. "You didn't think it was a little odd that a newborn just showed up as available when it takes years for people to get a newborn?"

"I hear the judgment in your voice, Agent Foster, and I don't appreciate it. You don't know our story or our journey, so please keep your judgment to yourself," Barbara-Jean snapped, in spite of her husband's attempts to keep her under control.

Dakota's cold smile had the power to put the fear of God into the most hardened criminals but Barbara-Jean was oblivious to the danger she was in. "I'll ask one more time—where were you on the night of April 8, 2006?"

"Not murdering people in a Whitefish apartment, if that's what you're asking," Barbara-Jean shot back, her chin lifted. "This is…outrageous. We have the documentation. We did everything we were asked. You have no right to keep us from our daughter."

Ellis rose and Dakota followed his lead. "Until we can determine whether or not you had anything to do with the murder of Nayeli Swiftwater, we're taking you into custody for further questioning."

"What?" The word escaped Barbara-Jean's mouth in an explosion of incredulity but Dakota was already pulling her arms behind her and fastening the handcuffs. "What is happening right now?" she gasped in a shrill tone, looking to her husband. "Are you kidding me? You're arresting us?"

The husband, shaking his head, realizing it was futile to argue, calmly allowed Ellis to handcuff him. "We'll get it sorted, Barbara-Jean," he assured her. "We've done nothing wrong. Just calm down and don't make it worse."

"It can't possibly get worse!"

That cold Dakota smile surfaced again as she quipped, "Oh, I assure you, if we find out you had anything to do with Nayeli's murder, it most certainly can and will."

Dakota knew the kind of woman Barbara-Jean Grojan was the minute she walked into the room—overbearing, stubborn and rigidly certain her way was the only way— so it didn't come as a huge shock that Barbara-Jean put up a fuss as soon as she realized they weren't going to let her get near Zoey.

Their story might be legit—desperate people willing to look the other way when a baby became available wasn't farfetched—but Dakota would never understand how anyone could just accept an infant without question and expect nothing illegal was involved.

Babies didn't just fall from the sky.

It seemed the height of selfishness that people would

turn a blind eye to the possibility that their precious bundle might've been ripped from the arms of its birth mother without consent.

Coordinating with local police, the Grojans were transported to the police department where Ellis and Dakota could continue their questioning in a more controlled environment, which was a relief to the hospital staff as their presence on the wing was already a disruption.

Dakota sent the Grojans' details to Shilah to run background and Shilah was quick with the information.

"According to public records, the Grojans were your typical American couple, paid their taxes and otherwise were pretty average until 2006 when they simply dropped off the grid," Dakota shared with Ellis. "Ned Grojan was an accountant and Barbara-Jean a dental hygienist. One day, they both quit their jobs, liquidated their accounts, including their 401(k), and disappeared."

"That's not suspicious," Ellis joked. "Totally normal."

"Exactly. Something tells me there's more to the Grojans than meets the eye," Dakota said.

"Mmm, my favorite kind of suspect. Let's see how long it takes for them to spill their secrets."

"My money's on Ned. He looks the least likely to cling to a story."

Ellis agreed. "My guess is that after being married to Barbara-Jean for almost twenty years, a nice long stay in a quiet cell might feel like a vacation."

Dakota chuckled and followed Ellis into the room where Ned awaited. He was still handcuffed and secured to a special bolt in the metal table. His wife was in a holding cell elsewhere in the building.

"Where's my wife?" he asked as soon as they entered

the room. "She gets anxious in new surroundings. She's probably very upset right now."

"Probably," Dakota agreed, settling in the chair opposite Ned and continuing without a missing a beat. "Okay, so let's get back to the truth. If you're truly innocent, you're going to need to be more forthcoming about how you acquired a stolen baby."

"Please stop calling Zoey a stolen child. It makes me feel sick to my stomach," Ned implored. "To us, she was a gift from God. We had no idea that she'd been taken from her birth mother."

"Sure, that's possible but it doesn't negate the facts— *Cheyenne* was *taken* when her birth mother was murdered and given to you and we need to know by whom."

Ned's eyes sparkled with tears. "I swear to you, we didn't know anything about that."

"Who facilitated the adoption?" Ellis asked.

Ned hesitated, torn between saving himself and protecting the person involved. Impatience sharpened Dakota's tone. "In case it wasn't clear, without information proving your innocence, you're our number one suspect in a murder/kidnapping case, so I suggest you find your way clear to giving up some names."

"We're not guilty of murder or kidnapping," Ned stubbornly maintained.

"Prove it," Ellis countered.

"How?" Ned asked, licking his lips, confused. "How can I prove I didn't commit murder?"

"Let's start with the basics. Explain to us why you went off-grid at the exact time, or near to it, that Nayeli Swiftwater was killed,"

To refresh Ned's memory, Dakota said, "You liquidated all of your accounts and basically disappeared. Why? In our experience, the only people who do that are usually running or hiding from something or someone. Why would an accountant and a dental hygienist leave behind everything they'd worked for—" she snapped her fingers "—like that unless they were trying to run from something?"

"You've got it all wrong," Ned said, shaking his head. "We weren't running from our lives, we were closing a chapter and starting a new one, a fresh one with people who shared our values. Do you believe in God, Agent Foster?"

Dakota hated that question. After her sister's gruesome murder, she'd lost a lot of her faith. "Get to the point," she warned.

"Barbara-Jean and I realized a long time ago that the world had lost its way and we were tired of trying to right the ship. We prayed about it and realized the best use of our energy would be to find those who shared our faith and start over. That's when we met Zachariah."

That was a new name.

"Zachariah who?" Ellis asked. "Is he your pastor or something?"

"He's so much more than a pastor. He's our mentor, leader, friend, trusted confidant...and miracle worker."

"Tall order for a single man. Does he walk on water, too?" Dakota quipped.

"You joke because you can't possibly understand our calling. Zachariah formed The Congregation in the hopes of creating more space for like-minded people who simply want to be left alone to live cleanly off the land, supporting one another and raising our children to love God."

Dakota suppressed the shudder. In her line of work, often when cults reared their ugly head it was never as innocuous as it sounded on paper. There was always something dark working in the background. She suspected this would turn out to be no different. "Sounds like paradise," she quipped. "We need a name."

"If you could just let me make a phone call—"

"Name," Ellis cut in, getting impatient. He had just as much tolerance for zealots as Dakota. "Give us a name."

Ned clearly didn't want to but when he realized neither Ellis nor Dakota were interested in playing any games, he relented with a sigh, sharing, "Zachariah Deakins."

"Great," Dakota said. "And an address for Mr. Deakins?"

"10045 Sommerset Road. The Congregation owns a thirty-acre place outside of Stevensville."

"See? That wasn't so hard, was it?" Dakota said, rising and knocking on the door. A uniformed officer appeared. "Officer, please escort Mr. Grojan back to his cell and bring Mrs. Grojan in."

"Wait—I thought—"

"You thought wrong," Ellis cut in as the officer took Ned down the hall. To Dakota, he said, "You thinking cult?"

"Yep." Dakota was already texting Shilah the details so she could run backgrounds on Zachariah Deakins. "And those are rarely as 'Kumbaya, my Lord' as people want others to believe."

Ellis grinned. "*Amen* to that, sister."

Chapter 5

Barbara-Jean's eyes, red and puffy from tears, blazed with indignant fire the instant she was ushered into the room and restrained to the metallic table. Her voice, although strained, boomed with a fusion of frustration and demand. "This is outrageous. We have rights! This is America, not a third-world country, and I demand to speak with my husband. You have no right—"

Ellis interjected, curtailing her tirade with a firm yet calm demeanor, allowing little space for her to further erupt. "Let's streamline this discussion for the sake of efficiency," he advised, maintaining unflinching eye contact with the older woman. "You are being lawfully detained while we conduct an inquiry. We aim to ascertain whether you should be charged with the murder of Nayeli Swiftwater and the kidnapping of her infant daughter, Cheyenne. Your cooperation would be in your best interest."

In the silence that ensued, the weight of Ellis's words hung heavily in the air, trapping Barbara-Jean in a predicament where her next words could dictate the path forward and one wrong move could land her in hot water.

Deflated, Barbara-Jean whimpered, her eyes flicking between Dakota and Ellis, attempting to discern the sincerity in his statement. After a moment, she gave a terse nod, signaling her reluctant agreement to cooperate. "Ask your questions. The sooner this charade is over, the sooner I can be with my daughter," she declared with a shaky voice.

"Great. We appreciate your cooperation," Dakota responded, flipping open her notebook. "Can you tell us how you came to adopt Cheyenne?"

"Her name is Zoey!" Barbara-Jean snapped back, her voice laced with a mixture of defiance and protectiveness. "You will call her by her proper name. Do you understand? Her name is *Zoey*."

Barbara-Jean seemed on the verge of losing her emotional stability. Ellis recognized that if they pushed her too hard, she might collapse under the pressure and they would lose any opportunity to extract answers from her. He exhaled softly, choosing to employ a gentler approach. "Mrs. Grojan, may we get you something to drink?" he offered, presenting a disarming smile. "Perhaps a coffee or some water?"

"A water would be nice," she admitted with a stiff upper lip, shooting Dakota a sour look. "You've no cause to treat me so poorly. I didn't have anything to do with the death of that woman."

Ellis glanced at Dakota, prompting her to exit the room. She returned shortly with a bottle of water, which she opened before handing it to Barbara-Jean. Accepting the water with an air of it being the bare minimum they could do, Barbara-Jean nevertheless took a sip with apparent gratitude. Her hands trembled as she awkwardly lifted the bottle to her lips, the handcuffs inhibiting her movements.

After a drawn-out moment during which Barbara-Jean seemed to regain some composure, she began to speak with a reluctant tone. "For years we tried to have a child naturally, but God didn't bless us that way. We attempted to adopt through the foster care system and various charitable organizations but couldn't find a suitable match. We were looking to raise an infant, while most available children were part of sibling groups or were older."

The foster care system was brimming with children in need of stable homes, but many of them came with emotional challenges that numerous prospective parents were ill-equipped to handle. Securing an infant for adoption was considered the pinnacle, often unattainable without substantial financial resources—the damn Holy Grail of adoptions.

Given this context, Ellis queried, "So, understanding the challenges of being placed with an infant, didn't you find it peculiar when one miraculously became available to you?"

"No, we believed God had answered our prayers," Barbara-Jean responded, her voice devoid of deceit. She seemed to sincerely believe that they had been recipients of a divine miracle.

Blind faith gave Ellis indigestion. He didn't need to see Dakota's expression to know that she felt the same. They were different in a lot of ways, but the same in others.

"And who was this miracle worker?" Dakota asked, looking to cross-reference what Ned had shared.

But unlike her husband, Barbara-Jean didn't hesitate. "Zachariah Deakins," she shared with a hint of reverence in her tone. "He came to us with our beautiful Zoey, blessing us with the most incredible gift, and we'll forever be grateful. She's been the brightest blessing of our lives and I will never apologize for that."

Ellis didn't sense any subterfuge from the woman or guilt. She truly believed what she was saying, but why would Zoey run away from a happy home?

Dakota picked up his mental thread without missing a beat. "Let's set that aside for a minute. Help us to understand why Zoey was so anxious to get away from your *blessed* home that she ended up wrecking in her haste to escape?"

Fresh tears filled Barbara-Jean's eyes as she broke down. "We never wanted her to know she was adopted but she found those blasted papers in Ned's desk. I told him we should've burned them but Ned insisted that we keep them, saying they were official documents that Zoey might need at some point in her life. I told him it was unnecessary because Zoey's life was with us, on the farm, not out with the worldly people."

"Zoey was upset at discovering she was adopted?" Dakota asked.

"Terribly," Barbara-Jean admitted mournfully. "I think her heart was shattered. She was so angry with us for keeping that secret. I thought it would pass but then we woke up one morning to find the car and Zoey gone. We've been looking for her ever since she left. You have to believe me, we were devastated to learn she'd gone and we were worried sick. Zoey had never left the farm in her life. She had no idea what horrors awaited her out there."

"The car was registered to a man who died years ago. Why did you have possession of the vehicle?"

"The car belonged to The Congregation," Barbara-Jean said. "Everyone had access to it, should they need it."

"But it hasn't been registered to anyone in five years. The original owner is listed as deceased."

"The car was gifted to The Congregation and Zachariah handles the finances and paperwork. You'll have to ask him about the registration details. All I know is that when we needed transportation, we all had use of the vehicle but we rarely went to town unless it couldn't be avoided."

"And why is that?" Dakota asked.

"Because worldly people are a contagion of the spirit. Godlessness can be catching. It's best to limit contact."

Dakota looked like she was biting her tongue in half and Ellis couldn't blame her.

"So Zoey ran away because she discovered she was adopted?" Ellis summarized.

"Yes."

But was that the whole story? Seemed likely not. Zoey didn't seem the dramatic type. "Are you sure that's all that sent her running?"

"What are you implying?" Barbara-Jean asked sharply, her gaze narrowing. "If you're asking if we abused our daughter, you're out of line."

"You've never hit Zoey?" Dakota asked.

"In anger? Absolutely not. But discipline is not abuse. We disciplined our child, in accordance with God's law, and I won't be made to feel as if I've done anything wrong. It's our job as parents to raise our child to be kind, loving and respectful of God's word."

"And what does that mean exactly?" Ellis pressed. "Because some of the Old Testament stuff is pretty harsh."

"I'm not going to justify my parenting decisions. I've answered your questions and now I wish to see my husband or a lawyer. One or the other."

Barbara-Jean was finished cooperating and there was little point in keeping her. The officer returned the woman to her cell while Ellis and Dakota traded notes.

"She's clearly rigidly religious and some of those types of people have been known to be physically abusive in the name of God, so maybe we need to go back to Zoey and see if she remembers being abused at the hands of her adopted parents," Dakota said, scribbling down her notes. "What do you think?"

"Agreed. Although her husband seems more levelheaded, more mild-mannered. I'm not getting a killer vibe from either of them, though."

"Me, either. More's the pity," Dakota quipped. "That woman could do with a little time behind bars. I think it might humble her into being a nicer person."

He chuckled. "Maybe, or it might make her meaner. I've seen it go both ways."

Dakota sighed. "Well, at least we have a lead. Shilah is running background on this Deakins character. In the meantime, we don't have anything we can hold the Grojans for so we're going to have to let them go but they aren't leaving with Zoey. I'll take that as a small victory."

"We gotta take them where we find them, right?"

She smiled in response, adding, "I'd like a guard posted to keep them from having access for the time being. Until we know more about the quality of Zoey's childhood, I don't want them around her."

"Fair enough," Ellis agreed, pausing before sharing, "You're still sharp as a tack in interrogations. Impressive."

Dakota shifted against his praise, as if uncomfortable with how it made her feel, and he immediately wished he'd kept his feelings to himself, but she moved on quickly, saying, "I'm going to head back to the hotel and do some more research on this Congregation and see what I can find. I'll let you know if anything important pops up."

"Great. I'll let the officers know they can release the Grojans for now," he said, taking her lead.

Dakota didn't linger. She scooped up her notebook and left him behind.

The picture of cold efficiency.

Damn it, Ellis, should've kept your mouth shut.

* * *

It was such a small thing—a compliment between colleagues—so why was her heart hammering to a wild beat inside her chest?

It shouldn't matter what Ellis thought about her personally. She didn't live for or need his praise. And yet, a sweet warmth spread beneath her breastbone at the simple words as if it *did* matter to her how he felt about her.

Get a grip, you're embarrassing yourself.

She detoured to the grocery store to pick up something to eat—the hotel room had a tiny refrigerator and she disliked eating out too much when on assignment—and then after changing, headed to the hotel gym.

The best way to calm a disordered mind was to sweat out the extra noise.

Shilah was still running background so she had time to kill.

She went straight to the treadmill, popped her headphones in and set the pace. The best thing about most hotels was that it was easy to find an open station on the gym floor. Most people didn't go on vacation to sweat unless it was beneath the hot sun while sipping a margarita. The only people using the gym were like her, traveling for work, and on the job.

There was only one other person, another woman, using the facility and after perfunctory smiles, they were happy to leave each other in peace.

The treadmill helped her to think. There was something calming about the rhythmic motion of her feet slapping the high-grade rubber belt as her pace ate up imaginary miles.

The case immediately came to mind. As much as it would be an easy win if the Grojans were guilty of murdering Nayeli, her gut didn't support that theory. They might have extremist beliefs, but they didn't give off a killer vibe.

And her gut was always right.

Sweat rolled down her temple as the first wave of heat flushed through her body. She welcomed the punishing pace she set for herself, accepting the discomfort of fatigued muscles because it meant she was feeling something.

She started running after the death of her sister. Not on purpose, but one morning a week after Mikaya was found brutally murdered, she stepped outside her mother's house and, suddenly, she was running barefoot down the dusty road, numb to the fact that rocks were digging into her feet and tearing her soles. Tears had streamed down her cheeks as her rage and grief coalesced into fuel for her muscles and running had helped her manage the pain churning inside her.

After that moment, she became addicted to the release that running provided for her emotionally. She ran track in high school and later college, but now, she laced up to deal with stress that came with the job.

The other woman finished her run, wiped down her machine and left. Minutes later, a large man entered, choosing a treadmill uncomfortably close to her own when there were plenty of available machines.

Dakota's sense of awareness sharpened, dampening her enjoyment of her run. "You're quite the runner," he observed, trying to make conversation while he started his own jog. "You staying here at the hotel?"

Dakota ignored the man, giving him the cold shoulder to communicate that she wasn't here to chitchat, but at the same time, she was highly aware of his every movement. The red flags were flapping and Dakota never ignored what was flapping in her face.

"Oh, I see how it is, too good to talk to me, huh?"

Dakota swore beneath her breath and cut her run short. Shutting down the machine, she hopped off and wiped down, going to the hang bar to do some quick pull-ups before returning to her room.

One of the largest failings of ingrained patriarchal conditioning was women's reluctance to appear rude, which often caused them to ignore that inner voice when something wasn't right. Dakota didn't give two shits about seeming rude. Maybe if Mikaya had been a bitch to whoever killed her, she'd still be here.

From her peripheral vision, she caught movement and saw that the man had left his machine to head her way. His energy was arrogant and mildly predatory. Dakota summed him up within minutes. Older, traditionally good-looking, accustomed to getting what he wanted because of his looks, probably frequently told women to "smile more" because their worth was based solely on how screwable they appeared to him, and his ego was bigger than his sense of self-preservation.

And he thought Dakota was an easy target because she was a petite woman alone in a deserted gym.

Wrong.

"I love a woman with muscle," he said, openly leering at Dakota as if ogling a complete stranger without invitation was appreciated. "Pretty strong for such a little girl. I bet you're tight all over."

Final straw.

Dakota met his gaze, staring him down. "If I'd wanted to talk to you, I would've when you first interrupted my gym time. Take the hint and leave me alone."

He chuckled as if Dakota's firm warning was cute. "I find women like you just need a man to show them how to be soft, how to be feminine. You don't want too much muscle, sweetheart. A man wants a soft lady to cuddle up with at night."

"Last warning, mind your business, and stay out of mine."

"Or what, Pocahontas?" He made the mistake of trying to caress her cheek as if it was his right to touch her and Dakota reacted with the lightning-quick reflexes of a feral cat. She snatched his hand away from her jaw and cranked his fingers in the opposite direction they were made to go and drove him straight to his knees. He garbled a sharp yell, the agony keeping him locked in place as one more move and she'd snap his fingers in two.

"I get that you're from a generation that embraced casual misogyny, classism and blatant racism but let this serve as an educating moment—if a woman isn't interested in your attention, don't force it on her. Also, Pocahontas was a real person who suffered unimaginable horror as a child at the hands of a white man, who probably looked a lot like you, so keep her name out of your mouth unless it's spoken with the respect it's due. Now, my guess is that you've gotten away with this kind of disgusting behavior in the past, which has emboldened you—"

The man interrupted her with a wild swing with his free hand, shouting, "You stupid whore!" landing a lucky glance against her cheek, but it was only enough to throw her momentarily. Dakota snapped the fingers in her grip, breaking the bones like cracking a carrot in half, sending him writhing to the floor.

"Never mind. You're too stupid to learn," she said, rubbing at her bruised cheek. "You messed with the wrong girl. I'm a BIA agent and you assaulted a federal officer. Hope you didn't have plans for the evening because your ass is going to jail."

The man groaned, cradling his mangled fingers, and Dakota used the gym phone to call the front desk for security.

As the man was hauled off by two burly uniformed security officers, Dakota was surprised to see Ellis walk into the gym facility, apparently with the same idea of blowing off some steam, but when he saw Dakota, his expression darkened. "What the hell happened here?" he asked, his gaze going straight to the gathering bruise on her cheek.

She shook her head. "Nothing. Some jerkwad thinking he could get handsy with me. He'll think twice about doing that again."

"Did you break his fingers?" Ellis asked with a knowing expression.

"Yep."

"You okay?"

There was that warmth again. She stuffed it down and away, jerking a nod, shrugging as if it was no big deal. "I'm fine. I'm more embarrassed than anything that he got a lucky shot. I was off my game."

A smile curved the corner of his mouth, as if he were impressed and proud, even if he wasn't supposed to acknowledge that kind of thing between them. "Go put some ice on that bruise," he said, shaking his head. "You don't want to scare Zoey tomorrow."

She grinned in spite of her resolve to keep it professionally distant between them, then winced as the bruised flesh protested the motion.

Ouch. Ice was a good idea.

"See you tomorrow."

"Bright and early, Mike Tyson," he quipped, heading for the treadmill.

She chuckled and left him to his workout.

Chapter 6

Zoey wouldn't be available until later in the afternoon, so Dakota and Ellis decided to convene in Ellis's room for a Zoom meeting with Shilah.

Dakota, with a faint purple-and-blue bruise subtly discoloring her cheek from the gym altercation the previous day, opted to ignore her better judgment and brought along Ellis's favorite muffins—poppy seed. She did this as a self-assurance that she wasn't treating Ellis any differently than she would other colleagues in the field. Admittedly, the choice of poppy seed might have been slightly indulgent.

Ellis's eyes sparkled at the sight of the muffins. "How did you read my mind?" he inquired, eagerly reaching for one.

"You've never encountered a poppy seed muffin you didn't want to devour," Dakota said. "No matter the place or its source. I've watched you eat a muffin from a gas station convenience store, even when it was past its sell-by date."

"Are you implying my mind is easy to figure out?" he quipped, relishing each bite of the muffin with unabashed enjoyment.

The essence of Ellis lay in his steadfast appreciation for life's simple pleasures. While far from a simple man, the things that brought him joy were endearingly uncomplicated: the innocent sound of a child's laughter, the serene blue skies on a summer day and the taste of a freshly baked poppy seed muffin.

Dispelling a moment of nostalgia, Dakota pivoted toward the task at hand, opening her laptop for the scheduled Zoom meeting with Shilah. "I was thinking last night—"

"Was that before or after your impressive Special Ops takedown of that dumbass in the gym?" Ellis interjected, his grin teasing.

Suppressing a chuckle, she shot back, "You have seeds in your teeth," gracefully deflating his jest. "And for the record, he got what he deserved. I regret nothing."

Her words lingered in a space where lighthearted banter met the underlying pulses of their shared past, a balance that felt dangerously delicate. It was too easy to fall into a comfortable place with Ellis and that's what made her pull back.

"How's your boss gonna feel about it? The paperwork will probably be hitting his desk today."

Dakota laughed ruefully because she didn't know how Isaac would react but she still didn't regret a thing. Some men remained predators until someone made them stop. Dakota was happy to be the stopping point. "He thought it was okay to touch me without my consent. He learned the hard way it wasn't."

"No argument from me. I'm kinda tempted to get the surveillance footage just so I can watch the show."

"Surveillance footage of what?" Shilah broke in, sliding into her window screen. "What am I missing?"

"Just Dakota breaking fingers and righting social injustices one misogynist at a time," Ellis quipped.

Shilah laughed. "Well, that sounds like fun. What happened?"

Dakota rolled her eyes, giving Shilah the quick summary, and when she finished Shilah was hooting with appreciation and support. "Yesss, girl! Although, I probably wouldn't have stopped at his fingers. The man would've been sporting a broken jaw, too."

Dakota chuckled. "Well, hopefully, he's learned a valuable lesson and it'll encourage him to be less of a shit person in the future."

"Not likely, too old at this point, but worth it, I say," Shilah said.

"You're probably right," Dakota agreed, adding, "Still not sorry."

"I don't blame you. All right, I did some digging into your Zachariah Deakins but I don't think you're going to like what I found."

"What do you mean?" Dakota asked, frowning.

"I mean, he's seemingly clean as a whistle. Not even an outstanding parking ticket. I was really hoping to find some tax evasion or something but nothing juicy. It's pretty boring. Definitely not the picture of a crazy cult leader getting ready to pass out spiked punch."

Shilah put up a picture of Zachariah Deakins on the screen and Dakota agreed. He looked like the host of a children's television show about nature, meditation and respecting the earth.

"I don't trust anyone who can pull off a haircut that should've been made illegal after the seventies," Ellis said. "I mean, c'mon, who is this guy? That bushy beard should be a crime in itself. There's probably birds nesting in that thing."

Dakota barked a laugh, forgetting how funny Ellis could be. She sobered quickly. "Looks can be deceiving. We have an address for The Congregation. We'll have to schedule a meeting."

"You're not worried about leaving Zoey alone?" Shilah asked.

Ellis quipped, "Even if we didn't have an officer on guard at her room, I doubt anyone could get past Dr. Patel. The man is very protective of his patients."

Dakota nodded. "No one is getting past the good doc. We're going to talk to Zoey later this afternoon. Hopefully, we can get a better idea of why she was truly running away in the first place."

"Didn't the mom say it was because she discovered she was adopted?" Shilah asked.

"Yeah, but that seems flimsy. I don't know, something seems off. I'm hoping she can trust us enough to tell us what really happened," Dakota said.

"How's her head injury?" Shilah asked.

"Better each day. I think she's holding back because she's afraid of something," Ellis answered. "She's really a sweet kid. Now that we know a bit more about The Congregation, it makes sense that she seems a little naive. The kid has lived her entire life isolated on a farm with a bunch of people who believe outsiders are bad."

"Exactly, so why would such a sheltered kid run like a bat out of hell away from the only life she's ever known?" Dakota pondered, then decided, "Yeah, something's not adding up."

"I emailed you both the Deakins background details. You can go over it and see if anything stands out that I might've missed."

"Thanks, Shilah," Dakota said. "We'll be in touch."

Shilah waved and ended the meeting.

Both Ellis and Dakota took a minute to peruse the file from their email. Ellis asked, "Ever wonder what makes a person go from completely typical to 'I think I want to create my own cult'? Do they wake up one morning, eat some cornflakes and decide, 'Today is the day I walk away from normal society and rewrite the rules to suit my personal vision of how the world should be run.' Honestly, if it were me, I think I'd come up with a better name than The Congregation."

"Is that so? And what name would you pick?" Dakota had to ask.

The second she saw his immediate grin, followed by his answer, "Ellisville, of course," she didn't even try to stop the laugh even though nothing about their case was funny.

Still, it felt good to joke with Ellis again.

Even if it shouldn't.

That laugh, her smile, the way the corners of her eyes crinkled with true amusement, it was like a lightning bolt straight to his heart.

Man, their breakup still hurt. He missed her more than he was allowed to say. She left for a good reason but he should've been honest about why he didn't fight to keep her.

No one ever talked about how being noble sometimes sucked ass. He'd like to say that nobility had kept him from chasing after her, but that would be a lie.

His pride had stuck in his craw, too.

He'd been embarrassed by his lack of control and scared of being too much like his old man to drag Dakota down with him while he figured things out.

But, damn, the last two years evaporated in the sunshine of that smile.

Dakota sobered and their gazes met. That electricity that seemed to spark whenever they were around each other started to snap. He wanted to kiss her. The pull to taste her lips, to feel that familiar brush of her soft mouth across his, created a physical ache that shouldn't be real but he felt in his bones.

Shake it off. Don't blow it. She doesn't want you and she's made herself pretty clear on that score. Focus on the case.

It took superhuman strength to pretend that he wasn't feeling a damn thing as he pulled away on the guise of cleaning up his muffin crumbs, saying, "All right, so we have about an hour before we can head to the hospital. I'm going to run some errands beforehand and meet you there, yeah?"

Dakota blinked as if momentarily caught off guard by his not-so-subtle hint that it was time for her to go but she recovered quickly. She gathered her laptop and stuffed it in her bag with a short nod. "Yes, sounds good," she said and quickly left.

The energy between them was palpable. There was no way she didn't feel it but she'd made it very clear that she wasn't interested in the reunion tour of Ellis and Dakota and he'd never disrespect her boundaries.

He liked his fingers the way they were.

Speaking of, he wasn't joking when he said he'd love to see the surveillance footage. The thing was, Dakota was a badass. She didn't look it but she was tougher than anyone gave her credit for. A compact package of lean muscle and hard attitude with a mouth that—yeah, best not to revisit those memories.

But the memories were riding him hard.

His body buzzed with pent-up energy with nowhere to go. Was it too late to run down to the gym and punish himself with a quick workout? No, he couldn't take the chance of running into Dakota when he said he was going to run errands. He'd just have to let it dissipate on its own, knuckling down on the urge to catch up with Dakota and spill his guts in the hopes that she'd forgive him and they could repair what he'd broken.

Ah, hell, what a pipe dream and a waste of time. Dakota wasn't like any woman he'd ever known. She didn't waver, didn't give second chances, and once her mind was made up, it was a steel trap that nothing could force open.

Give it up, man. What you had was great, but it's gone. Focus on the case.

Grabbing his keys, he resigned himself to hitting the mall. Perhaps he could find something for Zoey. Everyone liked getting gifts—especially sheltered kids who rarely got chocolate and never left their compound.

He didn't know the details of Zoey's life on the compound but it was hard to imagine it as anything less than dull. Kids were meant to go to Disneyland, have sleepovers, play sports or something. Childhood was over in a flash. Why shorten the experience by sucking all the joy out of it?

Not that he'd know what it was like to have an idyllic childhood but maybe that's why he felt so strongly about it. He knew what it was like to live in fear, not knowing if that uneven footfall down the hallway would stop at your door, as the old man swayed on his feet staring into your darkened room, deciding whether or not he had the wherewithal to deliver a random beating to the kid shaking silently in his bed.

Had Zoey's childhood been like his? Was the Grojans' idea of parental love peppered with harsh discipline?

He thought of Nayeli, the young mom who'd been doing her best to be a good provider for her infant, only to have her life cut short for reasons they didn't understand yet.

His cell rang and it was a buddy still in Narcotics. He hesitated to take the call. When he was forced out and demoted, he'd cut off most ties, believing everyone had turned against him from his old division, but that'd been his pride whispering lies in his ear.

Thankfully, Harlan was a stubborn son of a bitch and he hadn't let Ellis off the hook so easily. If anything, the man had stalked and harassed him until he agreed to talk, ultimately saving their friendship.

Picking up, he answered, "This better not be a call bragging about your latest case or as soon as I'm back in town, I'm going to kick your scrawny ass."

"Dream big, kid," Harlan returned with good humor. "You couldn't kick my ass if I came to you half-broken and drunk from the night before."

Maybe so. Harlan was about ten years older than him but he was built like a brick shithouse. The man was unnaturally strong, an ox with a badge and laughing eyes that perps often underestimated right before he rearranged their face.

"So, how's it going?" he asked, going straight to the very topic Ellis didn't want to touch.

Ellis deliberately misunderstood. "Not much to go on just yet. The girl is still suffering from head trauma so her memory is spotty but we've got some leads to chase down."

"Not the case, dumbass. Your girl."

Harlan was also there when it all went sour with Dakota. He also was a secret romantic with a bleeding heart. The man should really get a hobby.

"She's not my girl," Ellis reminded Harlan. "Just a colleague and it's going fine. Dakota is a consummate professional."

"Aw, c'mon, don't feed me that crap. You've been holding a torch for your lady since the day you crawled out of her life with your tail between your legs. You can't tell me that the second you have a chance to actually say your piece, you've gotten all tongue-tied."

"What can I say, I'm a shy guy," Ellis quipped darkly, to which Harlan called immediate bullshit.

"And I'm the pope," Harlan countered derisively. "You've always been in love with the sound of your own voice so there's no way you've suddenly found the value in silence."

"People change," Ellis said, but Harlan wasn't buying it, nor should he because Ellis was lying. "Look, even if I was of a mind to crack that book open, Dakota ain't having it. She's not interested and I don't blame her. It's been two years, she's moved on, and I respect her for it. We're colleagues working together and that's all we'll ever be again. I'm good with it. Really, I am."

"Who you trying to convince? Me or you?"

"Stop busting my balls. The day I take advice from a man who's been married and divorced three times is the day I have my head examined," Ellis groused.

"I'm exactly the person you should take advice from— I know what don't work. Each wife teaches me something different. I can't wait to find out what wife number four has to teach me."

Ellis shook his head. Harlan was impossible but you had to love the guy for his irrepressible optimism. Or was that stupidity? Sometimes it looked the same.

On a whim, Ellis asked, "Carleton mention my name at all lately?"

"Sorry, not to me," Harlan answered with a touch of understanding. He knew how badly Ellis wanted to get back to Narcotics and how Carleton was dangling that carrot. Maybe Ellis was delusional in hoping that Carleton wasn't just stringing him along so he'd stop pestering him. "Hey, what you're doing... It truly matters. Remember that. You and me both know that there ain't nothing that's going to change the flow of drugs on the streets. It's a game of whack-a-felon. But what you're doing... That shit's real. Kids, man. And you're good at it. To be honest, I think you're where you're supposed to be."

That wasn't what Ellis wanted to hear. Frustrated, he exhaled and bit down on his urge to snap at his friend. Instead, he said, "Hey, man, I gotta go. I'm supposed to meet Dakota at the hospital in an hour and still have to run an errand. Stay safe out there."

"Yeah, yeah, of course. Right back atcha."

They clicked off and Ellis fought the wave of anger that always threatened to swamp him when he thought of how he'd been kicked from the job he loved the most.

He didn't believe for a second he was where he belonged and it pissed him off when Harlan said shit like that.

He was doing everything he could to get back to Narcotics—and nothing was going to stop him from getting there.

Chapter 7

Dakota and Ellis, united by a shared mission yet carrying unspoken memories, headed toward the hospital's private room section, their steps shadowed by the looming visit to The Congregation compound the next day.

A knot of anxiety twisted in Dakota's stomach as they prepared to unveil harsh truths to Zoey, a girl who'd already been through enough in her young life. Their goal was clear: navigate the difficult waters of revelation with utmost empathy and care.

Upon being cleared by Dr. Patel, whose firm reminder of Zoey's vulnerability echoed in their ears, they ventured toward her room, where the security, a silent sentinel, verified their credentials before permitting entry.

Zoey, her eyes momentarily brightening at their appearance, greeted them with a small smile, her spirit temporarily lifted by Ellis's predictable gift-bearing.

He handed her a soft, stuffed raccoon, its neck adorned with a shiny red bow, offering a gentle, "In my experience, something soft and cuddly goes a long way when you're feeling crummy." Ellis, always thoughtful in peculiar ways, found an odd charm in what Dakota playfully deemed "trash pandas," much to her initial amusement. "I hope you like *trash pandas*. I feel like they have more character than a regular teddy bear."

Dakota smothered a laugh, only because she'd given Ellis a hard time for picking a raccoon of all animals, saying a teddy bear was traditionally cuddlier. Then she'd quipped, "No one looks at a trash panda and says that looks soft and sweet and lovable. No, they usually think about throwing something to get it out of their trash can."

To which Ellis had countered, "Speak for yourself. Raccoons are just misunderstood night bandits with a bad rap."

"They bite," Dakota returned flatly.

He'd shrugged. "So do bears—and bears do a lot more damage."

As Zoey clutched the raccoon, Dakota, despite earlier jesting at Ellis's unconventional choice, surrendered a genuine smile, recognizing his uncanny ability to read the emotional pulse of the young victim. Zoey's approval—"I love it!"—further validated Ellis's gift choice.

Dakota smiled, shaking her head with a subtle motion, realizing Ellis had the jump on her when it came to understanding the emotional nuance of their injured teen victim and she'd just have to go with whatever he thought was best in this case.

The room, dimly lit and carrying the faint sterile scent characteristic of hospitals, seemed to pause as Ellis broached the topic of Zoey's healing, his voice an attempt to blend cheerfulness and admiration. "The doc says you passed all your tests with flying colors. Of all his patients, he said you're top of the leaderboard. Personally, I think you must be some kind of superhero with how fast you're healing. Pretty incredible."

Zoey's innocent curiosity surfaced with, "What's a leaderboard? Is it a sport thing? Father Zach didn't approve of open competitiveness. He said competition created negative energy." Her upbringing under Father Zach's strict, competition-adverse doctrine shadowed her understanding of such concepts. The shared glance between Dakota and Ellis carried unspoken agreement: it was time to delve deeper.

Father Zach. Cue the all-over ick shudder. Dakota shared a look with Ellis, silently giving him the cue to start the real reason they were there.

"Yeah, it's a sport thing. Suffice to say, you're winning," Ellis answered as he dragged a chair to Zoey's bedside. At Zoey's grin, he prompted, "Tell me more about Father Zach and what it was like to grow up with The Congregation."

"What do you want to know?"

"Anything you'd like to share," Dakota offered. "It's something we're not familiar with and we'd like to know how it's different. Such as... You mentioned you were homeschooled. Did you enjoy it?"

The purposefully soft entry into their questioning served its purpose as Zoey's shoulders lost some of their tension as she nodded with a genuine smile. "I didn't mind it. We had one schoolroom so it was all of the children at the same time but the older kids were able to help the younger kids and I liked that part. We're not supposed to have favorites but Georgia and Wesley were my little shadows. They're six and seven."

"Are you the oldest child in the Congregation?"

Zoey nodded, admitting with a touch a guilt creeping into her gaze, "I wasn't thinking about how my leaving would affect the little kids who look up to me and I didn't mean to crash the car. My actions were selfish and I'm embarrassed by what I've done. My parents must be so ashamed of me."

"We all make mistakes, kiddo," Ellis said, sharing, "One time I stole a tractor and drove it down the street because my buddy dared me. Definitely not my finest hour—or my best driving, either. I crashed into a neighboring fence and part of my punishment was spending my summer repairing it."

A giggle escaped Zoey, even if she knew he was commiserating to cheer her up. Even with the past between them, Dakota was humbled by Ellis's innate ability to empathize.

Dakota shared a smile with Zoey, saying, "Your parents seem to love you very much. I'm sure they're more relieved that you're okay than concerned about what happened to an old car."

Ellis nodded, his easy smile fading as he tackled the bigger issue. "Zoey, I need to ask you something that might be difficult to answer. I need you to know that you're not in trouble and nothing you say will be used against you, okay?"

"Okay," Zoey acknowledged in a small voice. "What do you need to know?"

"Did your parents or anyone within The Congregation ever hurt you or any of the other children?" Ellis asked.

Zoey's expression of shock was genuine. "Hurt us? How? No."

Dakota explained gently, "Sometimes in our line of work, we see organizations such as yours that normalize the abuse of children, both sexually and physically, and we want to make sure that's not happening where you live."

Zoey shook her head vehemently. "No, nothing like that. No one has ever hurt me like that. I swear it."

Ellis absorbed her answer, murmuring, "That's good to hear," but added, "When you first saw your parents, you looked scared. Are you sure you're telling us everything? I promise we can protect you if you're in danger or afraid."

Zoey swallowed, hesitating for a minute, chewing on the side of her cheek as if trying to decide how much to share.

"My mom… She has a temper but she's never hurt me like what you're asking. My dad has never even spanked me."

Dakota was relieved but surprised. Switching gears, she said, "Your dad said that you found something that upset you. Can you talk about that?"

Zoey nodded, tears welling in her eyes, her cheeks flushing as she admitted, "After everything that's happened, it seems so awfully terrible on my part but I was so upset I couldn't stand being there another minute. Everything I'd ever known felt like a lie and I needed to get away." She paused a minute, staring down at her fidgeting fingers. "I never meant for all of this to happen, though. I should've taken a minute to breathe and calm down before I let my emotions get the better of me. Father Zach is always saying I need to be more mindful of my actions." She looked guilty, adding, "Sometimes, I can be very thoughtless and a terrible example to all of the littles that look up to me."

Dakota didn't believe that for a second and was instantly defensive on Zoey's behalf. "I'm sure that's not the case," she assured the girl, making sure Zoey didn't take on unnecessary blame. "Big emotions sometimes bubble up and cause us to do things that we might not otherwise."

As the words left her mouth, she instantly flashed to the night that ultimately destroyed her relationship with Ellis. The sound of shattered crystal echoed in her memory and she had to drag her focus back to the moment. Forcing a gentle smile, she reached out and squeezed Zoey's hand. "What matters is that you're okay," she reminded her.

Ellis agreed, though the somber set of his jaw suggested that he remembered that night, too. It was the elephant in the room between them no matter where they went—reminding them that some things were too big to ignore for long.

* * *

Shame over his actions from that night washed over him. His anger management therapist always reminded him that no one could go back in time and change something that already happened so beating yourself up over what's been done was a waste of energy. Focus on moving forward, changing behavior for the future, was the win.

But it still didn't lessen the guilt.

He'd lost the love of his life that night.

C'mon, man, there's a time and place and this ain't it.

Shaking off his inner turmoil, he focused on Zoey. The poor kid was twisting herself inside and out for acting out over something traumatic. He knew better but he was starting to feel a soft spot for the girl and he felt protective over her well-being. "Zoey, I want you to know that we're not going to let anything bad happen to you. We're here to protect you. You know that, right?"

She nodded.

Ellis drew a deep breath, preparing to drop a bomb on her. "But we'll also always be honest with you, even if it's hard. Do you understand that?"

Zoey nodded again, though she seemed apprehensive. "I know you say it's nothing to worry about but resources in The Congregation are shared with everyone. We only have two cars and now we're down to one." She shook her head with a heart-broken expression that made Ellis want to slay dragons on her behalf. "Leaving like I did was so selfish. My parents are probably embarrassed, too."

Ellis stopped her from spiraling with a grave shake of his head. "That ain't it, kiddo. I can promise you that the car is the least of your parents' concerns."

"What do you mean?"

Ellis drew a deep breath, meeting Zoey's gaze. "I'm

going to need you to be brave and strong because I have to tell you something that's going to change your life going forward."

Zoey paled but bravely waited for the other shoe to drop.

Ellis shared a look with Dakota before he continued. "The reason we're here isn't because you crashed your car. Seventeen years ago, a six-week-old infant girl was kidnapped from her mother in the dead of night. Whoever took the baby also killed that poor young mother. She was only nineteen, working as a housekeeper at a Whitefish hotel. Authorities never found the baby girl." He paused and Dakota finished for him.

"Until you crashed your car and ended up here."

"Turns out, you're that baby girl that disappeared seventeen years ago," Ellis said.

"What?" Zoey shook her head in denial, unable to wrap her head around the information. Ellis didn't blame her—it was a lot to take in, especially after everything else that'd happened. "No, that can't be. There has to be a mistake."

"Hospitals take blood and fingerprints of newborns when they're born. When emergency personnel brought you to the hospital with no identity, they ran your DNA. It flagged the FBI database. It's definitely, without a doubt, you," Dakota explained, gentling her tone. "DNA doesn't lie."

"I don't understand," she said, her voice barely above a whisper, as if invisible hands were curled around her throat. "What are you saying? My parents…did they…" Her voice caught and she struggled to get the words out. "M-my parents…"

Dakota rushed to ease the panic she saw building in Zoey's gaze. "Honey, we don't know enough about your parents' involvement to say for sure. They could be victims, too, if they didn't know anything about how you came to be available for adoption. Let's not jump to conclusions just yet, okay?"

"That's why you asked me if they were abusive?" Zoey asked.

"Well, we had to cover all our bases," Ellis said. "There are still a lot of questions that need to be answered but when you were strong enough to hear it, we wanted to be honest with you about your situation."

Zoey jerked a nod, visibly gathering her courage. She clutched the stuffed raccoon to her chest, asking in a tremulous voice, "Can you tell me about my biological mom?"

It was a big deal to discover you were adopted and then in the next breath that your biological mother was murdered, but Zoey was brave and strong and as far as Dakota was concerned, handling the news like a boss.

Unexpected tears jumped to Dakota's eyes as she looked away under the guise of pulling up the one photograph they had of Nayeli Swiftwater from the file on her phone. She handed the phone to Zoey and watched as the girl laid eyes on the woman who'd given her life.

After a pregnant pause, Zoey looked up, her eyes sparkling with tears as she half laughed, half cried as she said, "I have her eyes," and Dakota nodded in agreement, realizing it was the first thing she'd noticed, too, but couldn't say anything.

"She was beautiful," Ellis said. "And so are you."

But even more important than that, Dakota said, "She loved you more than anything—and we're going to find out who did this. I promise."

Chapter 8

Dakota's grip tightened on the steering wheel, her knuckles turning an eerie shade of white as the car sped through the seemingly endless stretch of road toward Stevensville while Ellis sat in the passenger seat, glancing her way every now and again, his sharp gaze flickering with a mixture of trepidation and concern.

Agreeing to ignore the past and only focus on the here and now was like sliding a bucket beneath a dripping pipe and expecting the bucket not to overflow at some point.

Shouldn't they at least get some things out in the open, share apologies even as a start? Although, Dakota might say she had nothing to apologize for—and maybe she was right—but he'd sure like to know what was brewing behind those dark eyes.

Dakota was the kind of person who internalized her emotions, whereas he wore his feelings on his sleeve. When they'd been together, they'd served as a complementary yin and yang, balancing each other out. An unpleasant memory came to him—she'd told him on day one that she was seeing someone but he hadn't seen any evidence to that claim.

Not that he expected her to parade her man in front of him—Dakota was too private for that kind of show—but she hadn't mentioned her relationship since that day, which led him to believe she'd been lying.

And why would she lie?

Because she wanted him to feel that she'd moved on? To make him jealous? Maybe both. How screwed up was he that he took that possibility as a positive sign that she wasn't over him. *Pretty damn screwy.*

Frankly, he was surprised Dakota agreed to carpool when he'd half expected her to meet him at the compound, leaving him in the dust like she'd been doing this whole time.

The tension in the vehicle was palpable, underscored by the distant murmurs of the radio, spouting occasional weather updates and soft rock tunes.

"We could talk about it—" he ventured but she shut him down real quick.

"Unless it's about the case, there's no need to dredge up the past," she cut in with the short, polite smile she reserved for waitstaff. "No need to add water to a dried-up patch of mud."

"I guess not," he conceded, though he was just keeping the peace. He wanted to talk about it but if she wasn't ready, it would just be him talking to an unresponsive brick wall.

Throwing him a conciliatory bone, Dakota said, "I had my doubts but I think we're working well together. You're not half-bad as a partner."

That was high praise given their painful history. Hell, he'd take it. He released a short chuckle, forcefully shelving his feelings for the time being. "You're not half-bad yourself. I was worried you might've gone soft since I saw you last."

She barked a short laugh that ended with an indelicate snort. "Sure. Just ask Mr. Touch-A-Lot how soft I am. My boss said the guy needed surgery to reset his hand."

Ellis felt no sympathy. "Well-deserved," he said, but even as they bantered, there was a pocket of pain that remained lodged between them and he didn't know how much longer he could pretend it wasn't there.

They fell back into silence as Dakota's car ate up the miles between them and Stevensville, pulling into the compound property before noon. A wooden painted sign advertising fresh fruit, vegetables and canned goods directed them down a long dirt driveway. Ponderosa pines flanked the driveway, swaying in the cool autumn breeze. The crisp scent of pine, spruce and fir rode on the fine layer of dust from the tires as they rolled slowly into the compound.

The Congregation's compound, enshrouded in lush greenery, radiated a peaceful, idyllic ambiance that belied the underlying suspicion that both Ellis and Dakota shared about communal living in a cult-like environment. Some might say they were jaded but they'd seen too much in their line of work not to be.

"One thing's for sure, it's not hard on the eyes," Ellis murmured, surveying the area, taking in every detail, realizing that the compound had possibly served as a summer camp, back when it was in fashion to send your kids off for a few weeks in the care of complete strangers. The wooden cabins were equally spaced apart and a large main hall veered off to the left. They parked and headed to the tables laden with seasonal vegetables and fruits, as well as rows of canned items.

"Welcome to Eden's Bounty," a sturdy middle-aged woman of Hispanic descent with soft brown eyes greeted them with a gentle, engaging smile as they approached her table. "My name's Lina. Are you looking for anything in particular? We have butternut squash that'll melt in your mouth and honey crisp apples that will make you see stars. We also offer samples of anything you see here."

"Actually, we're here on official business," Dakota said

as she flashed her credentials. "We'd like to speak with Zachariah Deakins."

Lina's smile faltered in confusion but she nodded, flagging down a passing member. "Howie? Can you take our guests to see Father Zach?"

Howie, a tall and lanky man of roughly seventy, could have passed for a decade younger if not for his wild, coarse white hair. He nodded and gestured for them to follow, saying good-naturedly, "Promise me you won't leave until you try our homemade grape jelly. Or take some dried figs for the road." Patting his trim stomach, he added, "Good stuff. Keeps you regular."

"I'll keep that in mind," Ellis returned with a congenial smile as they walked to the main building. Howie opened the wooden door as it creaked on its hinges, gesturing for them to follow. The hall was busy with various people doing individual jobs, while the sound of children playing echoed off the thick walls.

They detoured to another room where the smell of incense pricked his nose and a group of people sat on ornate matted squares while another man, similar to Howie, sat cross-legged in a meditative pose, breathing in and out in a measured and purposeful way.

A burning stick of Nag Champa incense clouded the air with a single curling ribbon of scented smoke from a brass dragon holder while a gurgling water fountain created a calming white noise that immediately reminded Ellis's bladder of the long drive.

It was a peaceful room if you liked that sort of thing.

Howie bent down and whispered in the man's ear and then said to Ellis and Dakota, "He'll be with you in a few minutes. Intentional prayer is nearly finished."

Intentional prayer? That's a new one.

The short delay enabled them to observe as the man finished whatever it was they were doing. While Howie and Zachariah Deakins were likely similar in age and build, there was something about Deakins that was wildly different.

Ellis wasn't the woo-woo type but Deakins definitely had something about him, like an aura of energy that commanded respect yet at the same time elicited calm, which Ellis found distinctly dangerous. He was the kind of man who could sell ice cubes to an Inuit.

It was men with this particular gift that often turned out to be the worst kind of people.

Dakota's investigative instincts kicked into overdrive as they awaited an audience with Zachariah, a man of unassuming stature and disarmingly gentle demeanor. His long gray beard flowed like a river from his chin but his blue eyes glittered with a shrewdness that sent a chill skittering down her spine.

Ellis, always keenly perceptive, sensed it, too—an insidious undercurrent beneath Zachariah's charismatic exterior.

Or maybe they were seeing what they wanted to see. Maybe he was just a magnetic man grown weary of a broken society trying to create a better one for his pocket of people—it wasn't a crime to want better than what you had.

It would be great to be wrong, but her flagging faith in humanity put her squarely in the pessimistic side, especially when her gut turned out to be right.

Finished, Zachariah murmured, "Namaste," bowing low and dismissing the group. As the people filed out of the room, Zachariah climbed to his feet, smiling in welcome. "Agent Foster, Agent Vaughn." Zachariah's voice was smooth, honeyed and a particularly low dulcet that aimed to relax and disarm. "Welcome to our home. How may I help you?"

Dakota took the lead. "Is there somewhere we could talk in private?"

"Of course, though we hide nothing here. All of The Congregation are equal as we shoulder the burden and the bounty of our people. However, we have a room over here if *you* would feel more comfortable."

"Yes, I think that would be best," Dakota said, smothering that all-over ick that threatened to further color her bias. Just because it wasn't her cup of tea didn't mean they were up to no good.

The idea of living like this gave her immediate hives.

Zachariah led them to a quiet room down a long hallway, which seemed to be the old director's office, and Ellis commented, "I can't help but notice the vibe to this place... Am I off-base or did this used to be a summer camp of some kind?"

Zachariah smiled and winked, approving of Ellis's observation. "Good eye. This place was once Camp Serenity Pines, a beloved summer spot for families and youth groups from 1969 to the late eighties. A variety of factors caused its gradual decline over the years." His expression turned somber as he continued. "A string of misfortunes, including a tragic drowning and a fire that ruined the main recreation hall, marked the end for this magnificent place. Lawsuits, financial hardships and falling enrollment buried it until we stepped in. It had been closed for five years when we bought it in 1995."

"I'm surprised it was still standing," Dakota murmured, thinking of how much it must've deteriorated in that time.

Zachariah chuckled ruefully, recalling, "Oh, it was barely standing at all. A pine beetle infestation had nearly wiped out the surrounding trees. In fact, one damaged tree had fallen and crushed one of the southern cabins to bits. We had to rebuild it from the ground up."

"So you've lived here since 1995?" Ellis asked.

"Indeed. The old place had good bones but it needed a good, firm hand to put it to rights again. Much like people. Every person here in The Congregation has come to us with the need for healing—and we deliver with God's help."

"You're Christian?" Dakota asked, surprised. "I thought, with all the meditation and incense and general vibe—" she gestured all around "—you might subscribe to a New Age metaphysical, earth-based belief structure."

"Religion is man-made. God, Great Spirit, The Creator— is everywhere and everything. I prefer the term *spiritual* rather than religious. We embrace spirituality and follow God's laws at the same time. It's a blending that works well for us."

Ellis smiled and said, "It seems very peaceful here." His smile faded as he continued, "Unfortunately, I wish we were here to buy some of your homegrown goods."

But Zachariah already knew. "Ned and Barbara-Jean Grojan. You have questions regarding their daughter, Zoey."

"Yes," Dakota responded, her expression revealing surprise. Both she and Ellis were caught off guard by Zachariah's composed demeanor, which displayed neither indignation nor shock at their statement. "How did you know?" she inquired, her curiosity piqued by his smooth transition in the conversation.

"I told you, we have no secrets here. The Grojans called as soon as they were prevented from seeing their daughter. We've been apprised of the situation from the start. How can we help so that the Grojans can reclaim their daughter and come home?"

"That depends," Ellis returned, regarding Zachariah with a keen eye. "How did the Grojans come to adopt Zoey?"

"From what I understand, the circumstances of Zoey's birth were sad and tragic but the Grojans have blessed that child with an enviable life of security, spiritual wellness and happiness. A silver lining in an otherwise heartbreaking situation."

Dakota's eyes narrowed, her breath held in anticipation, hoping Zachariah would confess to knowing something about Nayeli's murder. But instead, he said, "Drugs are the nation's scourge and the true poison afflicting our humanity. If only more resources were devoted to recovery rather than punishment, maybe stories like Zoey's mother's would have different endings."

"Are you saying you knew Nayeli Swiftwater?" Dakota asked.

"Sadly, no. I like to think that if I'd been there, she might have found salvation instead of exiting this world in the way she did," Zachariah responded.

"Murdered?" Ellis interjected, his eyebrow arching. "Because that's how she died. Someone took her life. Are you implying that drugs were involved?"

This time, Zachariah was the one caught off guard. "Murder?" he echoed, his brow furrowing in confusion. "What are you talking about? Zoey's mother was a teenage drug addict. She died from an overdose." His voice reflected genuine surprise, revealing that the notion of murder was new and unexpected to him. "I'm sorry, I need a minute to process this information. Sweet Zoey, her poor mother. There must be some kind of mix-up. This is horrifying." Zachariah bracketed his head with his fingertips, taking a full minute to collect himself. When he finally composed himself, he said, "Now I understand why the FBI and BIA are involved with the Grojans' case. I can assure you, no one from The Congregation had anything to do with the death of Zoey's biological mother. We're a peaceful people who abhor violence. Just ask anyone here and you'll find happy, wholesome families living clean lives."

Dakota's gaze fixated on Zachariah. "Ned Grojan informed us that you played a key role in facilitating Zoey's adoption. Could you provide more details on how you helped make the adoption possible?" she asked.

Zachariah nodded in agreement, though he appeared distinctly rattled. "Of course," he said, trying to maintain a composed demeanor. "I have a copy of Zoey's paperwork in my office. I'll retrieve it for you." He gestured around them, adding, "In the meantime, please feel free to converse with anyone here or try a sample of the pear jam. It's a personal favorite of mine."

"Thank you," Ellis responded, his eyes tracking Zachariah as he walked away, navigating past a long line of cabins before vanishing into the distant building.

Dakota swiveled toward Ellis, her voice taut with skepticism. "Do you think he's bluffing?"

Ellis fell into a pensive silence, pondering for what seemed like an eternity. Eventually, he shook his head, his voice carrying a trace of begrudging admiration. "I don't think so. Unless he's the most skilled liar I've encountered in a while. He seemed genuinely taken aback about Zoey's birth mother."

A tense pause lingered between them, laden with unspoken thoughts and speculations, as they wondered whether Zachariah's shock was a masterful performance or a genuine reaction.

Either way, getting their hands on Zoey's adoption papers was the first step in discovering how little Cheyenne Swiftwater became Zoey Grojan after her mother breathed her last breath.

Chapter 9

Ellis's boots crunched on the gravel as he and Dakota strolled through the compound, the sunshine casting warm, inviting light on families playing together, groups of people chatting and children laughing as they ran across the open spaces. It was a serene picture, yet a knot formed in Ellis's stomach.

"Everything here seems so…happy," Ellis murmured, his brow furrowed slightly as he took in the scene.

"Yeah, too happy," Dakota replied, glancing around suspiciously. "Nothing's ever this perfect."

"How do they pay their bills? How did they pay for this property? Where's their income coming from?" Ellis mused, his gaze resting on the outdoor market that seemed to be catching a few buyers but wasn't exactly bustling with patrons. "We had a saying in Narcotics that seems to track here, too—follow the money. To run a place like this, they'd need more than what their little fruit stand can provide."

Dakota nodded, murmuring, "I'll have Shilah run financials and see what pops up," just as a young woman with a cascade of chestnut hair and a warm, albeit practiced, smile approached them. She wore a flowy summer dress, the kind that perfectly matched the carefree atmosphere of the compound, and a daisy tucked behind her ear.

"Hi there! You must be Dakota and Ellis, Father Zach's guests. I'm Annabelle Turner," she said, extending her hand graciously. Her eyes flickered ever so briefly when she mentioned Deakins's name.

Dakota shook her hand cautiously. "Pleasure. I'm BIA agent Dakota Foster and this is my colleague, FBI agent Ellis Vaughn. Mr. Deakins said we could take a look around the compound."

Annabelle's smile seemed to widen, but her eyes didn't quite match the enthusiasm. "Absolutely, I'd love to be your guide. Everything you see here, we're all one big, happy family. No secrets, no worries."

"The vibe here does seem that way," Ellis returned with a brief smile, adding, "I don't know how you do it, though. Managing all these different personalities would be a challenge for me."

"We're all like-minded so it's not that hard," Annabelle said brightly. "When you're bonded by love and respect, conflict is relatively easy to resolve. I've never been happier than when I pledged to The Congregation."

"Pledge? Is that like a baptism or something?" Dakota asked, curious.

"In a way, I suppose," Annabelle answered but didn't elaborate. Instead, she enthusiastically pointed toward the community garden. "This is our award-winning vegetable garden. Our zucchini and butternut squash took Best in Show at the Stevensville fair five years running. Honestly, sometimes it doesn't even seem fair to the other contestants when our produce is in the mix. We always win." She whispered conspiratorially, "I've been told the secret is in our composting. High-quality nutrients produce extraordinary results. Our carrots are sweeter than candy."

"Not really a vegetable fan," Ellis apologized. "I never

met a vegetable that could make me overlook a chocolate bar."

Dakota smothered a snicker; she knew all about his sweet tooth and his general disdain for vegetables. Annabelle didn't miss a beat, saying, "Well, then, you have to try our pear jam, it's to die for—and very sweet."

Despite her skepticism, Dakota couldn't help but be swayed slightly by Annabelle's charm. "Your community does seem quite peaceful."

Annabelle didn't hesitate, saying, "Oh, it truly is. What you see is what you get. We're all happy and content. Father Zach has made the success of The Congregation his life's work because quality of life matters. That's what's missing in today's world—true happiness."

"And that's what you found here?" Dakota said, gesturing around them. "By gardening and living in old cabins?"

Annabelle chuckled. "I know it's hard to imagine that giving up your material comforts could result in a better way of life but being free of the punishing drive behind late-stage capitalism is a gift you can't see but you can feel in your heart."

It all sounded bonkers to Ellis but Annabelle almost made it sound worth it. *Almost.* "What did you do before you came here?" he asked.

"Same thing that I do here—art," she replied cheerfully. "I'm a freelance graphic artist. I help create The Congregation's pamphlets and printed materials for Eden's Bounty."

"Don't you need technology to do that?" Dakota asked.

Annabelle offered an understanding smile, clarifying, "We don't shun technology here at The Congregation, but I know it's easy to assume we're *that* kind of group because we try to be as self-sufficient as possible. We have solar panels, we grow our own food, have our own livestock and school our children right here on the property, but high-speed internet is something we haven't figured out how to create on our own terms. We have a community Wi-Fi hub but in keeping with our beliefs, the hub is shut down by nine each night. Nothing is so pressing that it interferes with time that should be reserved for family, or personal wellness. There are studies that support the theory that too much technology actually dulls our brains."

"Believing what you want to see can be dangerous," Dakota commented softly. Annabelle heard her and replied with a faint, somewhat condescending smile, "Changing one's perspective is challenging, but worth it."

Ellis jumped in before Dakota got them kicked off the compound. "Sounds very healthy," he said, shooting Dakota a quelling look. "And I definitely want to try that pear jam."

Suddenly, Deakins found them, a folder in hand. "Got the paperwork," he announced, handing it over to Ellis. "Everything we have on Zoey's adoption is here."

"What are you doing?" Annabelle's demeanor shifted to concern. "That's private information."

"Whatever we can do to dispel any shadow of guilt on The Congregation, we're eager to provide," he replied with an even smile but his sharp look to Annabelle quieted any further protest. "Belle, would you mind helping Lina at Eden's Bounty? It looks like she could use a hand."

Annabelle didn't look happy being dismissed but she didn't refuse. Turning to Ellis and Dakota, she murmured a brief, "Pleasure to meet you," and then hustled off in a swish of her flowing dress to do as she was directed.

Deakins watched her go with a mix of indulgent pride like that of a father figure but his gaze lingered a bit too long on her backside to be completely innocent and Ellis was willing to bet the older man was sleeping with the younger woman.

Finally, something typical in situations like this. Primal human nature was hard to fight, especially when people were removed from the public eye and left to their own devices.

"If there isn't anything else I can provide…"

Ellis shook his head. "We appreciate your cooperation. We'll get this verified and returned as soon as possible."

Deakins nodded, clasping his hands together in a prayer motion, bowed and left them with a solicitous, "Lina has prepared a basket for the road. Enjoy."

"It's not often we're given gift baskets by potential suspects," Dakota said quietly as they trudged over to the open-air market. "Think it's safe to eat?"

"It's probably fine. It wouldn't be very smart to send agents home with a poisoned gift basket. Deakins is too sharp to make such a careless mistake," Ellis returned in a low voice before they reached a smiling Lina as she produced a beautiful wicker basket packed to the brim with a little bit of everything available for sale. Ellis accepted the basket with a smile. "This is very kind of you."

"We hope you enjoy," Lina said with a warm smile. "Perhaps when you return, it will not be under the guise of official business."

Dakota and Ellis just smiled and walked to the car. "You can drive," Dakota surprised Ellis, tossing him the keys.

Ellis chuckled, "You feeling all right?"

"Just drive," Dakota returned, the corners of her mouth turning up. "How else am I supposed to rummage through this gift basket?"

He laughed. "Ah, the true reason. You never could resist a good gift basket."

It was true. Every banquet with a silent auction Dakota

was there, putting in her bid if there were gift baskets on the line. She was also enamored with trial-sized items. If something came in trial-sized, she'd buy it. A weird compulsion, but not the weirdest.

As they left the compound, the laughter and chatter of the people behind them seemed to fade into an eerie silence. Ellis broke it. "All right, first impressions on The Congregation?"

Dakota barked a short laugh even as she rummaged through the huge basket of goodies. "My opinion stands— anyone trying to sell the myth of a utopia is usually hiding something else. Also, I'm pretty sure that Annabelle is sleeping with Deakins, which gives me an all-over ick but she's of legal age so it's not a crime."

"I'm surprised Deakins handed over Zoey's paperwork so easily," Ellis remarked, as Dakota took a careful bite of a carrot. "I was expecting him to make us get a warrant first."

"I thought the same," Dakota responded, chewing thoughtfully. "Either he's confident in the paperwork or he genuinely has nothing to hide. There's something off about The Congregation, though. I can't tell if it's just my bias against groups like these."

Ellis nodded in agreement. "Pass me one of those carrots," he said, intrigued by its supposed taste.

Handing him a freshly picked carrot, Dakota teased, "Never thought I'd see the day where you willingly eat a veggie, Ellis. Who are you now?"

Taking a bite, Ellis was pleasantly surprised by the taste. "It's definitely good. I get the hype—but it's no chocolate bar."

Dakota finished her carrot and her stomach growled loudly as if to protest such a paltry offering. "Let's stop in Stevensville for some food," she suggested.

Ellis, however, seemed preoccupied, his gaze fixed on the rearview mirror. Sensing his unease, Dakota glanced to the side mirror, spotting an old sedan trailing them. "Problem?"

Ellis's eyebrows knitted. "That car pulled in right after we left the compound. The consistent distance and speed... It's suspicious."

"Do you think they're from the compound?" Dakota inquired.

"Could be."

She swiftly moved her basket to the floor, drawing her sidearm. "Why would they tail us?"

Ellis looked thoughtful. "Deakins might not have been as forthcoming with those documents as he'd like to appear."

"Are they planning to chase us and retrieve them? Seems like a foolhardy move on their part." Dakota's body tensed, ready for any scenario.

"I doubt they're exactly criminal masterminds," Ellis remarked. Just then, as if to challenge Ellis's comment, the sedan closed in, tailgating aggressively.

Ellis kept his cool, noting, "They're really pushing their luck and testing my patience," he said, as the sedan pushed in so close they were practically in the back seat.

"Can you see the driver?" Dakota asked.

"The sun's glare is in the way. All I see is sunglasses and a hoodie."

"Tap the brakes," Dakota said.

"And brace for impact? No thanks. I don't have plans to spend the day nursing a whiplash headache." Ellis remained steady, unrattled, but they both knew the situation could go sidewise on a dime.

Before they could decide on a course of action, the sedan suddenly rammed into the bumper of their car, the impact causing the back end to get squirrelly. "Shit!" Ellis exclaimed, fighting to gain control of the vehicle.

Dakota braced for impact as a curve in the road worked against them. They were both trained in defensive driving techniques but sometimes all you could do was react in a way that would keep you alive.

The car left the road and skidded onto the shoulder in a spray of dirt and gravel. They narrowly missed slamming into the thick oak tree and their aggressor sped past them, leaving them in the dust.

Dakota coughed, waving away the dust cloud. "You okay?"

"So much for trying to avoid a whiplash headache, but yeah, I'm fine," Ellis groused, rubbing the back of his neck. "How about you?"

"I'm fine," she assured him, more irritated that she hadn't managed to catch the license plate. "Damn sun was in my eyes. I couldn't see the license plate numbers."

"A fact they probably knowingly used against us," Ellis said as he scanned the road ahead but whoever had run them off the road was long gone. "Maybe we can get a sample of paint transfer from the bumper, match it to the VIN and registered owner."

"I wouldn't get my hopes up. The Congregation doesn't seem real big on keeping up-to-date financial records."

Ellis agreed, saying, "Here goes nothing," as he tried to turn over the car. Miraculously, the engine sparked to life and Ellis was able to pull away from the soft shoulder and back onto the road with a grin. "I take back anything I've ever said about import cars not being able to take more than a tap without folding."

Dakota chuckled as she rubbed the back of her own neck. She was going to need a massage at some point. She remembered Ellis having good hands but pushed that memory aside as Ellis growled his next statement.

"I also amend my earlier statement—Deakins *is* a damn good liar. The man sent us off with a fruit basket and a smile all the while planning to send a couple of his people to run us off the road."

"We don't know for sure it's Deakins but yeah, I'd put money on that theory. You think it was just to scare us?"

"Probably," he answered with a dark glower. "But all it did was piss me off."

"Same," Dakota agreed but she switched gears quickly now, her stomach still growling. Nothing like a quick crisis to remind her belly that food was a priority. "Now I'm really hungry. Let's find a spot in Stevensville."

"You still want to get something to eat?"

Dakota blinked at his question. "Why wouldn't I?"

Ellis shook his head ruefully, his lips curving with amusement. "I mean, the whole car crash thing comes to mind…"

"It barely qualifies as a crash," she teased. "And maybe if you hadn't overcorrected when the other car tapped our back end…"

"Ohhh, those are fighting words," he shot back with a grin.

She laughed. Being able to joke with Ellis lessened the adrenaline rush of being run off the road. In their field, sometimes being able to joke about a bad situation made the reality of almost dying on a country road less daunting.

"All right, make yourself useful and find us a place to eat."

They entered Stevensville, a town exuding the charm of many settler-founded locales. Dakota found a cozy diner that boasted a country dinner for a reasonable price, and

Dakota knew how much Ellis loved homemade meat loaf. While Dakota was unfamiliar with Stevensville, she knew of its history with the Indigenous people uprooted by missionaries in the nineteenth century. Everyone who called the Flathead Reservation home knew of its sad origin story, which wasn't much different from most reservation beginnings. Land stolen equaled people displaced. End of story.

"Isn't your mom's place nearby?" Ellis asked.

"About two hours out," she replied, grabbing a menu. More than the past or her family, right now, she craved a juicy burger and a plate of fries. Dakota's relationship with her mother was complicated. Following the loss of her sister, family dynamics had shifted dramatically. Her mother had changed from an independent single mom to two daughters to an overprotective and paranoid parent of a surviving child.

The day Dakota shared she was leaving the reservation for college and a career in law enforcement was the day her mother broke down and begged her to stay and find a career less dangerous.

So, yeah, their relationship was strained to this day.

And it hurt to remember what it'd been like before.

Chapter 10

Ellis understood the delicacy of Dakota's relationship with her mother. It wasn't a lack of affection but the aftermath of tragedy.

Dakota seldom discussed the sensitive topic of her relationship with her mother, given the pain it evoked. Ellis quickly reported the incident to start a vehicle swap-out while Dakota pulled the file on Zoey's adoption as they awaited their server. Finished with the incident report, he clicked off and Dakota handed him the adoption paperwork, noting with a frown, "Everything seems legitimate."

Ellis quirked an eyebrow. "Yeah, I doubt they're going to list murdering the biological mother to get their grubby hands on an infant. We need more info on this agency."

Dakota shared, thinking out loud, "With the property's size, even if it was falling down like Deakins claimed, it must've been pricey. The land alone would've been worth a pretty penny. How does The Congregation fund such acquisitions? I don't care how good the pear jam is, I doubt they're selling enough to drop a couple hundred thousand."

Their young waitress, with her dark hair pulled in a disheveled bun with the name "Cora" blazoned across the dull surface of her name plate, piped up, "I know how they do it... They steal it."

That got their attention. "What do you mean?" he asked.

Despite her initial quip, Cora suddenly seemed reluctant to elaborate until Ellis quickly flashed his credentials. "We're federal agents investigating a local case. Anything you can share with us about what you know about The Congregation would be a big help."

Cora pressed her lips together for a minute before divulging, "My aunt Lina is with them. She left her normal life, gave away all her assets from her divorce to The Congregation and basically walked away from everything."

Ellis remembered the name but wanted to make sure they were talking about the same person. "Short, dark-haired Hispanic lady in her midforties?"

"Yeah, that's her," Cora confirmed. "Plus, there aren't many Linas around here."

Fair enough.

"We met her at the compound. She made us a fruit basket to take with us," Dakota shared. "Your aunt just...left everything behind?"

Cora's eyes sparkled with a mix of frustration and bewilderment. "Yeah, just like that. One day she's celebrating Sophie's sixteenth birthday, and the next, she's packing up and leaving, saying she's found her 'true calling' and she's going where people understand her. It was so abrupt, so out of character, but no one could stop her."

"Were there any signs—possible mental illness, depression—anything at all that could've hinted at this?"

Cora snorted, her tone bitter. "Hints? No. Shock? Absolutely. She abandoned a good job, her family... My cousin Sophie was devastated. My uncle? Broken. And for what? To live on a compound with strangers and give everything to that Deakins guy so she can can peaches and grow asparagus all day? C'mon, my aunt was an ER nurse. She thrived in crisis situations—always the cool head—but then this guy comes along, and suddenly she's walking away from everything and everyone she's ever loved and cared about? What would you do if it were your family member that did this? Would you just let them go without question?"

"Not at all," Ellis said. "I'd probably chase them down and make sure they weren't being coerced."

"Well, we did that and I think that was worse. She was doing it of her own free will. Like, it would've been easier to swallow if she'd been tricked or something, but no, she was happy to do it. I think that's the part that crushed my cousin."

Ellis tilted his head, "But why? There must've been something that drew her in, something they offered her."

Cora shot a glance to the manager, who was giving her a warning look, then defiantly turned back to them, lowering her voice. "Honestly? I think they prey on vulnerability. My aunt was going through something at work, a situation where someone died and she took it real hard. It changed her. And then her marriage started falling apart. So, I don't know, maybe he just said all the right things when she was in a bad place."

"You think they manipulate emotions, then?" Dakota queried, scribbling something in her notebook.

"Yes!" Cora exclaimed, slightly louder than she intended. The manager's stern gaze snapped to her again, and she lowered her voice. "*Absolutely*. It's like they have a radar for the vulnerable. And once they're in, The Congregation becomes their new family, their new world. It's creepy as hell, if you ask me."

Ellis looked deep in thought. "It's classic cult behavior, playing on insecurities and creating a sense of dependence."

Cora's face reddened, saying with a flash of spirit, "It's infuriating! And the worst part is, everyone just stands by.

Even when they see families torn apart. It's like they're blind. I literally don't understand why I'm the only one who sees it around here."

With a slight twitch of her lips, Dakota empathized, "It must be hard, seeing someone you love get pulled into something like that and feeling powerless."

"It is," Cora said, a mix of anger and sadness evident in her eyes. She then cast a defiant glance at her manager. "But I won't stay silent. People need to know."

Ellis smiled, admiring her spunk. "Stay strong, Cora. And thanks for sharing. It gives us more to work with."

The manager had reached her limit, motioning for Cora to get a move on, but Cora ignored her. "I hope you find a way to shut that place down. It's ruined enough lives already."

She gave a tight nod, her eyes conveying gratitude for being heard, and headed off to attend to other tables, every so often throwing annoyed glances at her disapproving manager.

After she left, Dakota speculated, "It's plausible. If all members give their wealth, coupled with smart investments…"

But for Ellis the numbers didn't add up, countering, "Given the compound's size and the modest potential assets, there must be another income source."

The manager approached, addressing Ellis with an apologetic smile. "I'm so sorry for Cora's behavior. We've talked to her about bringing her personal issues to work but she's young and sometimes she just does what she wants."

"I hope she's not in any trouble," Dakota said.

"Not any more than she usually is." The manager's reply suggested underlying tension. Ellis sensed that Cora could provide further information, given the right circumstances. He then ordered his meal, subtly shifting the focus.

"I'll get the double bacon burger with no tomatoes, lettuce or pickles, please."

"So, basically meat, cheese and a bun?"

"You got it," he said with a flirty wink. "And extra fries a little on the crispy side would make life worth living."

The manager, probably older than him by about ten years, reacted with a blush and a smile and Ellis hoped he'd distracted her enough to forget about chewing out the young Cora. He had a feeling Cora had plenty more to say about The Congregation and he was interested in hearing it.

The sight of Ellis ordering his usual "heart-attack special" stirred a pot of memories in Dakota. She had always chided him about his dietary choices, but that was just Ellis—stubborn and set in his ways about food.

As she contemplated teasing him, memories of their shared past rose to grab her by the throat. He might have a finicky taste in food, but his zest for life was contagious. And she had come to realize that maybe it wasn't just his energy she missed.

Maybe she missed him more than she cared to admit.

Don't muddy the waters, Foster.

She tried to refocus, but Ellis seemed to be on the same wavelength, looking nostalgic. "You remember that weekend we went camping at Glacier National Park? We'd set everything up, only to realize we forgot the ice chest with all our food."

Dakota chuckled at the memory. "Oh, that ancient granola bar at the bottom of my backpack? It tasted like cardboard but we were so hungry, we didn't hesitate to wolf it down."

Ellis laughed. "Yeah, but neither of us wanted to pack up and leave. We were determined to enjoy our rare free weekend together, even if it meant surviving on a stale granola bar."

Being federal agents with demanding jobs meant getting away for some quality "reset time" hadn't been easy.

"And the next morning, we ended up paying triple at a convenience store for food that was already waiting for us back home," Dakota remembered with a short laugh.

Ellis raised his eyebrows, playfully pointing at her. "It was your turn to remember the ice chest, wasn't it?"

She shot back, "No way, you were on ice chest duty. I packed the bedding."

His laughter was infectious. "All right, all right, you win. I should've known better than to try and question your memory."

Tapping her temple with a smirk, she quipped, "Like a steel trap, right?"

His soft chuckle resonated with her in an all-too-familiar way, tugging at memories of a shared past, and her cheeks flushed with warmth. That weekend, nestled in the cozy embrace of nature and the sanctuary of their tent, had created a red-hot connection that still had the power to burn.

Damn it, why couldn't she move on from him? She may have claimed to have a boyfriend, but the reality was no one since Ellis had barely registered and she wished it were different. It was a special kind of hell to be stuck in the past and unable to move forward to a new future.

But everyone else in comparison with Ellis was as enjoyable as the prospect of eating stale toast left out all night on the counter for breakfast.

Ellis's eyes danced with mischief, teasing her, "If my memory serves me right, didn't you leave some rather... wild marks on my back? It looked like I'd gone a few rounds with a bear. Or perhaps, a very hungry wolverine."

"Ellis!" she shot back, her cheeks burning, but yes, she remembered all too well. One thing they'd never fell short of having—chemistry.

He shrugged casually, unapologetic. "I'm just sayin'…"

Just as a playful retort danced on her lips, the demanding buzz of her cell interrupted them. As she glanced at the screen, Dakota's playful demeanor vanished, replaced with a mask of professional concern. "It's the hospital," she whispered before answering, "Agent Foster speaking."

"Agent Foster, we're facing an urgent situation." Dr. Patel's voice was grim. "Zoey's parents attempted to forcibly remove her from the facility."

A cold rush of panic hit Dakota. "Is Zoey all right?"

"She's safe now, and we've detained her parents with our security," Dr. Patel responded. "I think you ought to come to the hospital and assess the situation."

Drawing a deep, relieved breath, Dakota exchanged a brief, worried glance with Ellis, her eyes relaying the gravity of the situation. "I'll get the Butte Police to reassume custody. We'll be there in a few hours. Thank you, Dr. Patel," she said, ending the call.

She turned to Ellis, urgency in her voice. "We need our order to go. After being released, Zoey's parents headed straight for the hospital, trying to get her out by force."

"Damn it," Ellis muttered, "I had a feeling that woman wasn't going to let things settle before doing something stupid. She thinks she's above the law because of that all bullshit Deakins and his church has been shoveling down their throats."

"Yeah, well, she's just earned herself a night in jail to help her reevaluate her life choices. In the meantime, we need to secure a better place for Zoey for the time being. With jails as crowded as they are, I don't see Butte police holding the Grojans much longer than they did before."

Ellis agreed, signaling the manager to put a rush on their order. The faster they hit the road, the better.

Chapter 11

Dakota and Ellis arrived at Butte Hospital later that night, pausing briefly to speak with security before making their way to Zoey's room. Dakota's patience was wearing thin. "How did the Grojans get past your security?" she pressed. "There was supposed to be a guard at her door, always."

The security administrator, Mr. Forsythe, looked as if he'd swallowed a lemon. "Agent, we've gone above and beyond to safeguard your patient. Our team is overwhelmed and understaffed without adding additional work."

Dakota's temper flared and her words came sharp. "Overwhelmed or not, Mr. Forsythe, a breach occurred. How?"

Shifting uncomfortably, he admitted, "There was an unexpected lapse during the shift change."

"How long was the lapse?"

"It…lasted forty-five minutes."

Ellis' jaw clenched. "Nearly an hour? How is that even possible?"

The security manager shifted with discomfort as he struggled to justify an indefensible argument but in the end, he gave up and shrugged, lifting his hands with frustration, offering a weak, "We're reevaluating our shift change protocols to ensure this doesn't happen again," as if that should be enough to cool their anger.

But Dakota wasn't so easily mollified. "Zoey's bravery is the only reason she's still here. If the charge nurse hadn't been alerted, she'd be gone. Do you even comprehend what kind of danger you put Zoey in?"

Forsythe's face reddened, words caught in his throat as he garbled a mumbled apology of sorts. "As I said, we're re-evaluating our policies and making changes going forward. It was an unfortunate incident that won't happen again."

"You're damn right it won't happen again," Dakota growled, locking eyes with Ellis. "We have to move her. Can we get federal custody?"

"I can probably make that happen," Ellis said with a short nod, in lockstep agreement. "I'll make arrangements." Then, with a steely gaze to Forsythe, "We appreciate your... 'help.' We've got it from here."

As they exited the security office, Ellis sensed the storm of emotions within Dakota. She was on the brink of explosion. He grabbed her arm, making her face him. "Zoey's okay," he whispered, seeing right through her guilt and fear.

Her voice broke slightly as she said, "The what-ifs are killing me, Ellis. If they'd gotten to her—we don't even know the full involvement of the Grojans. What if they're more than what meets the eye and actually killed Zoey's mother? It makes me sick to my stomach to think of how close they came to snatching Zoey."

"You know the drill—the what-ifs will kill you if you let them," he gently reminded her. "We deal in facts, not speculation or fiction. We're back in control. Zoey needs us to be exactly as we've been from the start—calm, cool and collected. She's counting on us to feel safe when her entire world has been upended."

"But she was unprotected for *forty-five* minutes," Dakota protested. "Anything could've happened in that time and it would've been both our asses, not to mention how it could've affected Zoey. Zoey's been missing for seventeen years. It's not far-fetched to assume the Grojans would've disappeared into the wind if they felt threatened."

"But that's not what happened," Ellis said sternly. "Take a deep breath. Roll your shoulders. We're back in the driver's seat, okay?"

His words resonated. God, he was right. She was catastrophizing out of uncontrolled anxiety. *Get a grip, Foster.* She inhaled deeply, regaining her composure. Dakota had always been the overthinker and Ellis the one who shrugged off most challenges. She'd needed his perspective on this before she spiraled. She jerked a short nod as she sucked in a big breath and pushed it out with determination. *Calm, cool and collected.* She cast Ellis a grateful glance and by the time they reached Zoey's room, Dakota was the picture of composure and determination.

Zoey looked up as they entered the room, a combination of trepidation and relief in her wide eyes as she ventured, "You heard, didn't you?"

"Are you okay?" Dakota asked. "That had to be quite upsetting."

"You have no idea." Zoey looked miserable as she admitted, "I feel like I don't even know them right now. I've never seen them act like this before. It's like strangers took over my parents' bodies, forcing them to say and do things that are out of character. I know it's hard to believe but that's not how they acted back home."

"Your parents seem to be…unpredictable right now. Big stressors can alter people's personalities if they don't have the coping skills to manage the situation," Ellis said. "Try not to take it personally."

Zoey winced as her voice quavered, "Are they…in jail?"

Ellis hesitated, but Dakota answered, feeling honesty was best. "Yes," she said gravely. "But I don't want you to worry about that."

"How can I not worry? It's *jail*."

"I know it's probably upsetting but sometimes adults need time-outs, too. They can't just do whatever they want because they don't like how things are being handled. The fact of the matter is you're an important piece of a tragic puzzle that's been missing for far too long, and whether they like it or not, they're going to have to cooperate."

"My mom's pretty stubborn," Zoey admitted, the corners of her mouth lifting as if to say she didn't think her mom was capable of cooperating. "Even within The Congregation my mom was known for being rigidly stuck in her own ways. Father Zach was always counseling her to soften and bend but she struggled with the idea."

Dakota didn't like the idea of having anything in common with that shrewish woman but she could relate to not wanting to bend when she was certain her way was better. "Well, that's a problem for her to sort out."

"Why are you going to so much trouble for me?" Zoey asked, bewildered, clutching her stuffed raccoon to her chest. "I'm nobody."

Dakota's heart ached, feeling her isolation and vulnerability. No one should ever feel as if they were nobody. "You're the opposite of nobody, Zoey. I can promise you that your birth mother thought you were everything worth fighting for. That's another reason we need to make sure you're safe. Tomorrow, Agent Vaughn and I are going to talk with someone who knew your birth mother, Nayeli. We don't want to leave town until we know you're going to be well taken care of."

Zoey's eyes teared up. "Who?"

Dakota knew there was no way to soften the information. "We're going to talk with your biological aunt, Nakita. She lives in Missoula now."

Zoey shook her head trying to cope with the flood of information. Dakota couldn't imagine how jarring it must be to realize you have more family than you ever knew, especially if you were raised in such an insular bubble your entire life. "I have an aunt?"

"And a grandmother," Ellis added. "And when the time is right…and if you're interested in doing so, we'll arrange a meeting."

"Do they want to meet me?" Zoey's voice was small, vulnerable.

The first rule in investigations—don't let it get personal—used to be stamped on Dakota's spine but she felt herself slipping. There was something about Zoey that pricked at her sense of justice in a way that made being impartial almost impossible. It probably had something to do with the trauma of Mikaya's death but Dakota didn't have the time to puzzle it out.

"I'm sure as soon as they're aware of you they will absolutely want to be part of your life, but that will be your choice. It's a very complicated situation and we're all treading cautiously forward but I promise you, everything we do will be done with your safety and well-being at the heart."

Zoey nodded, wiping at her eyes, admitting, "I don't know how my parents will take me wanting to know my biological family."

Given their current instability, not well—but that was a problem for a different day. "Your parents need some cooling-off time. Meanwhile, we're moving you to a safer spot to help everything settle."

Zoey's eyebrows knitted in confusion. "Moving? To where?"

"We believe it's safer for you, considering everything, to be in a federal safe house," Dakota explained. "A nurse we trust will be with you. And your parents… They won't know where, for now."

Zoey's eyes shimmered with unshed tears. "I don't get it. My mom's never been this…unhinged. She genuinely scared me."

A pang of suspicion hit Dakota. How far had Barbara-Jean been willing to go for a child of her own? Desperation led people down dark paths. Had Barbara-Jean lied about knowing who Nayeli was? Had she and Deakins orchestrated the entire adoption scenario as a way to cover her tracks?

Too many questions and not enough information.

"I wish I never took that car," Zoey admitted in a hoarse whisper, practically disintegrating beneath the guilt. "This is all my fault."

Dakota reached for the girl's hand and squeezed it gently. "No, it's not. You're not responsible for the actions of others. I never used to believe that everything happens for a reason but sometimes it does. If you hadn't taken that car, crashed and ended up here, we never would've found you. That's something to hold on to. I don't know how your parents are connected but we're going to keep you safe, okay? That's a promise."

"My head is a mess. I don't know what or how to think about this entire situation. Suddenly, my life is so much more complicated than it ever was and I just want to crawl under the blankets and hide."

"Don't sell yourself short, kiddo. You might not believe this but you're handling things pretty well," Dakota said.

"But let's prioritize getting you settled. The other pieces we'll fit together later."

As Ellis approached, signaling a successful call with a thumbs-up, he quipped, "Five-star relocation service ready to roll. Just a quick chat with your doctor, then it's lights and sirens for you."

Zoey's expression crinkled into an unhappy frown. "Do I have to go in an ambulance?"

Dakota quickly jumped in. "I get it. Ambulances aren't the most fun. But we need to ensure your safety, especially with your injury. Think of it as a medical limousine—a sort of privileged transport. Ready to roll?"

Zoey sighed. "As ready as I'll ever be, I guess."

Dr. Patel signed off on the transfer with stern instructions for her aftercare as well as arrangements to get cleared by the FBI for weekly check-ins and Dakota felt a grudging respect for the crusty doctor. He might be grumpy and unfriendly to everyone else but he genuinely cared for his patients and that was a good quality for someone in charge of others' well-being.

Ellis pulled the car into the dimly lit parking garage of the boutique hotel, the weight of the day pressing on his shoulders. His head and neck ached from the accident but he wasn't going to complain. He'd take some aspirin when he got to his room. Dakota, eyes shadowed but determined, glanced out at the darkened streets. He could practically hear the wheels grinding in that busy mind that probably had the same pounding headache as him but she'd never admit it.

He knew how she shouldered the blame of the Grojans' failed hospital heist, even though it wasn't her fault. It was in her nature to be the one in charge, the one with the answers and solutions—a consequence of losing her older sister too young and ending up being the responsible one when her own mother crumpled.

"Zoey's safe now," he murmured, cutting the engine. It was late and they were both dragging at this point. All Ellis wanted now was his bed and at least four hours of solid shut-eye but Dakota was pensive.

"For now," Dakota murmured, already trying to prepare for the next obstacle or challenge, even though they didn't know how or when it might happen. "We're far from done and if anything, we're just as far from an answer as when Zoey first popped up on the radar. I can't explain it but I feel this sense of urgency that's pressing on my shoulders, whispering in my ear that we're running out of time."

"But we're not," Ellis said. "Aren't you the one who was always advocating slow and steady wins the race?"

Dakota's half-hearted smile as she quipped, "Don't use my words against me," gave him hope that Dakota would come around. For some reason this case had her spinning on her axis in a way he'd never seen before. He suspected it had something to do with her sister's death, but he was reluctant to go there if she wasn't ready. "But yeah, you're right," she chuckled ruefully, before admitting in a weary tone, "I'm off my game and that worries me. I've never felt so unsure of my every move like this. I don't know why this case is affecting me so much. I mean, I do know but that bothers me even more. I should be able to put everything in its place but I'm wildly off-balance right now."

Ellis drew a deep breath, hoping he was doing the right thing. "Nayeli's death was too close to Mikaya's and you were so young when it all happened. You're human, Dakota. You're allowed to have feelings."

"Not if they get in the way of my judgment," she returned with a frown. "I can't let my feelings muck up this investigation."

"You won't," he assured her. "If there's anyone I would never worry about in that regard, it's you. Don't be so hard on yourself."

He hated seeing her look so dejected and lost. He wanted to shake her and tell her to snap out of it, but also he wanted to hug her tight and reassure her that it was going to work out. He split the difference, playfully admonishing, "I never pictured you as the pity-party type, Foster. Even off your game, as you say, you're still a damn good investigator so cut yourself some slack, okay? Your instincts are sharp. You just have to listen to them. You're too busy second-guessing every move and you're smothering that spark that made you the right person for this case."

She was ever the overthinker, and he couldn't imagine the chaos inside Dakota's brilliant mind.

Dakota cast him a look full of grudging appreciation, murmuring her acknowledgment. "You're right. I am second-guessing myself and I need to stop."

"Sometimes things get messy even when we know to keep it clean," he said quietly and wasn't entirely sure that he was only talking about the work. The more he worked side by side with Dakota, the harder it was to remember to keep it professional.

If she caught on to the parallel, she didn't comment. Instead, she exhaled a long breath, taking a minute to re-calibrate.

They'd gotten Zoey transferred to the federal safe house, a fortress hidden in plain sight. But even as he cautioned Dakota to be wary of putting the cart before the horse, he knew there was more to the story, more threads to unravel. He felt it, an itch at the back of his mind.

Rubbing the grit from her eyes, Dakota shared on a yawn, "Shilah called while you were signing the paperwork for the transfer. She's got something worth looking into on Deakins."

"Yeah? What's she got?" He unbuckled his seat belt, turning fully to face her. "Anything good?"

"Possibly. I mean, it's definitely odd. The Congregation compound? It was purchased by a company that traces back to Montana senator Mitchell Lawrence."

Didn't expect that intel. "I've met Lawrence once before, some FBI benefit dinner. He was one of the VIP guests." Ellis's eyebrows shot up. "But Deakins and Lawrence? You're right, that's an odd pairing. But why? What's his play?"

Dakota ran a hand through her hair, tension drawing her features tight. "I don't know but it seems weird that a senator would have ties to a cult compound in the middle of nowhere."

"I'll add it to the list of questions attached to this case," Ellis said.

There was a moment of heavy silence as fatigue warred with restless energy born of too much adrenaline. Dakota's gaze was sharp, assessing. "If Deakins has enough influence and power to convince a senator to pony up the cash for the compound, we're not just fighting a cult. We're up against a system with deep pockets and dangerous connections."

Ellis grunted in agreement. Working in Narcotics for as long as he had taught him that dirty money found itself in many different hands, regardless of social stature, but the more powerful the connection, the more determined people were to keep their secrets hidden. Had Nayeli been mixed up with the wrong people, collateral damage in a danger-ous game?

A yawn found him in spite of his restless thoughts and he knew he had to hit the sheets. "Look, it's been a helluva day and we need to get some sleep—and some aspirin. We're no good to anyone if we're dragging ass in the morning."

"Second on that aspirin. Damn my neck is sore," Da-kota agreed with a nod as she climbed out of the car and he followed. "Thanks for driving," she said with a hint of a weary smile. "I'll drive tomorrow if you want," she of-fered with a wave before leaving for her room without a backward glance.

Of course, that's how it should be. No lingering looks, or hint that there'd once been something passionate and tender between them. Now, it was all about the job.

Why was he struggling to follow her example?

As ready for bed as he was, he stood for a minute, al-lowing the cool night air to kiss his face. Call it a moment of weakness but he'd give anything to be invited into Da-kota's hotel room so he could fall asleep with her body be-side him. That wasn't going to happen, but it didn't stop the longing from punching him in the gut.

How could he have lost such an incredible woman? He sighed inwardly. Those were not the questions to entertain when the tank was nearly empty, and self-control was low.

Because if he went down that rabbit hole, he'd end up doing and saying something he regretted and potentially screw up this case—and he wasn't willing to do that.

Too much was riding on the success of this case and he wished he could say it was only Zoey's well-being that mattered but his career was on the line, too.

Chapter 12

Ellis maneuvered the car onto the highway, making the journey from Butte to Missoula under a canvas of thickening clouds. Fall always brought unpredictable weather patterns. One minute it was sunny and warm; the next, a storm boiled on the horizon. Ellis kept his eyes on the road, his focused expression matching the tension Dakota felt.

Even as tired as she was, sleep hadn't come easily to her last night. Sitting in the car, enveloped in the cocoon of the car's shadowed interior, Dakota struggled against the powerful pull toward Ellis. His voice soothed her ragged nerves—something she hadn't realized she'd been sorely missing—and the simple scent of his skin made her want to lay her head on his shoulder and close her eyes for a brief moment.

Ellis had always had a way of making her feel emotionally safe—until that night had shattered everything between them.

She couldn't explain to anyone who hadn't experienced trauma in their life how precious a gift that feeling of safety was to someone with a soul torn in half, but it was equally traumatic to lose that security when it meant so much to you.

But there was a saying, "Dating someone you've already broken up with is like biting into an apple you already know is bad and being surprised when you eat a worm," that stuck in her head whenever she ventured too close to considering another try with Ellis.

Not that she should assume he was open to another try.

Needless to say, she tossed and turned, punched her poor pillow, kicked her bedding around a bit, all in effort to find sleep that didn't come until almost one in the morning.

Which made getting up bright-eyed and bushy-tailed when the alarm went off a challenge.

But caffeine paired with her driving sense of responsibility was a godsend because today was too important to waste on poor life decisions.

They were meeting Nayeli's younger sister, Nakita, not only to learn about Nayeli's past but also to share that her long-lost niece had been found. It was bound to be an emotional meeting and she needed all of her faculties on point.

Even though she'd offered to drive, Ellis had taken one look at the dark circles beneath her eyes and wordlessly pointed to the passenger seat. Any other time she might've pushed back but today she was silently grateful for his innate protective nature.

They pulled into Missoula in good time, making their scheduled appointment with a few minutes to spare, which was just how Dakota liked it as it gave her time to prepare.

"Ready?" Ellis asked.

She inhaled deeply. "Yes."

The modest suburban neighborhood was typical with tidy tract homes lining the streets and city-approved landscaping that looked copied and pasted from one house to the next.

They parked and walked up to the home, Ellis taking the lead to rap sharply on the front door.

Nakita knew they were coming, but not the full purpose of their visit. Dakota shared they were investigating new leads on Nayeli's case and asked if Nakita wouldn't mind talking to them. It was a way to gauge Nakita's interest and to see how open the family would be to finding out about Zoey.

Nakita had been eagerly open to talking about her sister's case and quickly invited them to talk, which was a good sign.

The door swung open, revealing Nakita—a petite woman with long dark hair that hung in two braids, and even darker eyes that were kind as a smile wreathed her face. "You must be Agent Foster and Agent Vaughn," she said, before they could even flash their credentials. Her dark eyes lit up as she ushered them in, anxious to hear details of the case. "I can't tell you how happy I am that you're reopening my sister's case. It's been so long I'd almost given up hope."

"Thank you for agreeing to talk with us on such short notice," Dakota said, showing her credentials even though Nakita didn't seem to need it. She was too excited to hear what they'd come to share.

She motioned for them to sit. "Can I get you something to drink? I have coffee, tea, juice boxes…"

Ellis waved away her offer with a smile. "Please, have a seat, Miss Swiftwater. The kind of news we have to share is best heard sitting down."

Nakita swallowed and sank into the chair opposite them. "Please tell me you've caught who killed my sister."

"Not yet but there's been a development in the case," Dakota said. "A pretty big one."

Nakita nodded imperceptibly, steeling herself for the news.

"A week ago, a seventeen-year-old Jane Doe was brought into a Butte hospital with major head trauma from a solo car accident. DNA revealed the teen to be your niece, Cheyenne."

Nakita cried out, her shaking hands going straight to her mouth as if trying to keep the storm of her emotions from spilling out further. Tears leaked down her cheeks as she tried to find the words. "Are you sure?" she asked, her voice choked. "Without a doubt?"

"The DNA match was conclusive," Ellis confirmed.

"Is she...okay? You said major head trauma?" Nakita said, her bottom lip quivering.

"She's recovering," Dakota said, hoping to ease Nakita's fears. "She suffered some short-term memory loss, but the doctor feels confident she'll make a full recovery with time."

Nakita nodded, relieved, but the floodgates opened and the questions came tumbling out. "I don't understand. Where has she been all these years? What happened? Does she know about her family? Where was she going when the accident happened? When can I see her? Oh my God, I have to tell my mom." She rose sharply, her hands fluttering as she tried to prioritize what to do first. "I need to make arrangements for my sons but I can be ready to leave in about an hour—"

"Miss Swiftwater—"

"Call me Nakita, please."

Dakota smiled. "Nakita, I know this is a lot to take in but I need you to take a breath. Your niece has been moved to a federal safe house given the circumstances of her abduction. We can't take you to her just yet, but I promise, when Cheyenne is ready... We'll facilitate that visit. For now, we need your help finding who killed your sister."

Sharply disappointed but trying to be cooperative, Nakita returned to her chair, sniffing back tears. "Of course, whatever you need. I'll help in any way I can." She glanced up, her eyes still watering. "But… Can you tell me something about her?"

Dakota nodded, pulling out her cell phone. "I can do you one better." She brought up a picture of Zoey holding the stuffed raccoon Ellis brought her. The smile on Zoey's face was similar to Nakita's, showing strong genes ran in the Swiftwater genetics. "This is Cheyenne…although she goes by Zoey now."

Nakita accepted Dakota's phone with trembling fingers, tears splashing down her cheek as she stared at the photo. "She's beautiful," she breathed, her voice clogged with tears. "She looks just like Nayeli."

"I was thinking she looks a lot like you," Dakota said with a smile.

"People always used to say that me and Nayeli looked a lot alike," Nakita admitted with a watery chuckle. "I guess they were right." She reluctantly returned Dakota's phone. "Is she okay? Does she know about us, her real family?"

"She knows now," Dakota answered with a kind smile. She could only imagine what was going through Nakita's head right now and it made Dakota freshly angry over the cruel nature of the situation.

"Does she…want to meet us?" Nakita's halting question pierced Dakota's heart.

Dakota chose her words carefully, trying to navigate a tricky situation. "Zoey's been through a lot and she's a bit overwhelmed. Until we can determine that her adoptive parents are innocent of any wrongdoing in regards to your sister's case, we're keeping Zoey in protective custody and they haven't responded well to that situation."

"I don't understand. My sister was killed and her baby abducted. Of course they had something to do with Nayeli's murder," Nakita returned, flabbergasted. "Why aren't they in jail?"

"Technically, they are, but for other reasons, and they're likely to be released within a few days," Ellis said.

Nakita didn't understand and Dakota didn't blame her. Logic and reason were difficult to manage when emotions were running high. She tried to return Nakita to the current situation. "Traumatic brain injuries take time to heal and it's best if Zoey focuses on what she needs for her health. It's all very confusing for her and we want to minimize the stress. I know you want what's best for Zoey, and right now what's best is trying to find out who killed her biological mother. I'm hoping you can help us find the clue that might've been missed the first time around."

That pierced through the fog of Nakita's pain and she nodded. "Yes, of course. Whatever she needs." She wiped at her eyes and rubbed the moisture away on the thigh of her jeans, drawing herself up and straightening. "What would you like to know?"

Ellis admired the strength of women. Time and time again, he saw instances of women rising to the occasion despite physical or emotional pain and it always awed him.

Today was no different. He just watched Nakita Swift-water discover her niece was alive after being missing for seventeen years and in the next breath, shelve her emotions so she could help find her sister's murderer when he knew all she wanted to do was hop in the car and drive straight to the child who represented the last living piece of her sister.

Seeing such emotional strength was humbling.

"Can you tell us about Nayeli's relationships, friendships?" Dakota asked.

"I can try," Nakita said, taking a minute to search her

memory, a flicker of pain crossing her gaze as she confessed, "Sometimes my memory isn't so good about remembering my childhood. After Nayeli died, I spiraled, lost myself in addiction." She swallowed hard, her eyes glistening. "It was the birth of my first son, born addicted, that was my wake-up call. I got clean. For my child. For Nayeli, who would've been an amazing mom. Once I was clean, I poured myself into bettering my life. I went back to school and got my counselor credentials. Now I'm a substance abuse counselor, helping others overcome similar challenges with addiction and loss."

"That's incredible," Dakota said. "I'm sure Nayeli would've been proud."

"I hope so. For a long time I didn't think I could pull myself out of the dark place I was in but somehow I found the strength. I liked to think that Nayeli was there beside me in spirit, lifting me up when I stumbled," she shared with a mild blush. "We were raised to believe that the Great Spirit is everywhere but it was my sister's spirit I needed most."

Dakota's own belief structure leaned more toward science, finding solace in the tangible rather than in faith. After Mikaya was killed, it was hard for Dakota to embrace the concept of a higher power when there was so much evil in the world.

Shaking off her personal thoughts, she murmured, "I understand," shooting a glance at Ellis. "Anything you can remember might point us in the right direction."

Ellis pressed gently, "What about Nayeli's romantic relationships? Perhaps a past boyfriend we could talk to?"

Nakita chuckled, shaking her head. "Childhood friends, yes, but a boyfriend? Nayeli was very shy around boys. She wasn't like some of those girls who are so eager to get attached. She was quiet, kind and always had her nose in a book. She loved to read. Me, not so much. I used to tease her that she was going to end up an old auntie with nothing but cats to keep her company when she got old. She said she didn't care because a cat in her lap wouldn't stop her from reading whenever she wanted." She chuckled at the memory, recalling with a pained frown, "That's why when she told us she was moving to Whitefish for a job, we thought she was joking."

"So that seemed out of character for Nayeli?" Ellis asked.

"Well, yeah, a little bit. She was painfully introverted and preferred to stay home than go out and she knew our mom needed her help here," Nakita said.

"Did she give a reason for leaving?" Dakota asked.

"From what I remember, she said it was the only way to make more money. She said there wasn't enough opportunity in Flathead and she knew that she'd need a better career if she was going to be able to take care of us."

"So Nayeli was trying to improve your family's financial status," Ellis said.

"She got an interview at that fancy hotel and said she wanted to work up the chain to manager." Nakita nodded but guilt remained in her expression. "She told me it was up to me to help Mom while she was gone and that she'd send money each pay period. I was supposed to help with the groceries and day-to-day stuff but I was a kid and I didn't want that kind of responsibility. I resented Nayeli for leaving."

Ellis digested that information. "Did she follow through and send money?"

Nayeli nodded. "Like clockwork. She would even send extra if we were short. Nayeli never complained or said no. She just fixed whatever problem happened. Especially if I was the one being the problem," she admitted.

Ellis could read between the lines. Nakita, a resentful kid unable to understand why she was being asked to shoulder a heavy burden for the sake of her family, probably helped herself to some of the funds as compensation but then that created a shortfall in the family budget.

Dakota asked, "Once she moved to Whitefish, did she mention having a boyfriend?"

"Not that I knew of," Nakita said, shaking her head, pausing as she recalled something. "Though she mentioned a frequent hotel guest. Always polite, always kind, even helped her out a few times. She got a flat tire one time and he bought her all four new tires. I think… I think she had a crush on him. But she never named him. I was too young to think about pressing any harder, and honestly, I was self-ishly preoccupied with my own stuff."

"You were a kid being a kid," Ellis reminded her. "Being asked to carry a heavy load for an eleven-year-old." But his thoughts were stuck on the mysteriously generous stranger in Nayeli's life. Four tires were costly. Whomever Nayeli was talking to, they had money to throw around.

Nakita cast a grateful smile his way. "That's what my therapist told me, too. It was a long time before I accepted that truth. It's still hard, to be honest. It always feels like somehow it was my fault what happened to Nayeli, even though I've processed that it wasn't. Emotions are tricky."

"That they are," Dakota agreed with a murmur. "Thank you, Nakita, for talking with us today. We'll be in touch," she said, handing Nakita a business card with her personal number scrawled on the back. "As soon as we know more, you'll be the first call."

They left Nakita's with a list of old contacts and possible connections back at the reservation and climbed into the car, but Ellis was still thinking of the mysterious hotel guest.

"We need to find out who Nayeli was seeing," he said. A connection, however faint, gave them a direction to investigate further. Human beings, no matter how private and reserved their personality, craved connection. Nayeli was seeing someone long enough to get pregnant. It was possible whoever got her pregnant…was also the killer.

Dakota was on the same page. "Beautiful, shy Native girl with a kind heart and a generous soul alone in a city full of predators… Yeah, I have a feeling someone took advantage of a naive girl and then snuffed out her life when she became inconvenient."

Ellis agreed. Did a younger Zachariah Deakins set his eyes on Nayeli or was there someone else lurking in the shadows of the past thinking they got away with murder?

Chapter 13

Taking advantage of the fact that Flathead Reservation was only an hour and a half from Missoula, they immediately returned to the road after leaving Nakita's place.

Again, Dakota let Ellis drive but this time it was so she could put her emotions in check. She rarely found reason to go home again, and the guilt always sat like a stone in her stomach.

The rusty hues of fall painted the landscape, accentuating the beauty of Montana's sprawling vistas. However, the trees shedding their golden leaves only served as a stark reminder of time passing, of seasons changing, and of the wounds that never quite healed.

She rested her head on the open window frame, closing her eyes as the wind blew her hair back and caressed her face. The sun bathed her upturned cheeks and the scent of evergreen, wild things, and the hum of nature plucked at her soul.

As she knew they would, the memories hit her hard and fast. Her home was beautiful but a well of grief simmered beneath the pretty picture, creating a lump in her throat even as she tried to push it away.

When would the pain end? Shouldn't there be a statute of limitations for the sharp stab of emotional damage? She saw herself, at sixteen, lost and shattered, needing the strength of her only parent—but her mother was drowning in her own pain and had nothing left to offer her youngest—and remaining—daughter.

Dakota reopened her eyes in time to see the diner where Mikaya used to work—a sad shack off Highway 93, closed and boarded up for a long time now—yet still standing as a painful relic of the past. If it were within her power, she'd bulldoze the place to the ground and scorch the earth where it stood. *Oh, Mikaya, I miss you so much.*

Nineteen was too young to die. Dakota blinked back tears. It was always this way when she came home. The tears lay in wait, bubbling in her heart, just waiting to spill over at the first opportunity.

Ellis, sensing Dakota's internal struggle, squeezed her hand. "You okay?"

Not even a little. She took a deep breath, letting the cool fall air fill her lungs. "Yeah, just… It's a lot coming back here."

He nodded. "I know it's hard to be home."

Hard to be home. Bittersweet was more like it. Flathead Reservation was good-sized with more employment opportunities than the nearby Macawi Reservation—the casino and the sale of timber drove the economy—but there remained an undercurrent of inequality and financial insecurity that fueled much of the social problems affecting the tribes.

Alcoholism, domestic violence, drug abuse—they were common enough among the Native people as an aftereffect of generations of subjugation at the hands of settlers and missionaries with an inflated sense of entitlement.

But home was still achingly beautiful to eyes that misted from a bone-deep homesickness that no amount of avoiding could smother.

A sigh escaped her lips but not Ellis's notice. "How long has it been since you've been home?"

"Too long and not long enough," she answered wistfully watching the scenery pass by in a colorful blur. "It's been about five years, I think."

Saying it aloud made her feel worse. It was easy to lose track of time when you were busy with your life and that life included a time-consuming career but it was so much more than that simple answer. She avoided this place—and her mother—because this place held her dreams and her nightmares clutched tightly in its fist.

Being honest with herself, she didn't know if she'd ever be able to return home without suffering the feeling of being smothered beneath the weight of the past.

But today wasn't about her—it was about Nayeli.

She realized the same hope she'd harbored as a young, grieving teen following Nayeli's case still burned inside her. In seeking justice for another, maybe she could find some semblance of closure for Mikaya.

"What's the best memory you have of living in Flathead?" Ellis asked, his arm crooked out the open window.

She shook her head. "I don't want to play that game."

"C'mon, it could help. Sometimes we let our minds paint over the good times and all we end up remembering is the bad stuff. I need you to hold on to something good so you can stay focused."

Dakota shot Ellis a dark look. She didn't like being managed, but there was a certain level of logic to his suggestion. She'd never returned to Flathead on a case and it mattered how she reacted to being home again. She needed her head on straight, not struggling to breathe because the memories were being shoved down her throat.

Drawing a deep breath, she pulled a memory free—

something she hadn't dared to think about since she was a kid.

The dappled sunlight peeked in and out of the passing clouds, casting dancing shadows across her face.

"It was one of the hottest summers I can remember," Dakota began, smiling grudgingly. "We were wilting like houseplants left in the sun. Mikaya talked our mom into letting her borrow the car, even though she didn't have a license yet, so we could go swimming at Flathead Lake. We packed the car with a blanket, some towels and sandwiches, and headed out. We played the music loud, laughed and felt like grown-ups. That day on the lake was almost perfect. I thought my sister was the coolest person on the planet and I wanted to be just like her. I still remember her purple bikini top and how beautiful she was. I thought, if I turned out to be half as pretty as my sister, life would be damn good. I idolized her." She trailed off, weathering the inevitable wave of pain that always followed a memory of Mikaya. "The smell of coconut suntan lotion always reminds me of that day on the lake." She wiped at a sudden tear, nodding. "It was a good day."

That day had been the catalyst of Mikaya getting a job at the diner. She planned to save enough money to buy her own car. She'd been $300 shy of her goal when she was killed.

A cold chill shook Dakota's frame, and she shot Ellis a short smile. "A goose walked over my grave."

"Those damn ghost geese are a menace," Ellis joked, teasing a more genuine smile from Dakota.

"I'm glad you're here with me," Dakota said, ignoring all of the boundary rules about keeping things professional. "I think you're the only person who would truly understand how difficult returning home is for me."

Ellis sobered, acknowledging her comment with a grave nod. Words would just muck things up and he seemed to understand that. *Let the moment be, whatever it needed to be, and then move on.*

They had a list of contacts to start with, all of whom had remained in Flathead, so they wasted no time in going down the list.

First up, Evelyn Redhawk, one of Nayeli's closest friends growing up. Evelyn and Nakita had remained in contact over the years, the initial connection being Nayeli, but they'd since grown close on their own terms. If anyone would know about a boyfriend, it would be Evelyn.

Evelyn worked as a tourism and hospitality manager at the casino, an integral cog in the tourism machine that drew people to the area, infusing much-needed cash into the region.

Nakita gave Evelyn a heads-up that they were coming and as soon as they arrived, Evelyn was waiting for them. A tall, graceful woman with long hair pulled into a stylish bun held in place with a beautifully beaded hairpiece, she ushered them into her on-site office and closed the door for privacy.

Her office was smart and tidy with enlarged historical photographs of Indigenous people at the turn of the century hanging on the wall. She smiled as she gestured for them to take a seat as she sank into the large leather chair behind the expansive desk. "Nakita called and told me you were coming and why." She inhaled a breath and shook her head, amazed at the turn of events. "After all this time…for Cheyenne to pop up like that… It's something of a miracle."

Dakota smiled. "Definitely a stroke of good luck at work. Nakita said that you and Nayeli were best friends growing up."

"Like sisters," Evelyn said. "I always liked to think we were perhaps soul sisters. The day she died, a piece of me died with her."

Dakota knew that feeling. "Nakita said it was a surprise when she took that job in Whitefish, out of character, even. Do you know if she was seeing someone there? Perhaps secretly?"

Evelyn chuckled, admitting, "It was a surprise to her family but not to me. We'd been talking about going into the hospitality business since freshman year in high school. We had a plan—I'd handle the tourist stuff, she'd handle the guest services. In a way, my job today is because of our long-ago dream."

"Why didn't Nayeli share her aspirations with her mom and sister?"

Evelyn smiled, shaking her head at the memory of long-gone squabbles between loved ones. "Nayeli was so close to her mom and little sister but she always knew she'd have to leave Flathead in order to make her dreams come true. She wanted to manage a large hotel chain. She'd been planning to take college courses in hotel management when she found out she was pregnant. Still, even realizing she'd have to work twice as hard, she always planned to return to school after the baby came. People always underestimated Nayeli because she kept her thoughts and plans to herself, but that girl had ambition."

"So Nayeli wasn't seeing anyone in Whitefish?" Ellis asked.

"Not anyone serious," Evelyn answered, though a troubled frown creased her forehead and there seemed to be something she wasn't sure if she should share, but upon Dakota's encouragement, she admitted, "It feels like gossip and that feels like a betrayal to my friend, especially when nothing became of it when I shared the information with police, but there was someone she was seeing casually that I thought might not have been a good idea."

Ellis and Dakota perked up. "Who?" Dakota asked.

"Someone we grew up with who always held a torch for Nayeli, though she never really saw him as more than a friend. However, he started visiting her on weekends, and then she admitted that one night they'd ended up sleeping together. She felt really bad and cut it off."

"And how did he take the news?" Ellis asked.

"According to Nayeli, not well," Evelyn admitted with a wince. "He got a little physical with her—I guess he pushed her against the wall but she kicked him out before things got worse. As far as I know, he never came back around, which was a good thing."

"Is he the father of Nayeli's baby?" Dakota asked.

Evelyn was unsure. "I never asked and Nayeli didn't say. I figured it was her business and if she wanted me to know, she'd tell me. Or maybe she didn't know herself and didn't care to know. We never really talked about the paternity of her baby."

"Curiosity never got the better of you?" Dakota asked. "That kind of secret would've driven me crazy."

Evelyn shrugged. "A lot of us were raised by single mothers. Sometimes all a man does is get in the way. I supported her decision and her secret."

"So, who was the man she rejected?" Ellis asked.

Evelyn hesitated, conflicted. "He's a good man and I'd hate to rehash old hurts for nothing, plus his father is an important member of the tribal community. If I tell you, I'd ask that you handle your questioning with sensitivity. At the end of the day, we all loved Nayeli in our way and losing her was a huge blow to the community."

"If he's innocent, he'll have no worries about talking to us. Ultimately, finding Nayeli's killer is our main concern," Ellis said, saving Dakota the trouble of sounding hard-hearted. "A name, please."

Dakota smiled, supporting Ellis.

Evelyn huffed a short breath and pulled up a name on her phone. "His name is Leonard Two Eagles but we all called him Lenny. He works odd jobs, as a handyman of sorts. His father is a tribal elder, and well-respected."

"Do you have a contact number for Leonard?" Dakota asked.

Evelyn sighed. "Yes." She scribbled down a number quickly and handed it to Dakota. "For what it's worth, I don't think Lenny was capable of hurting Nayeli. He truly loved her but it just wasn't meant to be."

Dakota pocketed the paper, appreciating the lead. "You said you shared the information with authorities?"

"Yes, I felt terrible doing it but it seemed the right thing to do." Evelyn's solemn answer seemed genuine, then she added, "When nothing became of the information, I was relieved. Like I said, Lenny is a good man who's had his struggles but he's worked hard to put all of that behind him."

Dakota shared a look with Ellis. There was no mention of Leonard in the original investigation. The follow-through on the case seemed half-hearted at best but there was nothing that could be done about that injustice now. All they could do was move forward.

"What if Cheyenne is Leonard's biological daughter?"

Evelyn held her ground. "If Nayeli wanted that information known, she would've shared it. It's not my place to do so. Not then and not now."

Dakota realized the woman was strong in her convictions but they had a lead to chase down. "We'll be in touch."

They left the casino and returned to the car, realizing they were going to have to spend more time in Flathead than she'd planned—another sign she was off her game.

Ellis, reading her mind, squinted into the slowly setting sun. "Well, I say we get a hotel, grab a pizza and regroup tomorrow. We're both tired, need to debrief and check in with Shilah about Deakins. Sound like a plan?"

It was a good plan. Solid. Except, there was one place she needed to visit before calling it a night—the one place she dreaded—and she didn't want to go alone. "I...uh... should probably pop into my mom's place before calling it a night," she said, her mouth suddenly feeling dry as dust. "I can drop you off at the hotel..."

Ellis regarded her with compassion, knowing the painful history between Dakota and her mother and how it tore at her. "Do you want to go alone or do you want backup?"

It was a simple question.

But somehow it felt heavy between them.

Her eyes welled up as she admitted in a barely audible voice, "I'd like backup."

And that's all he needed. Nodding, he tapped the roof of the car and said, "All right, let's do this," and Dakota never felt more supported by the man who didn't have to care anymore.

But he did anyway.

Chapter 14

Ellis could almost see the agitated energy rolling off Dakota in waves. He knew what it took for Dakota to admit she needed him to do this with her and he wasn't going to make it harder on her by drawing attention to her request.

Dakota had shared her childhood experiences with him when they were first dating, and he'd shared his, bonding through trauma and finding a kindred spirit in the shared pain. While his dad had been an abusive drug addict/alcoholic with no redeeming qualities, Dakota's mom had once been a good mother until tragedy ate her from the inside and the soothing burn of alcohol became her only solace.

Ellis thought that was the hardest part for Dakota—knowing that her mom had once been different. Being the child of an addict, sometimes the hope that they'll get better was the thing that broke you.

Except in Ellis's case, his dad had always been a piece of shit and he'd never harbored any delusion that he'd ever be anything but a worthless waste of oxygen.

When he died, Ellis hadn't shed a tear.

Best day of his life, actually.

"Does she know we're coming?" Ellis asked.

"No. I wasn't sure she'd be home if she knew I was coming. My mom pretends like she's not avoiding me, but I'm not the only one who can't handle the past. Aside from the obligatory phone call on birthdays, and the major holidays, mostly Christmas and Thanksgiving, we don't talk and we definitely don't visit."

"So, why today?"

Dakota shrugged, admitting, "I don't know, seems like the right thing to do. I mean, I'm here. I don't really have an excuse."

"Maybe she'll be happy to see you. Time has a way of healing old wounds."

Dakota's wry expression revealed her opinion on that adage. "We'll see. I'll just apologize in advance if she's not exactly a welcoming hostess. We won't stay long," she promised.

But he was willing to stay for as long as she needed. Dakota prided herself on being self-sufficient, independent and strong, but he knew the side of her she protected like a Doberman against intruders.

Ellis reached over, entwining his fingers with Dakota's. The gesture was silent, no words exchanged, yet it spoke volumes of the support and understanding he was offering her.

The drive continued in a quiet solidarity, the world outside passing by as the landscape gradually changed. The road stretched out, weaving through an expanse of open land with occasional clusters of homes and cabins as the beauty of the area exploded in brilliant colors like spilled paint from God's palette.

Every so often, Ellis would shoot Dakota a glance. Not the curious or probing kind, but the reassuring ones that said he was right there with her, ready to face whatever awaited them. Maybe he was overstepping but he felt Dakota's need and responded, damn the supposed rules.

Dakota took a deep breath, her gaze focused on the road ahead. "It's just past this bend," she murmured.

As they rounded the curve, a modest house came into view. The paint was peeling off in places, but it was tidy and well-kept, showing a certain level of attention to the small garden spilling over with bright, red tomatoes and large cucumber leaves shadowing green cucumbers ready for harvest.

"Your mom's a gardener?" he observed as they parked in the driveway beside an older sedan.

"Yeah, she's always had a green thumb," Dakota answered, climbing from the car, squinting against the sun as it played peekaboo with the passing clouds. "Something I didn't inherit."

Ellis chuckled. He remembered Dakota's black thumb. RIP to any plant she'd brought home until she finally accepted that silk plants were her only option.

Dakota bounded up the two short steps to the front door, but hesitated, her hand on the door handle. Her gaze darted toward the window of the house, as if half expecting her mother to appear. "You know, I've been preparing myself for this moment for so long, but now that it's here… I'm not sure if I can go through with it."

"Whatever happens in there, just remember you're not alone. I'm here with you."

Dakota met his gaze, her eyes glistening with unshed tears until she straightened her spine and cautiously opened the door, calling out, "Mom? You home?"

From his vantage point, Ellis could see a bedroom door slowly creak open to reveal a woman with salt-and-pepper hair, lines of age and hardship etched on her face. Her eyes, the same shade as Dakota's but weighed down by years of sorrow, widened in shocked recognition.

"Dakota?" Her voice was barely above a whisper, thick with disbelief.

Dakota swallowed hard, her posture straight yet hesitant. "Hi, Mom."

An uncomfortable silence stretched between them, as if each were stuck in a loop and unable to move past the glitch.

Attempting to bridge the gap, Ellis cleared his throat slightly and stepped forward. "Hello, Mrs. Foster. I'm Ellis, Dakota's…partner."

Dakota snapped out of her funk and picked up the slack with quick introductions. "Ellis, this is my mom, Amara Foster. Mom, meet my partner, FBI agent Ellis Vaughn."

"Partner…" she queried, sizing him up for a moment "…in life or work?"

"No, he's my colleague," Dakota answered for him. "I mean, we dated once before but that ended and now we're just colleagues…working a case."

One thin eyebrow shot up. "Oh, well, that sounds complicated."

Dakota's chin lifted, as if readying for a fight and preparing to counter any sling or arrow. "It's not. Perfectly professional between us. No problems whatsoever."

"Hmm…well, nice to meet you, Ellis," Amara said, gesturing toward the living room. "Come, sit. I have sun tea. Brewed this morning."

Both Ellis and Dakota declined as they sat on the faded gingham sofa. Time had frozen some moments; pictures of a younger Dakota with a bright smile, some with her sister and a few with all three in happier times.

"So," Dakota's mom began, her voice quavering with forced casualness, "how's the city? Still as busy and loud as ever?"

Dakota chuckled softly, "Even busier, I think. But it's home, you know?"

Her mom nodded, sinking into a chair, awkward in the space between them. "And the job?"

"Good. I made the new BIA Task Force. That's why we're in Flathead. We're working a local case so I thought I'd pop by."

A subtle frown of interest crossed Amara's features. "Local? Which case?" The faint burgeoning unsaid hope caused Dakota to hastily clarify.

"It's not Mikaya's case, a different girl. Her name was Nayeli Swiftwater. She was killed—"

"In Whitefish," Amara finished with a subtle stiffness of her mouth. "I remember."

Dakota didn't hide her surprise, murmuring, "I didn't think you'd remember much of that time period. It was only a few years after Mikaya died."

Amara didn't flinch as she said, "I remember far more than you think, far more than I'd like to. Being a drunk didn't save me from remembering a lot."

Dakota shot Ellis a look as if reaching her breaking point already, unable to bridge the gap between them. It killed him to see her trying to find common ground yet failing. "Well, speaking of… How's your sobriety going?"

"Each day has its struggles but I have my support group, my work and my garden. I'm managing."

"I'm glad to hear that, Mom," Dakota said. "You look good."

"Your garden is impressive," Ellis said, trying to find an inroad to a less painful topic. "Those tomatoes are better than what you can find in the store."

The first genuine smile wreathed Amara's face as she said, "I'll send some with you when you go. I always end up with more than I can use." She cast a hopeful look Dakota's way, adding, "I've been pickling, too. I can send you with a few jars of homemade pickles. I remember them being your favorite."

Dakota shared with Ellis, "I used to eat so many pickles as a kid. My mom makes the absolute best." To her mom, she said with a smile, "That would be great, Mom."

The air in the room seemed to lighten, as if the room itself released a deep breath, and conversation started to flow more easily.

By the time they wrapped things up, Dakota actually seemed glad they made the stop.

True to her promise, Amara fetched the jars of pickled cucumbers and a bag of ripe tomatoes. "For the road," she said, handing them to Dakota.

Ellis read the body language between the two women and he sensed something had shifted between them. It was small but it was a good start to something even better in the future.

They lingered longer than anticipated, sharing memories and skirting around certain topics. As the sun cast a soft glow over the garden, Dakota knew it was time to leave. She sent a silent, thankful look to Ellis and said, "We need to get to our hotel. Early start tomorrow."

Amara's eyes moved between the pair. "Had I known you were coming, I would've cleaned up your old room. It's currently storage for my craft supplies. I've a dream catcher workshop at the tribal center next week. Your room is filled with beads and frames."

Dakota smiled. "It's okay, Mom. We have reservations. Plus, I like sticking to routines during a case. Helps keep me focused. Tomorrow we're talking with Leonard Two Eagles and a few other people and I want to be mentally sharp."

Amara's eyes showed recognition. "Why Lenny? Is he all right?"

"I can't share case specifics," Dakota began, "but any insights about him you'd like to share?"

"He's turned his life around. Did a great job tilling my garden. I even hired him to paint the house next week. If you need a character reference, I'd back him."

Smiling, Dakota replied, "Noted. Thanks, Mom." They hugged awkwardly but what could you expect after a five-year hiatus from the mother/daughter dynamic? It was a start and Dakota would take it.

En route to the hotel, the atmosphere in the car was quiet, punctuated by the soft music on the radio. Pine Ridge Inn, their last-minute choice, was an old yet charming three-story building.

Pulling into the parking lot, Dakota spotted an oddity—a black sedan with dark windows. A sense of déjà vu hit her; she'd seen it near Amara's house earlier. As if on cue, the sedan exited the lot in a rush.

"That car seemed familiar, didn't it?" Ellis questioned.

"It was near my mom's. I found it peculiar then and now," Dakota admitted with narrowed gaze.

Her phone buzzed, displaying a chilling message: "Stop digging before someone gets hurt."

"Damn it," she swore under her breath. "Look at this," Dakota said, showing Ellis the message. "Brave keyboard warriors. Now I'll have to change my number."

"Forward that to your IT," Ellis said, surveying the surroundings. "You think it's Deakins's men tailing us?"

"Zoey mentioned they have two cars. Zoey took out one in the accident and the other was probably tailing us after we left the compound. That sedan might not be Deakins's," Dakota said.

"Which implies someone else is getting real uncomfortable about us asking around about Nayeli's case."

"That's always a good sign we're on the right track," Dakota quipped, shaking her phone playfully. "Thanks, anonymous keyboard warrior, for the validation."

Ellis chuckled and collected his key card. "I'd offer to share a room for safety's sake but I wouldn't want you to get the wrong idea that I was trying to get frisky."

"Frisky?"

"Yeah," he returned with a grin that sent butterflies dancing down her spine. "I said what I said."

A familiar warmth spread across her skin as memories of their "frisky" adventures flooded her brain and nearly stole her breath. A charged, playful silence grew between them and Dakota felt the tug to close the distance but she held back. The mantra "Keep things professional" seemed a distant echo as her fluttering heartbeat drowned out the good sense of that decision.

She'd underestimated the power of their chemistry when she'd naively assumed she could just ignore it.

Right now, ignoring the urge to reach up and pull him straight to her lips was like trying to yell into the swirling winds of a tornado to "back off," but that's what she needed to do.

Clearing her throat and breaking the spell, she scooped up her key card, joking, "Well, nice to know we have fans," and acted as if she hadn't been scorched by the sudden heat kindling between them.

They parted ways and Dakota let herself into her room, leaning against the door to take big, calming breaths, reminding herself that *she* was in control—not her hormones. Once she was sufficiently right in her head again, she focused on doing her usual safety checks before settling in her room for the night.

But alone in her hotel room, Dakota's emotional armor crumbled as she realized the threat might not be for her, but for the only family she had left behind on the reservation. And that thought was chilling—and aggravating.

Come for me all you want but leave my mom out of it.

She chewed the side of her cheek, sinking into the realization that she didn't want to be alone tonight but there was only one person she wanted beside her in that moment.

And she couldn't fight it.

Chapter 15

Ellis was barely settled when a soft knock echoed through the room. His pulse quickened, hoping it was Dakota. When he saw her, a rush of warmth surprised him, a surge of relief and happiness all at once.

"Is something wrong?" he asked, trying to appear chill when all he wanted was to pull her close and forget the world outside.

Dakota hesitated. "Could we…maybe get some pizza?"

It wasn't just her words, but the depth in her eyes that caught him off guard. The vulnerability there mirrored his own tumultuous feelings. They stood on the precipice of something deep and irreversible, and he felt his resolve waver.

From the look of it, so did hers.

It wasn't pizza she hungered for—and he was caught between giving in to what they both wanted in that moment and being the stronger person and shutting her down.

Dakota saved him from making that choice—taking control herself.

"I know we've agreed to keep things professional and I know I'm going back on my word but I don't care. I need you right now. Can we just pretend for a minute that the last two years didn't happen and just be who we used to be with each other?"

Was it possible? Was it wise? Hell, he didn't know the answer to either of those questions. All he knew was that his body needed hers like his lungs needed oxygen and he was tired of pretending otherwise.

Ellis reached for her hand, drawing her slowly into his room and shutting the door. "Are you sure?" he asked, their fingers intertwining. "It's not too late to change your mind."

Dakota lifted on her toes, pulling his hands and hers around her back as he drew her close. "I'm not changing my mind."

Ellis felt a spark of something familiar, something electric that made his heart race. He leaned closer, their faces just inches apart, their breaths mingling. This woman knew him like no one else, understood the private pain he carried from his childhood and gave him space to be who he needed to be. She was a kindred spirit, even if life had wedged them apart.

He didn't want to waste another minute second-guessing what was between them. He wasn't naive enough to think there wouldn't be consequences but his brain stubbornly refused to let that voice into his mental theater.

His lips found hers in a kiss that was soft at first but quickly intensified. Dakota's lips parted, welcoming him in with a moan that escaped her throat. Their tongues tangled, danced, as if they'd never stopped kissing. Heat built between them, igniting the desire they'd both done their best to smother.

Hands explored each other's bodies, as if reclaiming what had been lost. She shivered as his rough stubble scratched against her soft skin. Her nails dug into his shoulders, leaving small marks of possession. It was intense, passionate and all-consuming.

He'd dreamed of this moment but his imagination paled in comparison.

Dakota's small gasps poured gasoline into his soul as he devoured her from head to toe, lingering on the swollen peaks of her upturned beautiful breasts, suckling the areolas, using his tongue to swirl the tightened tips until she writhed beneath him, thrusting her hips toward the hard shaft between them.

"Ellis," she cried in a breathy groan that sent powerful surges throughout his body until he was nearly mindless with the need to feel her clasp around his length.

The scent of their sweat-slicked bodies drove him mad, desperate to sink deep between her hot wetness. Ellis pushed himself inside Dakota, instantly groaning with pleasure as she tightened all around him as her legs wound around his waist, drawing him deeper inside. He could die right now and leave this plane a happy man.

God, he'd missed her. Not only the sex—but her. Everything about Dakota made his heart sing. Even when she was being a stubborn ass, he missed her presence in his life.

He thrust against her with deliberate care, remembering the exact angle that always sent her straight to that sweet place of total oblivion.

"God, yes, Ellis," she groaned, clutching at him with mindless pleasure. "That's the spot..."

Pride and pleasure mixed with overwhelming emotion as he ground into her, rocking her body with each push. Dakota stiffened as she cried out, the sound of total abandon releasing his own climax.

"Uhhhh, Dakota..." Tears blinded him as her name exploded from his lips as he came hard, creating a confusing explosion of ecstasy and loss that he was helpless to stop. Burying his face against the sweetness of her neck, he gasped as he finished, his soul leaving his body as he lay completely spent.

He reluctantly rolled off her, surreptitiously wiping at his eyes. The last thing he needed was Dakota knowing that having sex with her had brought him to tears. He rose and grabbed a towel, handing it to her, much like old times. She smiled shyly, accepting the towel, but asked, "Would you mind if I showered instead? You could join me if you want."

"I'll start the water," he said, not about to give up the chance to be naked with Dakota a few minutes longer. They both knew they were acting on borrowed time. What existed outside of this moment wasn't a reality where they ended up together, but in this bubble, they were free to do and be whatever they wanted.

The intimate memories of Ellis filled her senses. Memories she'd tucked far away, though they lingered close to the surface. She missed being a part of his life and vice versa. People liked to say that you don't know what you've got until it's gone but Dakota always knew that losing Ellis would hurt for a lifetime. And so far, she hadn't been wrong.

While Dakota had moved on in the years apart, no one had made her feel quite like Ellis did. No one understood her like he had, or seemed able to hear what she was saying, even if she hadn't said a word. He had a special kind of magic that caressed her soul with the soft touch of a lover and she desperately missed that connection.

"I need to tell you something," she whispered as they stood close in the shower, her fingers tracing the contours of his body. His gaze remained fixed on her, expectant. "I don't actually have a boyfriend."

A soft chuckle escaped him. "I figured."

She raised an eyebrow, handing him the soap. "How?"

Ellis, gently lathering her skin, replied, "You are honest to a fault—and because of that—you're a terrible liar."

She accepted that judgment. "Guilty as charged." A weighty pause filled the air before Dakota murmured, "Being with others never felt the same. You were hard to replace."

Ellis's expression softened. "The feeling was mutual." Pulling her under the spray, he continued, "But we can't change the past. That incident, my outburst… I saw myself turning into my father. I needed help. You were right to leave."

Dakota's voice was laced with pain. "You're not him." And she believed that, but she'd been so shocked by the sudden explosion of violence from him that it'd thrown her world into a panic. "But I was afraid in that moment," she admitted quietly.

"I'm not him," he agreed, adding somberly, "but I was on that path."

Had he been, though? She'd had a lot of time to think about that day and sometimes she questioned whether she'd thrown in the towel too early. No one was perfect, so why had she given up on Ellis so quickly? She drew a deep breath, admitting, "Maybe I was too harsh that day. You'd been under a lot of stress—"

"No, don't do that, Dakota," he cut in with a warning, shaking his head adamantly. "I won't have you make excuses for what I did. There's no justification for that kind of behavior, ever. You knew that then, and deep down you know that now. Don't second-guess the right decision just because it hurts to remember what we had."

What we had. Past tense.

"But what if it was a mistake?"

"It wasn't."

How could he say that so easily? Was he relieved that they weren't together anymore? The thought stung. "You seem pretty sure that breaking up was the right thing to do," she said, trying to keep the hurt from her tone. "I wish I had the same confidence."

"Dakota, I saw myself through your eyes that day and I was sick to my stomach. I swore I'd never be like that bastard and yet, in that moment, I was just like him."

"You could never be like your father," Dakota protested, hating that he was carrying that guilt. "Never."

"You don't get it. I was him in that moment. My rage blotted out everything. I didn't care about anything. I reacted and I broke something that belonged to you—something irreplaceable. My dad did that shit all the time but it all starts somewhere. One act leads to another and then another. You were right to leave me. I deserved it."

"But you've changed, I can see it," Dakota said. "One mistake shouldn't ruin any chance in the future, right?"

"Dakota… What if it's a part of me and it's just lurking beneath the surface? As much as I've worked to change the parts of myself that are too much like my dad, he's still in there. I can't stomach the thought of you seeing me like that again. I just can't."

What could she say to that? Nothing. She wasn't going to argue the point but she shared in a small voice, "Being without you, it's been hard. I feel like a piece of me is missing. When does that feeling go away?"

"I wish I could say. Maybe it never does."

God, she hoped that wasn't the case. Dakota didn't like admitting a weakness but Ellis was her Achilles' heel. She needed to find a way to get over him if this was all they'd ever have. "How did you do it?"

"Do what?"

"Forget about me."

Ellis swore beneath his breath, shaking his head as if she were being deliberately difficult. He bracketed her against the cold shower wall, leaning in, kissing her hard and almost desperately. Their tongues tangled in an emotional dance that rang of heartbreak and loss but never new beginnings, and it was enough to split her in half. "Does that feel like I've forgotten about you?" he asked huskily, pulling away, his gaze tortured but laced with frustration. "You're the one person I'd do anything for. I'd give you my last breath if you needed it. Don't think for one second that I'm over you or that I ever will be because it ain't happening."

Dakota knew it was wrong of her to need to hear that from Ellis but the idea of suffering alone made her twist in on herself. Misery loved company, she supposed. "So, what does that mean for us?" she asked.

"It means if you ever need me, I'll be there."

Her eyes watered. What if she needed him right now? But what he wasn't saying was that there was no putting the pieces of their life together. She should've been grateful for his wisdom but she wasn't. If anything, she felt her heart cracking all over again and that made her want to howl at the moon for opening a box that should've stayed closed.

"You're an incredible woman. I'll always cherish what we had," he said.

That was the last thing she wanted to hear but she nodded, accepting the sentiment at its face value.

"So what happens now?" she asked, her voice choked.

"We solve this case and we go back to our lives. If this case goes well, I could return to Narcotics. It's what I've been working toward since Carleton bounced me from the division."

Dakota felt a pang of dread. Narcotics had changed him

before, dragging him into dark places where his demons felt too comfortable to play. She knew this was a touchy subject for Ellis but the idea of him returning to Narcotics made her sick to her stomach. She had to try and be the voice of reason. "But you're doing so well in Missing Persons," she argued gently. "Maybe that's where you're truly supposed to be. You're a brilliant investigator with a warm heart. I didn't say anything before but I peeked at your record since joining Missing Persons and you've received nothing but accolades from your superiors for your investigative skills. At least with Missing Persons you can see the good you're doing, unlike Narcotics, where it's just a day-in and day-out, never-ending stream of drugs hitting the streets and killing people."

"What are you saying? Narcotics doesn't do any good for the general public?"

"No, of course not, but you've got to admit, no matter how many drugs you take off the street, there's another shipment coming in on another boat. The war on drugs is never going to end. Hell, sometimes I think they ought to just legalize everything and tax the shit out of it like a legitimate business. That might be the only way we make any progress on the epidemic of drug trafficking."

Under normal circumstances, the conversation would've been entertaining. It wasn't the first time they'd joked that legalizing drugs might be the answer, but that was during better times when they were together.

Now, it felt like she'd insulted him and thrown a gauntlet by the way a curtain slammed down behind his eyes. He stiffened, shutting off the water. "Narcotics is where I belong. Even if you don't think we're making a difference, I believe that we are, and the work is important."

Dakota knew his narrow-minded vision to return to Narcotics had everything to do with the hatred he harbored for his dad. Before Ellis's dad ate a bullet, he'd been a street dealer and he hadn't been discriminate about whom he sold drugs to. Ellis had shared that his dad had thought it was funny to watch kids get high for the first time. One kid had OD'd. He'd only been twelve. "I'm not saying the work isn't important," she persisted, struggling to say the right thing. "I'm just saying—"

"Let's let it go," he said, wrapping a towel around his mid-section and handing her a towel, but gone was the warmth and tenderness of only a few moments ago—as was any hope of grabbing a pizza and eating it together while watching a movie like they used to.

Damn you, Ellis. Sometimes you're as stubborn as a mule.

Silence hung between them as they dried off. The emotional gulf was palpable. Dakota backed down reluctantly. "I guess you know what's best for you."

Looks like it was vending machine surprise and a heart full of regret for dinner tonight.

Chapter 16

Ellis slept fitfully, haunted by dreams of a future that never had a chance to happen. When the alarm pierced the darkness, he rose unsteadily and went through the motions of starting his day. Over bitter coffee, he pushed aside tangled thoughts of last night with Dakota and tried to focus on the case.

They'd agreed to be professional, but the charged air between them in the lobby said otherwise. Dakota's eyes were shadowed, proof she'd fared no better rest-wise.

"Shilah got the warrant for Deakins's financials," she said as they walked through the lobby and into the parking lot. Her distant tone held zero warmth, a complete 180 from the woman she'd been in his arms last night. "She said we've got enough to pull a warrant for The Congregation's financials but it wasn't easy. The judge said we were walking a fine line and we'd better have a good reason for poking into Deakins's church business. Now that we know that Deakins has friends in high places, makes me wonder if Deakins was tight with the judge, too."

"Probably a coincidence but I'll file that away as a possibility," Ellis said, pausing as Dakota purposefully went to the driver's side. It was a silent but loud assertion that they were going back to professional mode, and he couldn't say that he was glad, but he knew it was for the best.

He hated the distance between them but it was better this way. Did he want to be with Dakota? Hell yes. Was it healthy for either of them to forget the past and go blindly into the future when he couldn't promise the ghost of his father wouldn't show up again? No, he couldn't take that chance. He loved her too much to bank on a hope and a prayer buoyed by good intentions. Dakota deserved so much better.

Besides, what she said about him going back to Narcotics really punched him in the gut. She was wrong about Narcotics being a never-ending cycle that didn't do any good. Every shipment they took off the streets was potentially someone who didn't get addicted or die trying it.

When he was fresh on the detail, a case stuck with him that to this day chased his sense of duty. A sixteen-year-old kid died after trying meth for the first time. What the kid didn't know was it was laced with fentanyl and the tiny dose was enough to put the kid into the ground. He'd been the one to tell the kid's mother that her child was gone. You never forgot the sound of a mother's heart breaking.

That case had triggered the memory of the twelve-year-old who'd died because of his dad and it'd nearly crushed Ellis. Another street kid who died on a dirty couch in an abandoned warehouse, whose body wasn't found until two days later by construction workers getting ready to demo the building.

That kid had had a name, a future.

How could he explain that being on the streets, fighting the war on drugs helped him keep the darkness inside him in a manageable place? She knew his childhood was shit—but she only got the highlight reel. He'd never told her all the bad things that happened and he probably never would. Some things needed to stay private.

But every time he dragged a drug dealer off the street, confiscated a shipment of product or stopped a kid from throwing their life away—he was giving his old man the middle finger.

He wouldn't give that up—his sanity needed it. His therapist had suggested too many times he needed to share those dark things because light chases away shadows, but burdening Dakota with his bullshit past seemed unfair then and definitely not appropriate now.

"I also talked briefly to Zoey this morning."

At the mention of Zoey, he shoved his personal thoughts aside. "Yeah? How's she doing?"

"She said the food is much better at the safe house and the nurse is really nice but she's worried about her parents. The kid has such a heart of gold. Even though she knows her parents screwed up and lost their minds for a minute, she doesn't want them in jail."

"She's a good kid," he agreed, hating that Zoey was in the middle of a war she didn't start. "I really hope her adopted parents didn't have anything to do with Nayeli's death. Maybe they're victims in all of this, too, and just overreacted to the stress of the moment. I've seen it happen before."

"Yeah, maybe. I'm trying not to let my personal feelings get in the way. I really don't care for Barbara-Jean. Just goes to show there are difficult people anywhere you go—even off-grid."

He chuckled. No argument there.

"I called ahead. The receptionist said that Leonard Two Eagles always mows the grass on Wednesdays. He should be easy to spot."

As they pulled up to the parking lot, they saw a man on a riding lawn mower, wearing large ear-protecting headphones and focusing on the task. They exited the vehicle and headed toward him, waving to get his attention.

Leonard cut the engine warily and removed his headphones. His dark eyes were hard, distrustful. "Main office is down that way," he directed, but before he could replace his headphones, Ellis caught his attention.

"Leonard Two Eagles?" he asked, and the man nodded slowly, regarding them with suspicion. "I'm FBI Agent Ellis Vaughn and this is my colleague, BIA Agent Dakota Foster. Can we talk for a minute?"

Leonard nodded, though he didn't look like he trusted either of them, which wasn't surprising given his record. When he couldn't sleep last night, Ellis had logged on to his laptop and accessed Leonard's file.

A garden-variety criminal—drugs, petty theft, vandalism and assault and battery—the man had been through some things, but according to Evelyn and Amara he'd turned his life around. Ellis was more concerned with what might've happened seventeen years ago between him and Nayeli. Sometimes guilt was a powerful motivator for change, too.

"What do you want?" Leonard asked.

"We understand that you were once close with Nayeli Swiftwater. Can you tell us what the nature of your relationship was?"

"Haven't heard that name in years," he said. "She's with the spirits now."

"Are you a spiritual man?" Dakota asked, curious.

"I didn't used to be," Leonard admitted, wiping at his forehead. Even though it was brisk, he was sweating. "But when I was in trouble a lot my father told me I needed to sweat out my demons, to ask the ancestors for help. I had nothing to lose at that point so I started going to the sweat lodge ceremonies. Each time I came out a little bit stronger. Now, I go regularly. Does that make me spiritual?" He shrugged. "But I know I'm better because of it." Leonard used the break to resecure his long dark hair in the hairband away from his face. Tribal tattoos crawled up his neck and spilled onto his chin. "So, why are you asking about Nayeli?"

"The case has been reopened," Dakota answered. "And your relationship?"

"We were friends."

"Just friends?" Ellis queried. "We heard you were dating."

"And what if we were? Are you talking to all of her friends?" he asked defensively. "Or are you coming at me because I have a record? I haven't had no trouble with the law in five years. Not a single thing. Ask my probation officer—he'll tell you. I've been toeing the line like I'm supposed to."

"No one is accusing you of anything," Dakota clarified, regarding him without emotion. "Is there a reason you feel attacked?"

"Yeah, because that's all you cops ever do. Doesn't matter what badge you're wearing, you're all the same. You see my record and assume I'm the problem."

"No one is assuming anything," Ellis returned calmly. "We heard that you and Nayeli had a romantic relationship that ended badly. Can you tell us about that?"

"Yeah? What about it?"

"Tell us about the last time you saw Nayeli," Ellis said.

When he hesitated, Dakota said, "If you have nothing to hide, you have nothing to worry about."

"I know what you want me to say—"

"We only want the truth," Ellis said.

"No, you want someone to take the rap for what happened to her, that's what you want. Well, it isn't going to be me. I didn't kill Nayeli. I would never. I loved her. You want the truth? That's the truth, I loved her more than anything on this earth but she didn't feel the same way about me."

"How'd you handle that?"

Leonard's mouth seamed as if ashamed. "Not real good. I was still drinking and stuff then. I think that's why she didn't want to be with me—and I really don't blame her for that—but at the time, it really crushed my heart, you know what I mean? And I didn't know how to handle my feelings."

"Did you hurt her?" Dakota asked.

"I pushed her around that night but I never hit her or nothing like that."

"And that night, was that the last night you saw her?" Ellis followed.

Leonard nodded solemnly. "Sometimes I think maybe if I'd cleaned up before it all happened, she might still be here and we'd be together."

"Do you remember when that was? The date, specifically."

"Of course I remember. It was August 25—I remember because I was arrested for drunk driving on my way back from her place that night."

Ellis did the math. That would've made Nayeli about two months pregnant.

Ellis and Dakota exchanged a glance. If the dates matched up…

"One more thing," Ellis said casually. "Would you consent to a DNA sample?"

* * *

They left Leonard with their contact cards and instructions to stick around town or else they'd have a talk with his probation officer. Leonard looked visibly shaken by their question about the DNA sample. Had it never occurred to him that the kidnapped infant could've been his?

"I don't think it's him," Dakota admitted, disappointed. "I mean, I've seen plenty of guys guilty of killing their significant other trying to play it off as innocent, but Leonard doesn't give off that vibe. He looked genuinely stricken at the idea that he might have a child he didn't know about."

Ellis agreed. "He's got a chip on his shoulder from years of being on the wrong side of the law but that doesn't make him a murderer. Plus, he doesn't strike me as the type of man who could kill a woman in cold blood and sneak off in the night with a baby. It doesn't add up. He might be Zoey's biological father but I doubt he's Nayeli's killer."

"Well, DNA should clear up a few things at least. I'll have Shilah get the warrant for his DNA."

"I don't even think he'll fight it. I think he wants to know, too," Ellis said.

Dakota nodded absently, but her thoughts kept drifting back to last night—the same thoughts that'd kept her from falling asleep at a decent hour and made waking up a Herculean effort. The way he'd kissed her, touched her... It had resurrected feelings she'd spent a long time burying. But it was a mistake, one they couldn't repeat, and she was frustrated with her own lack of self-control for practically jumping into his arms when he gave her a chance to reconsider.

At least Ellis had been trying to do the right thing.

She forced herself to focus. "You're right, he seemed genuinely shocked about the baby. I don't think he's our guy."

Ellis agreed as they got into the car. Dakota gripped the steering wheel tightly, hyperaware of his presence next to her. The interior still held traces of his scent, evoking memories of heated passion in that cramped motel bed. She shifted in her seat, willing the memories away.

"You okay?" Ellis asked.

"Yeah, fine," she said sharply.

An awkward silence filled the car until it threatened to smother her. Dakota's mind raced as she drove. Why couldn't she find that professional distance that she'd mastered before? She wanted to hate Ellis for complicating things, but the truth was she'd created this mess and that bothered her a lot.

Was it her fault that they had a combustible chemistry, no matter how hard they tried to ignore it? *Deflecting and justifications. Nice, Foster. C'mon, you're better than that.*

Okay, so it happened, and it can't happen again. She refused to lose herself to him like she had all those years ago. This case was too important to let emotions get in the way. *Shake it off, put it in its place and move on.*

"About last night…" Ellis finally began and she nearly jumped out of her skin. Was the man psychic or something? Or was she just that transparent?

"We don't have to go there," Dakota said tightly. "It was a mistake. We can't change the past. Let's just focus on finding justice for Nayeli."

Ellis looked like he wanted to argue but finally just nodded. Dakota swallowed hard against the ache in her chest. She had to stay detached, despite her traitorous heart begging her to fall into his arms again.

The ghosts of the past would just have to wait in line.

This case came first.

Chapter 17

The drive back to Missoula was quiet, the air still thick with unresolved tension from last night. Ellis was glad when they pulled into the hotel parking lot. He needed space to clear his head.

"I'll get us separate rooms," he told Dakota. She nodded, her face unreadable. It was possible fatigue made her seem unreachable but it could also be because they were both struggling with the aftermath of what they'd done.

Without much further discussion, they got their keys, made quick plans to meet in the morning as usual and then went their separate ways. Once in his room, Ellis sat on the edge of the bed and scrubbed a hand over his face. Last night had been a mistake, but damn if it didn't feel good at the time. He wished they could go back to how it used to be, before life got so goddamn complicated.

Maybe in a different timeline, he and Dakota were living their best lives, married with a couple of kids, making the dream work, but in this timeline? Shit, they'd made a huge mess of things.

His phone buzzed with a message from his work email. He frowned as a photo of Senator Mitchell Lawrence, arm in arm with Zachariah Deakins, popped up on his screen. The message was sent anonymously through the FBI tip line. Senator Lawrence was known for hawking family values loudly and obnoxiously whatever chance he could get. Ellis always gave guys like Lawrence the side-eye. No one was that virtuous. If you had to yell it to the rafters how rigidly you walked the line of morality, chances were you were playing fast and loose with the rules.

But the anonymous tip was clear—the men were definitely connected somehow. What role was the senator playing in this little mystery?

He probably should've just called but he headed over to Dakota's room, rapping on the door.

She answered cautiously.

"We got a lead," Ellis said without preamble, showing her the photo. "Senator Mitchell Lawrence is tied up in this somehow. We need to talk to him."

Dakota's jaw tightened as she studied the image. "Guess we're taking a trip to Helena," she said, adding, "Oh, and Shilah told me that the threatening text came from an untraceable burner. Looks like whoever my keyboard warrior is was at least not stupid enough to use their actual phone."

Ellis expected as much. "I had a feeling that was going to be the case. You're definitely going to need to swap out your number."

Dakota looked annoyed but nodded. However, she waited a beat before saying, "You could've just called me about the photo. You didn't have to tell me in person."

Right, yeah, I know that. I'm just stacking up stupid mistakes by the bushel.

"I needed to get ice and it was on the way," he lied gruffly.

"Oh, sorry. I shouldn't have assumed anything," Dakota said, her cheeks heating. "My mistake. Good night."

He acknowledged her sentiment with a jerked nod on the pretense of heading to the ice machine but as soon as

Dakota closed her door, he changed direction and returned to his room, feeling like an idiot.

Ellis closed the door to his room and leaned against it with a sigh. Dakota was right—he didn't need to tell her about the lead in person. He just wanted an excuse to see her again, even though he knew he shouldn't.

Groaning quietly, he berated himself for acting like a lovesick teenager. They had a job to do. Personal feelings had no business on the playing field right now.

Still, seeing the faint flush on Dakota's cheeks threatened his resolve. He stood by his reasoning to keep things professional but that was his head talking, not his heart. That thing between them was a fire that couldn't be extinguished and was impossible to ignore but they had to try.

With a grunt of frustration, Ellis pushed off the door. A cold shower and a good night's sleep. That's what he needed to clear his head. In the morning, they would be focused, professional partners again—and they'd wash, rinse and repeat until this case closed.

Yet as he stripped down and stood under the frigid spray, he couldn't stop his thoughts from drifting back to Dakota. The silken warmth of her skin, the taste of her lips…

Get it together, man, he scolded himself. He ticked off the priorities: justice for Nayeli, answers for Zoey and getting back to Narcotics where he belonged. Too much was at stake. He couldn't afford distractions throwing him off course.

Ellis toweled off and sank onto the edge of the bed, dropping his head in his hands. Unwanted memories from two years ago surfaced, when he'd finally worked up the courage to see a therapist after Dakota left him.

After he'd acted like a psychotic toddler and destroyed her grandmother's crystal cookie jar in a fit of misplaced rage.

"Anger is a natural emotion, but violence is a choice," Dr. Singh had told him gently. "You cannot change how you were raised, Ellis. But you can choose to break the cycle of abuse. Be better than what came before."

At the time, her words had given him hope. But now, as his feelings for Dakota resurfaced, so did his deepest fears. What if the monster his father tried to turn him into was still lurking underneath the surface? Waiting to lash out and hurt those he cared for most?

Dakota had been right to walk away. She deserved someone uncomplicated, without so many broken pieces. Ellis was a chronic work in progress. Despite his best efforts, shadowy remnants of his father's cruelty still haunted him.

Although he no longer went to regular sessions anymore, Ellis kept Dr. Singh's number in his phone. Sort of like an "In case of emergency, break glass" situation.

He was proud that he hadn't yet had to use that safety lever but the fear that he could lose control again haunted him.

Again, he heard her voice, reminding him, "It's a process, Ellis. There will be setbacks. What matters most is that you keep getting back up."

Dakota was his weakness, but he had to stay strong—for both of them.

Dakota lay awake, staring up at the dark ceiling as sleep evaded her, yet again. The ghost of Ellis's touch still lingered on her skin, raising goose bumps. Her body ached for more, even as her mind pushed against her longing. She was stronger than this, wasn't she? She'd never been the type of woman to pine after a man, nor did she allow anything or anyone to cloud her judgment when it came to holding a personal boundary.

What made Ellis different from any other man she'd cut ties from in the past?

With a frustrated sigh, she kicked off the covers and went to stand by the window, gazing sightlessly over the parking lot. She shouldn't have let things go so far. She was to blame for what happened. Sure, it took two to tango, but she'd gone to his hotel room knowing full well what she was truly asking. She'd poked the sleeping bear and she couldn't be shocked that now that it was awake, it was hungry.

Well, what was done was done, right?

They had a job to do, and letting themselves get deeper involved would only end in heartbreak. Hadn't she learned that lesson already?

Resting her forehead against the cool glass, Dakota replayed every searing kiss, every hungry caress in her memory. Ellis had always been her weakness, a fire in her blood that nothing could quell. Much as she tried to resist him, desire won out.

But it was more than physical attraction. When Ellis held her, she felt a sense of homecoming, like the missing piece of herself had been restored. She had never stopped loving him, despite the bitter pain of their breakup years ago.

Dakota squeezed her eyes shut, remembering the shattered cookie jar, Ellis's uncontrollable rage. The yelling, the tears. Her heart had broken, but her will remained unbendable. She'd done what she had to and Ellis had agreed the decision had been sound.

But risking sounding like someone in denial, she could sense the change in Ellis. Was he the same man with a toxic well of rage percolating inside him, just waiting for the right moment to explode? Her gut told her that he wasn't but Ellis was afraid to test that theory. They'd never actually talked about that night, only the repercussions.

Resting her palm on the cool glass, Dakota considered reaching for her phone. One call, and she could feel the reassurance of Ellis's voice again. One call, and all her doubts might be silenced.

But she stopped herself. Tomorrow they would be professional partners once more. She was Dakota Foster—independent, uncompromising. Her spirit had been bruised but never broken. This was about justice, not burned bridges or second chances.

Dakota left the window and returned to bed. She would build an emotional wall between herself and Ellis, even as their bodies yearned to come together once more. Her heart had chosen self-preservation over the man who offered both boundless love and bottomless pain.

Dakota stared up at the dark ceiling, unable to quiet her racing mind. Could people truly change their nature, she wondered, or did the past leave permanent scars? Even though they both shared dark childhood moments, Ellis's childhood was the stuff of nightmares. His father had been a true villain, a man without any redeeming qualities from Ellis's point of view, and it took a lot for a kid to truly hate their parent.

Going through that kind of pain left trauma that never went away, no matter how you tried to bury it. Dakota still believed that working Narcotics had kept dredging up that poison until it was all that was left in Ellis's cup. She hated the idea of him returning to the very place that'd aggravated those wounds, but it wasn't her place to insert her feelings anymore.

She wanted to believe Ellis was a different man now—kinder, gentler. But a dark voice whispered warnings she couldn't ignore. What if she was wrong?

Being near Ellis again was emotionally exhausting. She

had to remain hypervigilant, continually tamping down her desire while keeping her walls up. The work of constantly analyzing her every word and action to maintain that professional distance was wearing on her in ways that she hadn't seen coming.

Yet she was drawn to him like a moth to light, despite the risk of getting zapped. His laugh made her heart clench. His subtle scent stirred memories that left her aching. Shutting out the truth was impossible—she still loved him, after everything.

Which left her guarded, confused, oscillating between hope and fear. Part of her yearned to melt into his arms again, rekindle what they'd lost. Another part wanted to run, to protect the still-mending pieces of her heart before it was shattered beyond recognition.

Could she ever let go of the past? Did she even have the right to, when Nayeli's spirit still cried out for justice? The fact that she was even losing sleep over this was selfish. She had to stop.

Exhaustion seeped into Dakota's bones, but sleep would be difficult to find. Too many ghosts jostled for prominence in the darkened bedroom for any decent shut-eye. For now, she could only take things one moment at a time. And try to quiet the ceaseless chaos in her heart.

In her misguided youth, she'd dated an older man in college. At the time he'd seemed so much more emotionally intelligent and wise than the men her age. She'd been awestruck by his solid sense of self and she'd eaten advice from the palm of his hand—which he was fond of feeding her at the drop of a hat.

One thing about Silas that'd been incredibly alluring was his unwavering sense of always knowing what to do in any given situation. She'd asked him his secret, and feeling intellectually superior—something she came to learn was his ultimate failing—he'd shared his method.

"Baby girl," he'd drawled, smiling down at her with indulgence as she rested on his bare chest, "it's simple."

She gazed up at him with pure adoration. "Yeah, how so?"

"I'm always right—even if I'm wrong."

Dakota had chuckled, believing him to be joking, but he was completely serious.

"When you believe your way is right, it always is."

"But no one is always right, all of the time," Dakota had protested, lifting up to peer at him quizzically. "At the end of the day, you're only human and humans make mistakes. Even you."

Silas just shook his head as if she were adorably simple and unable to grasp the concept that he was sharing but before they could dive into that discussion more deeply, he'd distracted her with an epic lovemaking session that'd lasted into the wee hours of the morning.

She'd been too exhausted to return to the topic, but eventually she realized Silas wasn't the man she thought he was and broke it off without ever looking back.

However, she wondered if maybe Silas had influenced her more than she realized.

When she made a decision, she never changed her mind, even when she was wrong.

Chapter 18

The bitter hotel coffee did little to wake Ellis as he and Dakota left early to make the long drive to Helena where Lawrence kept an in-state office. This case had him in the car more than any case he'd ever been assigned and it was starting to wear on his nerves.

"Sleep okay?" he asked, making conversation, but one short look from Dakota told him, no, she hadn't and she wasn't up for small talk, which suited him fine. He didn't want to chat about the weather, either. "Are you driving or me?"

"You," she responded, pulling her sunglasses from her bag, pushing them farther up on the bridge of her nose as she slid into the passenger seat. "I have a splitting headache and the sun is stabbing my brain."

Yeah, same. A tiny reluctant smile tugged at the corner of his mouth. He'd be willing to bet Dakota would sleep the entire way to Helena while he drove. Dakota had slept through more road trips than he could count, rising refreshed and ready to roll while he, on the other hand, had to prop up his eyelids with toothpicks. He didn't mind, though—not then and not now.

True to his prediction, Dakota was lightly snoring before they'd even cleared the city limits of Missoula, but knowing that no matter what lay between them, she still felt safe enough in his company to sleep like a baby when she needed it gave his masculine pride a much-needed lift.

They arrived at the slick, executive building in good time and an aide ushered them into Senator Lawrence's expansive office.

The heavy oak door swung open to reveal an office that looked more like a luxury hotel lobby than a public servant's workplace. Plush cream carpeting swallowed their footsteps as they walked past framed photos of Lawrence with other dignitaries.

Behind an imposing desk of highly polished mahogany, a wall of built-in bookcases stood packed with leather-bound volumes. Ellis noted the complete works of Shakespeare and other classics one would display to look cultured but likely never read, and he immediately started to get a vibe from the man that didn't bode well.

The sitting area held a crystal vase bursting with fresh lilies and ornate antique sofas upholstered in brocade.

Everything about the office shrieked of old money and privilege. Ellis wondered how many donations from struggling families could have furnished this ostentatious space. He glanced at Dakota and knew she was thinking the same.

The distinguished senator rose from behind his desk to shake their hands with a polite, concerned expression.

"You're lucky I'm in town this week. How can I assist the FBI and BIA today?" Lawrence asked mildly as he settled into the leather chair behind his imposing mahogany desk.

"We appreciate you making time for us on such short notice," Ellis said. "We'll try to make this as quick as possible."

"Anything I can do to help," Lawrence said.

Ellis opened by sliding the photo of Lawrence and Zachariah Deakins he'd had printed across the desk. If the senator recognized it, he didn't let on. Lawrence's stare was blank as he said, "By the looks of it, this is a publicity shot," Lawrence replied easily. "I've taken countless of these over the years. Is there a reason I should know this person?"

"His name is Zachariah Deakins. He's the pastor/leader of a minimalist group called The Congregation in Stevensville."

"Hmm, can't say the name rings a bell," Lawrence said. "Has he done something wrong?"

"Not that we know of, yet, but personally, I think people who run cults are always hiding something," Dakota said.

"You said it was a group, like a church," Lawrence said, confused. "Why are you calling it a cult?"

"Because it's very cult-ish," Dakota returned simply. "We visited the compound and it seemed deeply cult-like, and history has shown that cults are rarely a good thing, no matter how they like to paint the picture otherwise."

Lawrence chuckled with amusement at Dakota's judgment. "I see you have some strong personal feelings on the subject, but have they actually done anything wrong?"

"Not that we can tell," Ellis answered calmly. "But there are connections to the case we're working that are potentially serious."

"What case is that?"

"Seventeen years ago, a young Indigenous woman named Nayeli Swiftwater was found murdered in her Whitefish apartment and her six-week-old infant daughter, Cheyenne, was missing. The trail went cold and the case gathered dust until Nayeli's missing daughter showed up at a Butte hospital."

One brow went up. "Interesting. Where has the child been this whole time?"

"She was adopted by a family within The Congregation and living on the compound," Dakota shared. "But we haven't determined yet if the family who raised her are guilty of anything more than unknowingly adopting a stolen child."

"What a terrible tragedy," Lawrence murmured, shaking his head. "That poor girl. I hope she's all right."

"She's recovering," Ellis said, wanting to steer the conversation away from Zoey. "But that brings us back to you."

"Me? How?"

"Well, the compound was formerly a bankrupt summer camp known as Camp Serenity Falls, which was purchased by a company that traces back to you."

"Ah, I see," Lawrence connected the dots, quickly explaining, "my investment advisers are always making financial decisions without my involvement. All aboveboard, of course, but I leave the heavy lifting to the professionals. I own several companies, all funneled through my investment group. I couldn't even tell you all of the businesses in my portfolio. All I know is that my investments are robustly profitable, and for that I don't mind paying the exorbitant amount each year to my investment group for their labors." At that Lawrence smiled widely, unruffled and unconcerned.

But Ellis's investigative senses tingled.

"So you don't remember Nayeli's case?" Dakota asked. "It was pretty big news at the time. Being an upscale community, Whitefish isn't known for its violent crime."

For a split second, Ellis thought he saw Lawrence's genial mask crack. But the senator quickly composed himself, spreading his hands regretfully. "I'm embarrassed to admit that I don't remember the case. I take any crime committed against my constituency seriously—particularly violent crimes against young women—but I don't quite recall that one. I'm sorry."

Ellis supposed it was possible the senator missed the case because he hadn't actually been elected as senator yet when Nayeli was killed. At that time, Lawrence was still an attorney and serving in the House of Representatives and couldn't be expected to know about every murder case in his state.

Still, there was something about Lawrence that rubbed him wrong—or maybe it was just that Ellis felt all politicians, at some level, somewhere, had something to hide.

As they left Lawrence's office, Dakota felt the senator's eyes boring into her back. A warning, or a threat? Or was she seeing what her bias wanted her to see?

She shook off the ominous feeling as Ellis held the door for her. Still, unease lingered in her gut. Men like Lawrence weren't used to being questioned. For now he wore the mask of polite cooperation, but how long until it slipped?

"He's definitely hiding something," Dakota said quietly as they walked down the echoing marble hallway. "If he's involved in Nayeli's case…"

She didn't need to finish the thought. They both knew what was at stake. A killer escaping justice. And even worse, if Lawrence was involved, now that he knew Zoey was alive, her safety could be at risk.

"Just to be on the safe side, I'll beef up the security at the safe house," Ellis said.

Dakota unconsciously flexed her hands, longing to grab Lawrence by his expensive lapels and shake the truth out of him, not the politically savvy responses that might as well have been crafted by his PR manager.

But they had to move carefully. Lawrence was no petty

criminal. His wealth and connections could potentially make him dangerous, capable of burying inconvenient truths.

"Did you buy that?" Dakota asked, still chewing on the conversation. "Are we really supposed to believe that the senator doesn't have a clue what properties and businesses he owns?"

Ellis wasn't sure. "It's possible. He's a wealthy man and definitely enjoys his creature comforts. Priceless art on the walls, luxury furniture, and that suit probably cost an easy couple of Gs. From what I've seen, the super-rich go about business differently than the average person. You and I wouldn't let a group of people handle our big purchases but the super-rich don't think twice about it."

"Yeah and then they cry about it when their investment team or adviser ends up ripping them off for millions," Dakota quipped derisively. "Honestly, I have no sympathy for them when that happens. They're so far removed from reality that it's hard to work up a tear when they get taken advantage of."

"Being rich isn't a crime," he reminded Dakota with a grin.

She shrugged. "Try saying that to a kid who hasn't eaten in a few days. Sorry, but living on the reservation, you get a different view of people with more than most. Maybe I'm wrong for saying it but I'm just not a fan of uncontrolled capitalism."

Dakota didn't often share her particular views on economic issues but people like Lawrence triggered her childhood wounds all over again.

When her mom had sunk deep into her alcoholism, money had become desperately scarce. Amara had lost one of her two jobs for showing up drunk on-site and barely held on to the first. Dakota had picked up an after-school job to fill in the gaps but it was hard to focus when sheer exhaustion and hunger ate at your ability to function. She nearly dropped out of high school when her failing grades had threatened her graduation status.

Somehow she'd pulled herself together in the nick of time, graduating with good enough grades to get her to college, but she remembered those times like they were yesterday—and she wasn't alone. Lots of kids went without on the reservation and it was a serious problem of varying levels for all First Nations tribes.

"I'm just saying, the guy seems like a rich, entitled asshole and when he smiled at me with those perfectly white teeth, I felt like a crocodile had just grinned my way."

Dakota's unexpected comparison popped a laugh from Ellis. "A crocodile?" he exclaimed.

"Yeah, or something else with big, sharp teeth that'll take a bite out of your leg if you turn your back on him. A Komodo dragon would've worked, too. Those things are scary. I saw one on a nature documentary swallow a whole baby goat without blinking an eye—and then kept walking like it was just enjoying a leisurely stroll through the garden."

"I never realized you felt so strongly about the Komodo dragon."

She smothered the urge to grin. Ellis always had the ability to coax her away from a bad mood but she didn't want to let this go.

The opulent office, expensive suit and rehearsed charm had set her teeth on edge. Men like Lawrence represented everything wrong with the system—and maybe it rubbed her the wrong way that he had zero clue, nor seemed overly distraught, about Nayeli's case. Sure, he said the right things but true empathy had never actually reached his cool blue eyes.

Glancing over at Ellis, she knew he understood her cynicism, even if his own views were more tempered. Even though he'd experienced poverty when his dad was alive, he hadn't grown up watching the cycles of poverty and neglect on the reservation the way she had. Hadn't felt the bitter sting of injustice carved deep into her bones as there seemed to be one set of rules for one set of people and an entirely different set for her people.

"You really think he doesn't know exactly where his money goes?" she said, unable to keep the bite from her tone. "I think guys like him just play dumb when it's convenient."

Ellis shrugged. "Probably. But we can't make accusations without evidence."

Dakota breathed out hard through her nose. She knew he was right. Still, seeing such ostentatious wealth flaunted by men who ignored the suffering around them lit a fire in her gut—especially when that person was in a position of power and did nothing to help those less fortunate.

"I don't trust anything that came out of his mouth," she said bluntly. "You saw how rehearsed his answers were. He's hiding something."

But Ellis didn't fight her on her assessment, saying, "No argument there. We'll figure out his role in all this, I promise."

His calm certainty helped temper Dakota's simmering anger. In spite of their past sitting between them, she was grateful to have a partner who understood her fire for justice wasn't just recklessness.

Until then, she had to be patient, follow where the evidence led. For Nayeli's sake, and all the others failed by men like the senator. Even if it turned out that the senator was only guilty of being an entitled politician more interested in his career trajectory than the health and welfare of his constituency, the truth would come out.

Dakota would make sure of it.

Chapter 19

An unexpected complication popped up with the safe house location and the decision was made to move Zoey to a Billings location, which worked in Ellis and Dakota's favor because it meant they could return to home base for a few days at the very least.

By the time they got back to Billings, each going straight home for some much-needed recharging, Dakota was emotionally and physically exhausted.

After sifting through her mail, tossing the junk and placing the important mail in its own pile to go through later, she stumbled into her bedroom and fell into bed, instantly crashing, even though it was only late afternoon.

She woke several hours later to her apartment door buzzing from a package delivery. Disoriented at first, she stared blearily at the bedside clock, rubbing at her eyes when she couldn't make sense of what she was seeing. Eight o'clock? Had she really slept that long? Good grief, she was going to have a helluva time trying to sleep tonight after that epic nap. She climbed from her bed and walked with an exaggerated yawn to the front door, checking the peephole to see a package wrapped in brown paper.

She opened the door, grabbed the package and brought it inside, frowning when she saw no return address, her name and address handwritten in a hasty scrawl.

Using scissors, she cut the box open and immediately knew something was terribly wrong.

A wretched smell wafted from the open box the minute she cut the tape sealing the box. Decomp. Whatever was in that box was dead.

Rising, she grabbed her kitchen gloves and slid them on before returning to the box. She carefully pushed aside the crumpled newspaper to find the culprit—a long-dead rat, its insides oozing out of its slashed stomach, as it rotted into a pulpy, rancid mulch. Gingerly closing the box, she placed the box in her freezer and then called Ellis.

"Someone just delivered a dead rat to my apartment door," she said. "Seems my keyboard warrior just got a little more brave."

"Are you okay?" Ellis asked.

"Yes, I'm fine. I'm not scared of a dead rat."

"It's the fact that they got your personal cell and now your home address that concerns me. Whoever it is, they're escalating their threats."

Dakota refused to be intimidated. She was more annoyed than anything else. "Like I said, they're going to have to up their game if they think a dead rat is going to send me hiding in my closet. I'm well-armed and I'm trained to kill with my bare hands so they can take their chances and come at me if they're feeling lucky."

"Dakota, I'm serious. I don't like this and you're being too cavalier about it. I'm coming over," Ellis said. "Text me your address."

It was on the tip of her tongue to shut him down but she remained silent and texted him the address. "Bring a forensic kit. I have the box in my freezer."

"Will do. Be there in twenty."

Dakota paced her apartment, adrenaline still pumping through her veins after the disturbing delivery. She was angry more than afraid that this coward thought they could intimidate her with something so juvenile. A dead rat? *C'mon, that's child's play.*

When her buzzer rang, she checked the camera before buzzing Ellis up. He strode in wearing a stern expression, his sharp eyes sweeping the space as if to ensure her safety.

"You okay?" he asked first thing, clasping her shoulder. Dakota nodded curtly.

"I told you, I'm fine. But I want answers about how this piece of shit got my address." Gloved up, she went to the freezer and pulled out the box, handing it to Ellis.

Ellis, also gloved, carefully slid the box into an oversize evidence bag and sealed it quickly. "I'll get this to the lab right away, see if we can pull any prints or trace evidence. In the meantime, you should pack a bag just in case."

Dakota bristled at the suggestion of running. "I'm not going anywhere, I just got home."

Ellis sent her a hard stare that brooked no argument. "Don't be a stubborn ass, Dakota. Your home address has been compromised. It's not safe and you're not staying here."

"I'm sleeping in my bed tonight," she maintained stubbornly.

"The hell you are. Think about it, Dakota. Imagine this happened to a confidential informant. What would your advice be?"

Damn him for using logic against her. Of course, he was right. If the situation were happening to anyone else, she'd insist that they leave for someplace safer.

Ellis sensed her resolve slipping and pushed harder. "They're going to escalate when they realize you're not scared by what they've done so far—and that's how people get killed. I'm not taking that chance with your life. Pack your things."

"And where exactly am I going? I've just spent a week in hotels and I'm not about to spend another when I have a perfectly good bed of my own right here."

"You're not going to a hotel, you're coming home with me."

Dakota started to push back on principle but stopped. She was being childish and immature. Ellis was right—her place was compromised and if she didn't want to go to a hotel, Ellis didn't live far from her place so it made sense to bunk up. "Fine. I'll take the couch," she said, grudgingly accepting his offer.

"I'll take the couch, you can have my bed."

"That doesn't seem right," she said, frowning, but one look from Ellis and she didn't fight it. If he wanted to give up his bed, fine.

"Did you call your building manager when this came?" he asked. At Dakota's blank look, he sighed. "We should review security footage, see if they got the delivery on camera."

Chagrined that she hadn't thought of that, Dakota dialed the manager. Ellis's presence kept her levelheaded, focusing her adrenaline into constructive action instead of panic or rage. "I would've called, but I called you first," she admitted quickly before the site manager came on the line. She told the manager what happened and why she needed to see the hallway footage but his response wasn't great.

"Sounds like a prank," the manager said, dismissing her concern. "I wouldn't worry too much about it. If you want I can toss the carcass for you."

"It's evidence—and I still need to see the footage."

"Evidence? C'mon now, you're going a little far, don't you think, to bust a couple of bratty kids."

Dakota's patience was wearing thin. "My partner and I will be down in a few minutes to see the footage."

That's when the guy realized she wasn't messing around and wouldn't take no for an answer, causing him to admit sheepishly, "Yeah, about that… The cameras in the hallway don't actually work. They're just there to provide a deterrent. People see a camera and they think twice about vandalizing things but yeah, there's no actual feed."

Dakota was dumbfounded. One of the selling points of this complex was the seemingly robust security systems, and now she finds out it was all a marketing scheme?

"Sorry about that. Did you want me to throw away the carcass?"

"I told you, it's evidence, but I expect those cameras to start working real quick or else I'm reporting this building to the authorities for false advertising." She clicked off and percolated in silent anger. She met Ellis's questioning gaze, shaking her head. "Cameras are just for looks. They don't work."

Ellis nodded and said, "All right, grab your stuff. We need to get out of here, drop off this evidence at the FBI field office and then we'll head to my place."

Dakota didn't argue. His solid reliability comforted her, even as fury simmered beneath her calm surface at this violation of her home. She refused to be cowed by spineless threats but she felt a certain level of helplessness that rubbed her wrong. She wasn't the girl who needed saving, and yet Ellis was riding in, her white knight to rescue her.

"I don't need rescuing," she blurted out as she shouldered her bag.

Ellis chuckled and said nothing, simply leading out the front door, knowing she was right behind him.

But Ellis was the only person on this planet she'd ever allow even the semblance of rescuing her and that fact was not lost on her.

Ellis and Dakota dropped off the evidence at the FBI field office, filled out the paperwork and then headed to his place. Like Dakota, he'd only just moved to Billings in the last year, which made him the right choice for the task force collaboration, according to his supervisor.

Ellis tidied his sparsely decorated living room, trying not to focus on the reality that Dakota was there with him, in his space. The old, overstuffed couch and recliner were comfortable but shabby compared with Dakota's stylish place. Mismatched thrift store end tables held stacks of car magazines and the TV remote. After a quick tour of the apartment, he grabbed some extra blankets and a pillow for himself and tossed them to the couch. He'd fallen asleep plenty of times on that sofa to know that it was comfortable enough to fall asleep on, but the thought of Dakota sleeping in his bed made his pulse quicken, even as he knew it was the only sensible option.

He sighed, wishing he had art on the walls, fresh flowers or something to make it homier for Dakota. But he could barely keep his tiny kitchen tidy, let alone make a place warm and welcoming. That had always been one of her gifts. Well, she knew his place wasn't a contender for *Better Homes & Gardens* editorial and that hadn't changed.

"It still doesn't seem right to kick you out of your own bed," Dakota protested with a frown. He watched Dakota's throat move as she swallowed, eyes flickering with some interior debate. Ellis tensed, unsure if she would agree.

The wire-taut energy between them left no doubt this was intimate territory. Dangerous territory, given their history.

Ellis held her gaze, willing her to accept. "I insist. You need rest—a proper mattress will do you better than my lumpy couch. Besides, you'll be happy to know that bed set is brand-new and the mattress is one of those super-fancy ones that you were always trying to get me to buy."

"You pulled the trigger after we broke up?" she teased. "Nice."

"Yeah, and I'm a big enough person to admit you were right. Best damn purchase of my life. Turns out my aching back wasn't from my misguided childhood but just a really bad bed that wasn't doing my back any favors."

"Even more reason for me to sleep on the sofa," she protested. "I don't need your aching back on my conscience."

"You're taking the bed," he said decisively.

"If you're sure," Dakota finally acquiesced. Ellis let out a slow breath, ignoring the heat flooding his veins at the images her words conjured. Dakota, hair splayed across his pillow. Dakota, wrapped in his sheets. "I'm going to shower real quick, if you don't mind."

"Be my guest," he said, busying himself with making up his bedding, needing the distraction. This was about safety, nothing more. The distant sound of the shower tightened his groin as memories flooded his brain and he realized it would take the strength of a saint to stick to his guns, keep it professional and ignore the very real need to feel Dakota in his arms.

Especially knowing that someone was targeting her. It seemed some misogynistic bullshit that whoever was targeting Dakota hadn't also targeted him. Joke's on them— Dakota didn't scare easily.

One thing he knew for sure, if he got his hands on the

person trying to terrorize Dakota—he'd tear that person apart. They didn't know whom they were messing with, or the demons he held at bay.

Thoughts of Dakota's nude body, water sluicing over her curves, made his throat go dry. This was dangerous territory, given their history. But even more perilous was the escalating threat she now faced.

Ellis paced the living room, pausing to peer through the blinds into the dark parking lot. Were they being watched? Followed? Someone knew where she lived—someone with a sick mind.

The shower stopped. Ellis tensed, listening to Dakota's muted movements in the next room. He busied himself arranging blankets on the lumpy couch, trying to ignore his pounding heart.

When she emerged in a haze of steam, Ellis busied himself fluffing a lumpy pillow, avoiding looking at her damp hair and pink cheeks. *Don't go there*, he warned himself.

"Let me know if you need anything," he muttered, catching a trace of her lavender shampoo as she passed. He ached to pull her close, breathe her in, but resisted the urge. *Keep it professional.*

After brushing his teeth to have something to do besides imagine her in his bed, Ellis splashed cold water on his face. Gripping the cheap laminate sink, he drew a deep breath. He wouldn't fail her. This humble place didn't matter, only keeping her close, keeping her safe. He could battle his desire for her sake. For Dakota, he would stay strong.

And that meant going to that sofa, climbing beneath the blankets and pretending that it was just another night—and that the love of his life wasn't in the other room.

Chapter 20

While Ellis debriefed his people, Dakota debriefed hers. It felt like an age since she'd seen her team in person but this case was dragging them all over Montana and back with very little to show for their effort.

Dakota tried not to compare how her case was faring in comparison with how Sayeh and Levi's case closed with an epic capture, but Dakota was naturally competitive and the need to close this case was eating at her.

Of course, it was more than her competitiveness that drove her but it was an aspect of her personality that had always worked in her favor in her field.

They all met in the conference room and Isaac took the lead, wanting to know everything.

Dakota didn't sugarcoat anything, sharing everything they'd discovered so far, and even included the most recent delivery of the rat to her doorstep, but she stretched the truth about where she was staying, saying that she was staying with a friend.

"You can stay with me if you want," Shilah offered. "I've got a spare room that's just collecting dust."

"I'm good, thanks," she said, appreciative of Shilah's offer, but she'd slept better than she had in months last night. She wasn't naive—she knew the reason—but she didn't want to draw attention to it, even within herself. Denial could be useful at times. "So, now with Zoey here in Billings, we're taking a few days to regroup and make sure she's okay before heading back out into the field."

"What's the word on that rat delivery?" Sayeh asked, frowning. "That's some gangster-type shit."

Levi agreed. "I don't think you should dismiss that threat as nothing."

Dakota didn't like admitting that they were right but she also hated that someone had sent her running from her own apartment. She loathed weakness and she definitely hated feeling like the damsel in distress. "Well, the FBI has their forensics on it. The apartment manager thinks it was a kid prank but Ellis doesn't agree."

"I'm with Ellis," Levi said. "Especially after that text message. Someone's toying with you. The question is, why?"

"If it's because of the case, that must mean we're making people uncomfortable," Dakota said, taking that as a good sign that they were on the right track. She turned to Shilah. "What's the progress on getting Deakins's financials?"

"Still working on it. It's taking a little longer than I anticipated but we should have the financial audit in a few days."

Isaac grunted in approval, pleased with their progress. "You here for a few days?"

"Yeah, I need a break from the car."

"Take a few days off, recalibrate."

Ordinarily, having your boss tell you to take a few days off would be a godsend but Dakota didn't feel right resting when Zoey's future lay in the balance. Maybe she'd take a day but then it was back to the case.

But Shilah had news that definitely set her teeth on edge. "The Grojans were released from custody yesterday. There was nothing to really hold them on aside from malicious mischief, which is a weak misdemeanor at best. Their lawyer got the judge to dismiss the charges given their emotional duress. They went back to the compound."

"But we don't know their involvement with Nayeli's murder," Dakota protested. "What if they're guilty of killing Nayeli to get her baby?"

Shilah shrugged, as if she didn't know what to say. "The judge didn't seem to feel they were a threat and let them go."

Dakota swore under her breath. "Well, crap."

Maybe she wouldn't be getting that day off after all.

She knew as soon as Ellis found out that the Grojans were free he'd blow a gasket, too.

"How'd the interview with Senator Lawrence go?" Isaac asked, keeping the flow going. He was a no-nonsense kind of boss, something she appreciated, but she would've liked more discussion about the Grojans. Personally, she didn't feel it was responsible to let them go when a shadow of doubt clung to their potential involvement with a murder.

Dakota shrugged. "Fine. He's as cool as a cucumber and always says the right things but I didn't like him. I mean, he might be innocent but I just didn't like him as a person."

Sayeh commiserated with a chuckle. "I get that. Politicians always rubbed me wrong. It was always hard for me to believe that all of them weren't cut from the same cloth, but as much as I hate to admit it, Lawrence comes off as pretty clean."

"How so?" Dakota asked.

Sayeh pulled her paperwork, sharing, "Well, he donates every year to a nonprofit that helps orphaned children find homes. He and his wife are active in their church, big donors for all of the church-related functions, and they host an annual fundraiser at their home to help feed the homeless on Thanksgiving. I mean, as far as optics go, the guy is squeaky clean and well-liked."

"Ugh, I still hate him," Dakota muttered with a derisive grin.

Isaac didn't find the humor in the situation, though. "Keep your personal feelings under wraps. The last thing this task force needs is the accusation of an unwarranted witch hunt on personal reasons alone. It's already hard enough keeping interest in this task force past the initial honeymoon phase. Keep it professional and by the book."

Dakota didn't like being schooled. She kept her gaze lowered, jaw clenched, as irritation simmered just beneath her calm surface. She was the last person who needed to be reminded to keep things professional, but she was still new to Isaac and she didn't need to make enemies with her boss by mouthing off.

Satisfied, Isaac moved on, looking to Sayeh. "What have you managed to dig up on The Congregation?"

"Hate to disappoint but that field trip was even more boring," Sayeh said, passing copies of her research. "Zachariah Deakins formed The Congregation thirty years ago, started off with a few followers who agreed with his simplistic approach to life, going-back-to-nature kind of thing, and slowly he gained enough followers to purchase the summer camp two years later."

"But he didn't actually purchase the camp. Technically, the senator unknowingly did as an investment through his financial advisers," Dakota said. "Which is still weird to me, but whatever. Why would his advisers feel a bankrupt summer camp was a good investment for the senator? That doesn't make much sense to me."

"If I were you I'd head back to the compound and ask Deakins how he got the investment group to invest in his church," Levi suggested. "I mean, if Lawrence truly had no clue about his investing in The Congregation, then somehow Deakins managed to convince the senator's investment firm that he was a solid bet, and if that's the case, how?"

"Sounds like a bunch of magic beans to me," Sayeh quipped.

Dakota agreed, unless there was more to the deal than met the eye.

"If you're heading back to the compound to question Deakins, be careful. The charges against the Grojans were dropped but that doesn't mean they're not still dangerous, okay?" Isaac warned, gathering up his paperwork. "And I want you to take a few days. You look exhausted, Foster."

It was an order, not a suggestion.

As much as she wanted to decline, she knew it wasn't an option. She shared a look with Shilah but murmured her acquiescence.

Looked like a few days of R&R were on her plate— which meant she and Ellis were going to have to figure out how to share space without falling into old habits that included falling out of their clothes and back into bed together.

She groaned silently. Maybe it was better to get a hotel after all.

Ellis slid the pizza onto the kitchen counter, the savory aroma filling his small apartment. He'd grabbed Dakota's favorite toppings, hoping she was still fond of them after all this time.

Taking a steadying breath, he called out, "Food's here if you're hungry." He tried to keep his tone light, casual. This was just two colleagues sharing a meal. Nothing more.

Dakota emerged from the bedroom, hair damp, wearing an old academy T-shirt. He remembered plenty of nights like this in their past. Easy domesticity, passion simmering just beneath the surface. Did she have to look so effortlessly sexy?

He busied himself grabbing plates, hyperaware of her moving around the kitchen. Their banter stayed surface level as they dished up slices, but each laugh, each shared glance seemed weighted with history.

Sitting across from Dakota now, Ellis sipped his beer slowly, curbing the urge to reach across and tuck back the strand of hair falling across her cheek. To pull her close, get lost in her familiar warmth...

He cleared his throat, steering the conversation to safer waters—case updates. "My superior is putting a rush on the forensics on your rat," he shared.

She grimaced with a groan. "Don't call it *my* rat. I doubt they're going to find anything. Seems a waste of resources, honestly."

Ellis didn't agree. "You and I both know that even the most careful criminals forget something. With any luck, we'll find a print we can match in the system and I can personally introduce myself."

Dakota chuckled, biting into the pizza. "Mmm, you remembered. Mushrooms, black olives and pepperoni—"

"With the garlic white sauce, not red," he finished with a grin. "Yeah, some things are ingrained in my memory."

"Thank you. Glad to know I left an impression of some kind," she teased with a smile that threatened to reach into his chest and pull his heart out. God, he missed this. Her quick mind and wry humor drew him in like no other. That vibrant connection still sparked between them, if he let it.

"Tell me what you've really been up to since we broke up," he said, reaching over to wipe a smudge of grease from her cheek. For a tidy and organized person, Dakota was the messiest eater. She always ended up with something in her lap, on her shirt or on her cheek. It was adorable.

Dakota hesitated, a moment of vulnerability flashing across her expression, before answering with a small shrug, "Just work. I buried myself in the job. Seemed safer that way. When the task force assignment popped up, I jumped at it. It was exactly what I needed to keep my head on straight and focused. Gave my brain something to chew on instead of the constant overthinking that usually consumed my thoughts." She drew a halting breath, admitting, "My pride wishes I could say that I went out, dated a lot and easily moved on, but that would be a lie and we've already established I'm a terrible liar."

"You never have to lie to me, Dakota. I know you better than anyone."

"Then you should know that getting over you was the hardest thing I've ever had to do, and honestly, I can't say that I'm actually out of the woods just yet but I'm doing my best."

"I'm not over you, either."

"I know."

Just as she couldn't lie to him, the road traveled both ways. He wiped his own mouth. "So where does that leave us?"

"Confused."

Ain't that the truth?

She met his stare. "What are we doing, Ellis?"

"Besides torturing ourselves, I don't know," he answered with blunt honesty. "You tell me." He had to stay disciplined, guard his heart, but it was so much harder with her two feet away from him, her lips glistening, close enough to see the gentle beat of her heart beneath her skin.

He could fight this feeling, but he couldn't make it disappear. Not completely. Not ever. She still owned every bruised, battered corner of his heart.

"We both have our reasons for standing by the decision to break up," Dakota said quietly, though something in her tone made Ellis think part of her hoped he would argue. "Even if we could move past the past, I still believe you shouldn't go back to narcotics work and that would cause friction between us."

Ellis took in her words, sensing she spoke out of care, not cruelty. It took a minute to process that truth, but he couldn't find a hole in her reasoning. Further proof that it was best to keep things platonic—except, that decision tasted like cardboard in his mouth.

"You know I'm right."

He resigned himself to the fact with a nod. Her concern was valid. But why couldn't she see how important Narcotics was to him? He wasn't going to give up his desire to return to Narcotics and she didn't want to be with him if he succeeded.

All they could do was see this case through, then go their separate ways once more.

Even if doing so tore the ragged stitches holding his battered heart together.

Chapter 21

Waiting a handful of days as directed was excruciating for Dakota, especially when she and Ellis were tiptoeing around each other, trying not to take up too much of each other's space so when it was finally time to hit the road, Dakota was grateful.

They pulled into the dirt parking lot reserved for Eden's Bounty customers and headed for the main building where Zachariah Deakins kept his office. Unlike their last visit, the compound felt different this time, the air taut with tension.

They looked for Lina Vasquez, the nurse that'd been manning Eden's Bounty booths the last time, but someone different was assisting customers and they weren't as friendly.

"Not even a hello or an offer of a bag of nuts," Ellis joked as they walked into the building.

Zachariah Deakins's smile was cold when he greeted them, lacking its prior evangelical zeal. Dakota exchanged a wary look with Ellis. The chill coming off the man could freeze a penguin's privates.

"More questions, Agents? I'm quite busy today," Deakins said brusquely, his attention drifting. "I thought we clarified everything last time."

"A few follow-up questions as the investigation progresses is common," Dakota said with a professional smile.

Zachariah glanced at the small clock on his desk with a short nod. "What would you like to know?"

"We've recently discovered an odd connection between The Congregation and Senator Mitchell Lawrence that we'd like you to help us understand."

Zachariah's expression didn't change. "Which is?"

"Which is why would Senator Lawrence's investment firm pay for this compound? At first we thought perhaps you and the senator were friends but he claims not to know you, which only confused us further. How did you manage to convince the senator's investment firm that this compound—a bankrupt and defunct summer camp—was a good investment?"

Zachariah's annoyance returned but he answered calmly. "Our flock was growing exponentially each month with significant donations and the promise of more growth. As you know, religious organizations enjoy tax-exempt status so any properties owned by the church would avoid property tax burdens."

"And each congregant liquidates their assets and donates to the church," Ellis said, watching Zachariah's reaction.

Cool as ever, Zachariah didn't flinch or deny, simply nodded. "That's correct. We see to our people's needs, food, shelter, emotional sustenance—something the outside world doesn't care to provide—and in exchange our flock pours into The Congregation as we pour into them. And, in case you're wondering, yes, it's all voluntary and done without coercion. Ask anyone."

"We will, thank you," Dakota said with a thin smile. "Still, that's a significant investment based on a handful of members."

Zachariah shrugged as if the why didn't concern him. "The asking price was low enough to represent a good return on the investment in the event our improvements increased the property value, and if not, it would be a good tax write-off. The financial risk was relatively small but afforded excellent financial growth for the senator's portfolio. However, with that said, it's not my business to defend the firm's decision. I was simply grateful they saw the value and made the purchase."

"Do you pay rent?" Ellis asked.

Zachariah smiled. "No, but we do send a gift basket every Christmas to the firm address. I'm told it's always very well-received."

Even with that dispassionate and articulate explanation, it didn't make sense to Dakota. Still, Zachariah made an excellent point—one that would be hard to fight. It wasn't illegal for an investment firm to make a seemingly odd purchase.

And it definitely didn't point to murder.

Zachariah claimed to never know Nayeli and the senator couldn't recall her case.

This felt like a giant dead end.

"Was there anything else you needed clarified?" Zachariah asked.

Dakota looked to Ellis, hoping he had a reason to keep Zachariah talking.

And he did.

"We heard the Grojans were released from the Butte County Jail a few days ago. Are they here?"

Zachariah's gaze narrowed, his mouth tightening as he leaned forward, purposefully clasping his hands in front of him as if he needed to collect his patience with them. "The Grojans have been through a terrible ordeal. I won't have you heaping more emotional trauma on good people while you bumble your way through this investigation. The Grojans had nothing to do with the terrible crime that happened to Zoey's birth mother. They are as much victims in this as Zoey and her birth mother. Unless you have a warrant and just cause to drag them back down to the police station, I respectfully ask that you leave them alone while they grieve this situation."

Dakota caught a glimpse of compassion in Zachariah's stern decree. The Grojans were someplace on this property but no one was going to give them up without a fight. Seeing as they had no evidence that pointed to the Grojans' involvement, Dakota and Ellis had no choice but to walk away.

For now.

"You said that according to your sources, Zoey's mother was an addict who OD'd. Where did you get that information?" Ellis asked.

Zachariah stiffened, admitting, "Obviously, my information turned out to be false but I had no way of knowing that at the time and no reason to question. The private adoption agency supplied the information and I connected the Grojans with the agency. It seemed an answer to a prayer that I was humbled to facilitate."

"We followed up on the agency on the adoption paperwork but it doesn't exist anymore and we can't find any documentation stating it had ever filed for nonprofit status," Dakota said.

Zachariah didn't have an answer for that. He shrugged, as if, once again, they'd bothered him with a problem that wasn't his to solve. "I only worked with that agency once, for the Grojans. Everything seemed professional and organized. Why would I question the procedure?"

Fair point, Dakota realized with frustration. Was it possible she was hoping to find something that would point toward Zachariah's guilt because of her personal bias or was he really good at hiding a truly evil agenda?

Zachariah gestured to the burly men who appeared at the doorway. "James and Theo will escort you out. Good day, Agents."

An escort off the compound when last visit he'd practically given them the run of the place?

The little hairs on the back of her neck prickled as she rose, Ellis right behind her.

How could Zachariah say all the right things and still make her feel as if she'd just stared into the eyes of a shark?

Ellis chewed on Zachariah's distinct change in attitude toward them. One minute he was warm and effusive—the next, chill and curt.

What changed? Either he was offended on behalf of the Grojans for their recent treatment, or he was uncomfortable with Ellis and Dakota continuing to poke around. Maybe he hadn't expected them to keep circling back to him. Or maybe he felt the need to protect his "flock" from a perceived persecution.

They walked across the compound, toward the parking lot, and his gaze snagged on the Eden's Bounty booths. He paused, looking to their burly escorts with an apologetic smile, asking, "You don't mind if we make a purchase, do you? Lina gave us a gift basket full of goodies last time, and I've never tasted pear jam so good."

The one named James shared an uncertain look with his partner, but Theo grudgingly nodded, giving them permission but not before instructing gruffly, "Stick to the booths."

"Of course," Ellis agreed easily, moving to the first booth featuring an array of jams and jellies. Dakota followed his lead, shooting a look toward their escorts as they waited impatiently for them to finish. When they were out of earshot, Ellis pretended to peruse the wares but said under his breath, "We need to lose Frick and Frack over there so we can talk to people without a shadow."

Dakota nodded, turning to James with an apologetic smile. "Mind if I use the restroom before we hit the road? Long drive, small bladder."

James looked discomfited but relented, pointing toward another building. "Public restroom is over there. Come right back, and then it's time to leave."

"Got it, there and back," she said with a thumbs-up. To Ellis she said, "Pick me up a couple of goodies, too."

"Will do," Ellis said, returning to the person manning the booth, rubbing his hands with relish. "Now, I'd like to sample pretty much every jam and jelly you have on display. I have my credit card ready to spend."

Ellis knew Dakota would detour from the bathroom and wander around a bit, and he needed to buy her time. He made a show of tasting every sample slowly with appropriate enthusiasm, even asking questions as to how they got the flavor profile to explode in his mouth. Just as he expected, they were eager to talk about their work, and that ate up some more time as he pretended to care about soil conditions, fertilizer and crop rotations.

As he hoped, James and Theo soon became restless and, judging them as a nonthreat, drifted farther from their guard post until they were gone entirely.

Ellis paid for his purchases—he wasn't lying about enjoying their wares—and went to find Dakota.

He found her talking with a young couple in the large

greenhouse as they planted young seedlings with their two children.

Ellis smiled in welcome as he joined Dakota. "I love the smell of a greenhouse. Always smells so fresh and clean," he said.

Dakota introduced the couple she'd been talking to, "Ellis, this is Georgina and Ross Wilson and their four-year-old daughters, Hazel and Mabel. Twins."

"Adorable," Ellis murmured, ruffling the jet-black hair of the one closest to him. Then Ellis noticed there was no possible way the twins were biologically related to their parents. More adopted children in The Congregation? Strange coincidence or something else?

Georgina grinned as she saw his bag of goodies. "You have good taste. Eden's Bounty has spoiled us all when it comes to fresh produce and delicious things. Hazel can't get enough of the homemade applesauce."

Ellis checked in his bag. "Seems I missed that one. I'll have to go back and rectify that oversight. I haven't had applesauce since I was a kid," he lied. His dad hadn't given two shits if there was any kind of fruit in the house he grew up in. He was lucky if there was any kind of food in the house, but there was always plenty of beer.

Dakota said, making conversation, "Georgina was just sharing how she and her husband joined The Congregation. What an amazing story. Can you imagine being a defense attorney and an HR administrator in one life and in the next, minimalist churchgoers sharing resources? Amazing."

Georgina bobbed her head, smiling with true joy. "Best decision of our lives. I never realized how burdened I was by modern living. The rat race, as they call it. Before joining The Congregation, Ross's blood pressure was through the roof. He was on three different medications, and he could barely get through the day without crashing before eight o'clock. Now, he has more energy than men half his age, and he's no longer taking any meds. I used to say it was a conspiracy theory that the pharmaceutical companies want you sick, but now I believe it."

"Clean living, huh?" Ellis said, nodding as if impressed. "And here I thought stress was just part of the adult package."

"That's what late-stage capitalism would have you believe, my friend," Ross said solemnly. "I was guilty of it, too. I was in the thick of it, running on an endless treadmill until Father Zachariah showed us a better way. Know better, do better—that's the way to live your life."

"Your daughters are so beautiful," Dakota murmured, appealing to their mother's pride. "Those eyes are dark enough to lose yourself in for days."

It was a deliberate attempt to get either parent to admit they weren't biologically related to their daughters. Both Georgina and Ross had Nordic features with pale blue eyes; both girls were clearly Asian.

"Aren't they, though?" Georgina gushed with love in her gaze. "Sometimes I think they are perfect China dolls. We're so blessed to call them ours. Just another reason meeting Father Zachariah was meant to be."

Dakota smiled, interested. "How so?"

Georgina was only too happy to share. "I'm not ashamed to admit that I had fertility issues. We tried for years to have a baby of our own, but God had different plans." She looked to her husband. "Should I share our testimony?"

"I don't see why not," Ross answered, caressing his wife's cheek in a loving manner. "It's a beautiful story."

Georgina agreed as she launched into their testimony with her husband's blessing. "We were at our darkest moment. We had just left the fertility clinic after learning our last and final round of IVF had failed. We were devastated, but then Father Zachariah happened to see us crying and he approached us in the spirit of kindness. That moment changed our lives. He invited us here, to The Congregation, and we knew we'd found our place."

Ross's smile mirrored his wife's as he shared, "I know it sounds crazy, but we've found bliss."

What was in the water at this place? Ellis held his benign expression, even though on the inside he was starting to question if Father Zachariah was secretly dosing his people with Xanax. No one was this happy without chemical intervention. "So… You gave all your assets to the church and became members?"

"Once we saw what was possible, we didn't even hesitate. It was a relief, actually," Ross said. "No more chasing unattainable goals, running on a treadmill that never slows down so you can catch your breath. But even more important, we finally had our family."

That caught Ellis's interest. "How do you mean?" he asked.

Georgina handed each girl a bright red cherry tomato and directed them to start pouring potting soil in awaiting pots down the lane. Hazel and Mabel skipped away, hand in hand, giggling as they went.

"It's their favorite part of the greenhouse detail," Georgina shared, admitting with a rueful laugh, "But I think they get more potting soil on their clothes than in the actual pot."

"Seems like a small price to pay for those cute giggles," Dakota said.

"I agree," Georgina said. "I'm sure you can see that our daughters are adopted."

"Yes," Ellis said. "Interesting that there are two adopted children as members of The Congregation."

"Oh, there's more than that," Georgina laughed, looking to Ross for confirmation. "How many would you say? Ten or more? I've lost count, honestly. Just more proof that God directs Father Zachariah's hand and guides his mission."

Ten adoptions? "Are you saying Father Zachariah has facilitated all of the adoptions here at The Congregation?"

Georgina's eyes sparkled. "Yes. Isn't he wonderful? God has chosen Father Zachariah as his vessel, and he has humbly taken his role to heart. We owe everything to Father Zachariah."

Ellis's smile never faltered, but his mind was racing. He shared a look with Dakota, and he knew she was thinking the same—how the hell was Zachariah Deakins facilitating all of these adoptions? And why?

Chapter 22

Dakota stared at the corporate documents, adrenaline spiking. Senator Lawrence and Zachariah Deakins, partners in an industrial supply company based in Arizona. On the surface, Western Horizon Solutions appeared utterly mundane—a manufacturer of barrels, piping and containers.

"I'm telling you, these can't all be coincidences," Dakota said, sliding the corporate documents in front of Ellis. "I don't care what the senator says, he and Deakins are connected."

"Interesting that our distinguished senator seems to do a lot of business with a man he said he doesn't know." Ellis rubbed his temple as he read the docs. He frowned. "What's the connection? What are we missing? The land purchase for the compound, okay. But what's the senator want with an industrial supplier?"

"That's the million-dollar question," Dakota admitted with frustration. "I mean, just taking a guess, drug smuggling, human trafficking, selling weapons… The options are endless."

Ellis raised an eyebrow, chuckling darkly. "That's quite a leap. This is a business that sells plastic barrels and PVC piping. All totally legal."

"So they want us to think," Dakota quipped, ticking the facts off on her fingers. "Deakins is facilitating secret adoptions, Lawrence is lying about knowing him, now they own a company together? There's something bigger we're not seeing."

Ellis leaned back in his chair, considering. "I'll give you Deakins seems like a shady character. Zero doubt in my mind about that, but Lawrence? The guy has a squeaky-clean reputation and people seem to genuinely like him. As much as it pains to admit, Lawrence seems the real deal— a politician who is genuine about wanting to help people."

Dakota continued to chew on that bone, reminding Ellis, "Who's made some questionable business deals. Think about it. What if Deakins is moving illegal products under cover of this company? Lawrence provides protection."

"Using the business as a front and a way to launder money?" Ellis supposed, going along for the ride. "But what products? We'd have to find evidence that Western Horizon Solutions was doing shady shit to even try to connect those dots, and you and I both know, right now, what we've got is flimsy. I'm not even sure we'd get a judge to sign off on a warrant."

Yes, but flimsy was a start. "Oh, Shilah can get the warrant. She's magic with her requests. We get the records, we can connect the dots. Whatever they're hiding, it's big. My gut says we're on the right track."

"Look, far be it from me to question a gut instinct— hell, half of the reason I'm still alive is I listened to my gut when it told me things were about to go sidewise— but we're not dealing with some crusty drug dealer. We're talking about a US senator with a lot of connections. Connections that could seriously derail our careers if we bark up the wrong tree."

Dakota knew the stakes were high but she didn't care. She stubbornly held her ground. "When we get the warrant, the company records should give up the dirty laundry."

"If it's there at all," Ellis reminded her.

She thought of the adopted children at the compound, Deakins's slippery charm. Her skin crawled imagining what those supplies could facilitate away from prying eyes. "Either way, this is concrete evidence of a relationship between them—a relationship the senator previously denied," Dakota said.

Ellis couldn't deny that logic, tapping the table lightly with his index finger. "And where there's smoke…"

"There's fire," Dakota finished.

Ellis nodded, his brow furrowed as he sank deeper into thought, sharing, "This case feels a whole lot bigger than Nayeli's case. I don't see how it's all connected. I can see strands of suspicious activity but none that travels back to Nayeli, and that's what our original focus was when Zoey appeared on the radar. What if we end up spending all this time chasing leads that send us further away from solving Nayeli's case? Zoey needs to know what happened to her mom—and her."

"I haven't lost sight of what we're truly chasing. I believe they have to be connected," Dakota insisted, refusing to believe they were wasting their time and energy. "My gut says we just have to keep going. We're on the right track."

Ellis didn't seem as sure. She could sense his frustration and she didn't blame him, but Dakota knew they were pulling on the right threads. She gazed out the front window of her office, jaw tight. Whatever Deakins and Lawrence were up to, this company linked them together in it. She didn't know how yet, but those barrel drums made the hair on the back of her neck stand up.

Speak of the devil, Shilah walked by and Dakota flagged her attention. "Would you mind working your mojo and get a warrant started for Western Horizon Solutions? We need all financials, sales records and inventory logs."

"Yeah, sure. You getting some traction on your case?" Shilah asked hopefully.

"Maybe. It does seem like each time we catch a break, the case splinters into a bunch of new directions."

"Sounds exciting," Shilah said. "How's the kid doing?"

"We talked to her this morning. She's tough, hanging in there. She said she liked the cook at the other safe house better than this one. Apparently, Zoey has a sweet tooth but the new cook doesn't seem interested in doing much baking."

Ellis chuckled. "I say we drop by the safe house and rectify that little problem."

Dakota grinned, shaking her head. Ellis had such a soft spot for the kid. Someday, he'd make a great father. The intrusive thought caused her smile to freeze and her throat to close against the unwelcome grief that followed. The thought of Ellis making a life with someone else was more than she could handle right now and it was the worst time to sink into that way of thinking.

Forcing a chuckle, she acted as if everything was fine and her heart hadn't silently cracked in two.

Sleeping in his bed while he camped out on the sofa was weird. She tried to convince him to let her go back to her own apartment but he wouldn't hear of it—and to be honest, she hadn't tried all that hard to convince him, either.

Even though she'd like him lying beside her, there was an odd comfort in knowing he was in the other room—and she enjoyed having dinner with him each night, too.

That was an added emotional perk that buoyed her in ways that she truly needed right now.

Ellis watched Dakota pore over the files, her determination evident. He admired her tenacity, but privately worried this crusade against Lawrence could backfire. Dakota was letting the case get personal, too clouded by the shadow of her sister's death to realize she was riding the edge.

Usually he was the reckless one, while Dakota played it conservative. Now their roles had reversed. This case had lit a fire in her that was burning so bright they might all get burned.

Ellis understood her thirst for justice. But tangling with a powerful senator was risky without solid proof. He didn't want to see Dakota hurt if her hunch proved wrong.

And there was another fly in the ointment—one he wasn't ready to share just yet.

The lab results on the rat had provided zero usable evidence. Poisoned, mutilated postmortem, no prints or traces left behind. Another dead end.

Ellis was reluctant to tell Dakota, though. She'd insist on going back to her compromised apartment. And as much as he knew he should keep his distance… He wasn't ready to give her up just yet.

Having Dakota here these past nights was a double-edged sword. He treasured their easy camaraderie, her quick wit and laughter filling his small place. Each morning he found fresh excuses to linger over coffee, stretching out their time.

Yeah, talk about playing with fire—he knew he was prolonging the inevitable but he couldn't bring himself to push her out the door. He loved the stubborn woman but they didn't have a future together. Their history was too scarred, but he clung to these last stolen moments. Let himself imagine, just briefly, that she was here to stay.

Ellis swallowed hard, dragging his thoughts back to the case. He had to remain objective, no matter how his heart threatened to steer him off course. For both their sakes.

"We'll get the records," he assured Dakota, but tried to insert some caution into the mix. "But let's be smart. I don't want you hurt over this."

She cracked a grin, calling him out. "What's this? Ellis being the worrywart? Did we just jump timelines or something? C'mon, where's the reckless devil-may-care agent who laughed in the face of danger?" she teased.

But when it came to Dakota's safety, he wasn't laughing. "Maybe I've learned there's some value in being conservative. Not every situation calls for stupid bravery."

Her smile faded when she realized he wasn't playing around. "Are you okay?"

"I'm fine," he answered, but he wasn't really. He was on edge. Dakota didn't have the experience he did stepping into the arena with dangerous people. She didn't consider that tangling with Lawrence could kill her career—a career she loved and used to fill that emptiness left by her sister's death.

"Well, then enough with the sour face. We have a lead and we're going to chase it down." She leaned over with a sassy grin, adding, "And we're going to stop by that bakery and buy a ton of sugar cookies for our little federal hostage because we're part of the kinder, gentler federal government."

He chuckled in spite of the heaviness in his chest. The thought of a sugar cookie did make him smile, though. "All right, but only because Zoey deserves something sweet after everything she's been through in the last couple of weeks."

Dakota smiled, seeing right through his facade but letting him have it. "Any word from the lab about my rat?"

"Nothing yet," he lied. "Probably a few more days. They're backed up."

Dakota shrugged, letting it go. "It's probably going to come up with nothing anyway, but I suppose the sooner we know, the sooner I can get out of your hair. You probably want your apartment back."

Not really, but he smiled and let her believe what she wanted. If he had the balls, he'd admit that he loved having her around, that he selfishly wished he had a reason for her to stay and that he spent half the night wishing he was lying beside her when he was tossing and turning on his old sofa.

But he wouldn't say any of those things. They'd already agreed they had no future together and that the best they could hope for was a good working relationship built on a solid friendship.

Except he didn't want to be friends—he wanted to be the man he used to be to her, but who was that man? Did he even exist anymore?

Ellis didn't know. He was different now, changed in ways he couldn't even put into words but felt in his soul.

He feared he would never lose the thirst for the relentless adrenaline of narcotics work, even though, like Dakota had said, he was good in Missing Persons. But working Narcotics, he'd felt honed to a razor's edge, every nerve alive. Purposeful in a way civilian life had never matched.

Yet at what cost had that razor focus come? Softness eroded, vulnerabilities sharpened into weapons. Dakota used to quip he had ice water in his veins when he was deep undercover. But she'd never feared him—until the day that ice cracked.

Some changes were for the better—his hair-trigger temper now held in check, empathy where rage had once simmered. When he was moved to Missing Persons, he'd felt declawed, defanged. And that longing for the electric urgency of life had kept him on the edge, pushing for that goal to return to where he belonged.

Was Dakota right? Was it impossible to return to Narcotics without sinking back into those familiar dark places? Dakota didn't trust that he could and it wasn't right of him to ask her to try.

Ellis craved the clarity of his old life, before shades of gray blurred every line. Yet when Dakota looked at him now, he glimpsed a flicker of stubborn hope in her eyes that squeezed his heart.

Whoever he had been, whatever he became, some essential truth remained unchanged. She owned every battered, broken shard of his soul. Always.

And that was a problem that he couldn't fix without risking breaking them both.

So keep your ass on that sofa and don't make things worse by thinking you guys can fix what broke—because you can't.

Chapter 23

Realizing they had to rewind to the beginning, Dakota and Ellis made the long drive to Whitefish, to the hotel where Nayeli had worked before her murder, while Shilah chased down the warrant for Western Horizon Solutions financials.

The manager, an immaculately put-together woman with frosted blond hair and fashionable wire-rimmed glasses named Paula Simmons, greeted them politely, if not warmly, but her memories of Nayeli had faded with time. "Hmm, well, from what I remember, she was a strikingly beautiful girl but kept to herself mostly," she recalled. "We were all shocked when she admitted she was pregnant. Hadn't even known she was seeing anyone. Of course, we threw her a lovely baby shower and offered to help in any way we could. We're a family here at the Glacier View Hotel and Resort." Her expression dimmed. "We were devastated when we heard the news about her murder. It was simply awful to think of something like that happening here. Whitefish is such a safe community."

"So Nayeli never shared who the father was?" Dakota asked.

Paula shook her head. "Sorry, no, and it didn't seem appropriate to ask. Whoever it was, was no longer a part of her life so we didn't want to pry. She loved that baby so much. She would've made a wonderful mother."

Dakota's sinuses tingled at the sentiment. Was she emotional over Nayeli's loss or her sister's for never having the chance to have a family of her own? Dakota didn't know and there wasn't time to figure it out. She jotted down the notes but nothing seemed useful yet.

"May I ask why you thought the father was no longer part of Nayeli's life?" Ellis asked, curious.

"Well, I hate to talk about someone else's business, but right before the baby was born, I caught Nayeli looking at a pamphlet for a birthing class and I asked if the father was going to attend with her and she just shook her head with the saddest expression. That's when she shared that she'd be raising the baby by herself. I felt so bad for her."

Dakota imagined Nayeli had been devastated to discover she was alone in the biggest change in her life but she'd been trying to make a go of it. "Did Nayeli say she had plans to return to work after having the baby?"

"Yes, and we supported her decision to do so," Paula said quickly, as if fearing a human resource reprisal all these years later. "But unfortunately, childcare was an issue. She was nearing the end of her six-week maternity leave and still hadn't found an affordable childcare option. Placing an infant is difficult, from what I understand. I don't actually have children of my own."

Dakota wondered if money was tight for the new mom and she'd reached out to the father, hoping for some help. Sometimes that was enough to trigger a desperate person to act out in a murderous rage—especially if they weren't interested in being a part of the child's life.

"I'm sorry I'm not more help," Paula apologized. "Nayeli was such a lovely girl."

"We appreciate your time," Ellis said, handing her a

contact card. "If you remember anything else, please don't hesitate to call or email."

"Of course," Paula said, tucking the card into her sharp blazer before moving on to more pressing matters.

The Glacier View was elegant, sophisticated and rustic at the same time, similar to the Ahwahnee in Yosemite National Park, but much larger in scale. Dakota remembered Evelyn sharing how they'd dreamed of going into hospitality together and Nayeli had hoped to manage a hotel like the Glacier. She'd probably looked up to Paula as someone who'd achieved the very goal she was reaching for.

"Damn it," Dakota muttered in disappointment. "Looks like we came all the way here for nothing."

But as they turned to leave, a housekeeper who had been hovering nearby hurried over.

"Wait, wait!" she called after them in a hushed tone, motioning for them to follow her out of the main lobby. "I overheard you talking to Paula about Nayeli Swiftwater and I couldn't believe my ears. No one's talked about Nayeli in forever but I'm glad someone's asking questions again."

Ellis and Dakota shared a look, interested. "How did you know Nayeli?"

"We were hired at the same time, except I never expected to still be here all this time later and Nayeli had her eye on becoming manager someday. Funny how things work out."

"What's your name?" Ellis asked.

"My name's Holly Pickler but I don't want my name in any reports or anything. I mean, Nayeli's killer is still out there. The last thing I need is someone coming after me for talking."

"Do you know something?" Dakota asked.

"Well, I'm pretty sure I know who the father was," Holly said in a low voice.

A rush prickled across Dakota's skin. "You do? Who?"

"Nayeli had a boyfriend named Patrick who worked for that politician, Lawrence Mitchell. He's a senator now but he was just a congressman at the time. I think Patrick was his assistant or something because they were joined at the hip and Patrick got all the perks, like the hotel suite, an executive black card, you know, all the fancy stuff. They used to stay here campaigning, and that's how Nayeli and Patrick met."

Excitement flooded her veins. "Do you have a last name for Patrick?"

"Sorry, I don't remember that, but I remember him being real handsome but in a pretty-boy way, kinda like you." She pointed at Ellis.

Dakota bit back a snort of laughter at Ellis's expression. He was immune to being called handsome but pretty boy?

Ellis recovered, saying, "If he worked that closely with the senator we should be able to find out his last name easily."

Holly nodded. "Yeah, but I'm positive Patrick knocked her up. He was, no offense, too pretty. I mean, the man had more toiletries than any woman I've ever seen—and we know because we're the ones cleaning up after them. The stories we in housekeeping could tell…but we won't because, you know, we're professional."

"Why are you so sure it was him?" Ellis asked, puzzled.

"Because even though she tried to hide it, she always got super excited when the congressman's entourage were scheduled to check in. She'd go to extra lengths to pretty herself up, not that she needed much help in that department. And even though she said it wasn't for no man, the girl was so obvious. You'd have to be dumb and blind to miss that she was head over heels for that man."

"Thank you, Holly," Dakota said, handing her a contact card. "If you think of anything else, please don't hesitate to call."

Finally, a real lead—and one that tied directly to the senator.

Holly pocketed the card. "Well, I just hope it helps. Honestly, I just assumed the police probably already talked to him and I didn't really want to get involved but I think it's time to let that secret out."

"We do, too," Ellis agreed with a short smile.

They left with a solid description of Patrick and the SUV he drove at the time. Dakota's mind raced with the new implications as Ellis drove them back.

"This confirms the senator knew Nayeli, despite claiming not to remember her," she said. "If his aide got Nayeli pregnant, there's no way the senator was unaware."

But Ellis wasn't so sure. "That's a possible theory. Or he really didn't know his aide got Nayeli pregnant because Patrick probably hid that information from his boss."

Dakota liked her theory better. "Maybe," she allowed with a grudging nod. "But we need to find this Patrick guy, like yesterday, and I think we ought to start with the senator."

"On that, we agree," he said, that fierce light returning to Ellis's eyes. The one that made Dakota's pulse skip despite herself. They were close, she could feel it. All the twisted threads were intertwined, but the truth would come loose. She would make certain of it.

Ellis drove steadily back toward Billings, half listening as Dakota breathlessly rehashed the hotel lead. A secret boyfriend, tied to Senator Lawrence... It was certainly the best lead they'd had from the start, but doubts gnawed at the back of Ellis's mind.

The source was hearsay, the story nearly two decades old. Was it enough to justify the risk of antagonizing a powerful politician based on a tenuous connection? He knew Dakota wouldn't appreciate his skepticism, but he had to be the pragmatic one, which was an unfamiliar feeling. Was this how he'd made Dakota feel every time he went off half-cocked on a situation, high on adrenaline and the electric rush of the chase?

He didn't like it. Made him feel anxious and untethered—and not in a good way.

Ellis recalled one night in particular, seeing it from a different angle now. He'd been flush with excitement. A tip from an informant had the team gearing up in the middle of the night for a raid on a warehouse with a suspected huge haul of cocaine. It was the biggest bust of his career and he'd been in charge of the raid. Dakota had been a bundle of nerves, worried, asking him questions like, "Was the informant trustworthy?" (Not really) "Has the informant come through before with good intel?" (Never met the guy before that night) and finally, "Are you sure this is safe? I mean, don't you usually need more time to coordinate these things?" He'd brushed off her fears, ignoring the fact that her questions were valid. He'd been too hopped up on the possibility of getting that haul off the streets to pay attention. He should've listened. The bust had gone down in flames, the intel was bad, it was a trap—and he'd almost gotten his head shot off.

Not his finest moment. Eating crow on that detail had been tough but worse was seeing Dakota nearly throw up when she heard he'd narrowly missed meeting his maker. He'd always been the one to take the chances, without taking into consideration the toll it took on the person waiting for him to come home.

Dakota had always accepted that they both worked dangerous jobs, he more so than her, but he took unnecessary risks because it felt good—hell, he could see now that it wasn't fair.

Glancing over, Ellis took in Dakota's flushed cheeks and bright eyes, alive with renewed hope. She was lit up from within, her passion for justice radiating off her. It resonated deeply with his own determination, calling to him like a siren song.

Could this scrap of information finally break the case open? Or was it just one more severed thread leading nowhere? There was no way to know unless they ran it down. Dakota's hope was contagious—he wanted to believe they'd caught a real break but that hope was tempered by the possibility that it was another wild-goose chase.

Let her have this, a voice said. This case wasn't the same as her sister's but he sensed that Dakota was shadowed by a ghost. He didn't have any siblings—the one thing his son of a bitch father did right was get a vasectomy after knocking up Ellis's mom—but he saw how losing Mikaya had affected Dakota and he hurt for her.

So, yeah, for now, he was going to let her enjoy this reinvigorated lead before he brought pragmatism back into play.

"Secrets never stay buried forever," Dakota chirped, munching on her potato chips from the gas station. "No matter how much money, how many connections, eventually secrets surface, and when they do, there's always someone there to scoop 'em up like fishing in a barrel."

He chuckled. "I wouldn't go that far. Just because we've got a good lead doesn't mean the case is closed," he reminded her, watching her devour those chips like it was her last meal. "You still going to be hungry for dinner?"

"That's a stupid question, this is a snack," she said. "I've been thinking about that little sushi place. Spicy tuna roll, get in my belly."

"Sounds good to me," Ellis said with a nod, steering them closer to home as the sun dipped low on the horizon. They still had a long road ahead, but suddenly the shadows didn't seem quite so deep. If this lead panned out, maybe, just maybe, the long-silenced ghosts would finally rest. A stubborn bud of hope bloomed in his heart. He could only pray it wasn't misplaced.

Chapter 24

The next morning, Dakota and Ellis were back on the road to Lawrence's in-state office, determined to confront Senator Lawrence about his aide Patrick O'Malley before he left for Washington. Despite coming in late, Dakota and Ellis had stayed up late researching what they could find on the senator's entourage seventeen years ago. It wasn't hard to find the one aide named Patrick and even easier to track down his current whereabouts.

The slick former lobbyist had joined Lawrence's team early on, but left politics for the more lucrative finance sector several years prior.

The senator was visibly annoyed to see them again so soon. "Agents, I fear you've made a trip for nothing. I've already told you everything I can," he said as they walked into his office. "And my schedule is booked with prior appointments."

"We apologize for the short notice but we have another lead that you can help us with," Dakota said.

At that the senator's brow rose in a subtle question. "What kind of lead?"

"We received information that you had an aide named Patrick O'Malley seventeen years ago when you were still a congressman. You and your entourage stayed frequently at the Glacier View Hotel in Whitefish and a housekeeper remembered you and Patrick being close."

The senator leaned back in his chair, narrowing his gaze with deeper annoyance. "Pardon me, Agents, but how is this a lead? I try to have good relationships with those who work for me. It's just being a good employer, wouldn't you agree?"

"I work for the FBI, I wouldn't know anything about that," Ellis deadpanned. "Can you tell us more about your relationship with Patrick?"

Senator Lawrence checked his watch and blew out a short breath. "I think you're playing fast and loose with the term *relationship*. We weren't golfing buddies or even friends. I was his boss and we had a typical employee/employer relationship. He served in his position well enough, he switched gears in his career and I gave him an excellent reference. That was the extent of our 'relationship,' as you call it. Just as I've done with countless other employees."

Dakota watched the senator's expression for any hint of subterfuge but Lawrence was cool as a cucumber—an annoyed one, that is.

"Senator—"

Lawrence held up a hand. "I appreciate your dedication, but this is fruitless," he said. "Patrick left long ago and we didn't keep in touch. I'm sorry I can't be more helpful but please, I must be going."

But Dakota wasn't ready to let him go just yet. "Was Patrick dating Nayeli Swiftwater?"

"Who?" the senator asked, but quickly realized his mistake and apologized. "Right, the young murdered Native girl. Sorry, my mind is full of appointments and commitments right now." He took a minute to search his memory but ultimately came up empty. "I really couldn't say. I try to stay out of my employees' personal lives. Keeps expectations manageable. I'm sure you can appreciate how getting too close to an employee can look on the outside."

Ellis caught Dakota's gaze, signaling that they weren't getting anywhere with the senator. Frustrated that the senator hadn't even blinked weird, betraying nothing, Dakota grudgingly agreed to end the interview.

"Good luck, Agents," the senator said with a perfunctory smile as he grabbed his briefcase and began packing his paperwork, signaling that it was time for them to leave.

Back outside, Dakota fumed at the stonewalling. "I want to say he's hiding something but he didn't really give anything away. The man might as well have been talking about the valet. Of course he doesn't remember someone as inconsequential as an aide that's no longer with him."

Ellis agreed, but said, "We're here. Patrick O'Malley works in the area, so let's pay him a visit."

The Risen Financial Partners office tower gleamed like a pillar of polished granite and glass amid Helena's lower-slung buildings. Inside, Dakota's boots sank into plush carpeting as soft as a cloud. Behind the sleek walnut reception desk, an athletic blonde manned the phones with crisp efficiency.

"Good afternoon, how can I help you today?"

Both Dakota and Ellis flashed their credentials. "We're here to speak with Patrick O'Malley," Dakota said, glancing around the cathedral-like lobby, taking in the pervasive displays of wealth—massive floral arrangements, abstract sculptures, a trickling stone waterfall along one wall. *Fancy place.* Seemed Patrick gravitated to places that liked to show off their wealth, much like the senator.

This place was a temple to privilege, catering to the rich and powerful. Senators, CEOs, heirs and heiresses…the 1 percent who shaped worlds with the stroke of a pen. Men accustomed to doing as they pleased, without consequence. Dakota hated it instantly.

"Do you have an appointment?" the receptionist asked, adjusting her headset with a small, precise movement. "Mr. O'Malley has a very tight schedule and doesn't take walk-ins."

"He will for us," Ellis said, finished with this elitist bullshit.

The receptionist's indulgent smile was almost smug. "I'm sorry, there really isn't any wiggle room. Maybe you'd like to leave a business card—"

"How about this… Either he can talk to us now or we can make a big show of it and have him arrested in front of all of your fancy clientele. How's that sound? Think he can make time for us now?" Ellis said.

The receptionist's smile faded and she visibly swallowed as she quietly called Patrick's office. "Mr. O'Malley, you have federal agents Vaughn and Foster here to see you. They say it's…um, important." She listened and nodded. "Yes, sir. I'll send them right up." She hung up and smiled. "Fifteenth floor. He'll see you now."

"Well, look at that, there was some wiggle room after all," Dakota quipped, pushing off the marble counter to step into the elevator. "Amazing how that works."

In the elevator, Ellis said, "Remember, stay on your toes. Patrick might be wearing Italian leather but if he's guilty of Nayeli's murder, as soon as he realizes we're onto him, things could get dangerous."

Dakota grinned. "How cute, you're worried about me."

Ellis rolled his eyes, adjusting his holster behind his back. "Smart-ass. Just don't do anything stupid, okay?"

That was the pot calling the kettle black but he was so damn adorable in that moment that Dakota shocked him by sneaking a quick kiss on his cheek and said, "I'll leave the stupid up to you," before the elevator dinged at their floor.

She smothered a laugh at his expression. *Worth it.*

Goddamn it, Dakota. What'd you do that for? Now his head needed a reset. The elevator doors slid open, but Ellis still felt the warm imprint of Dakota's lips on his cheek. What did it mean? A playful gesture or something more? Ellis's pulse quickened at the possibilities, but he tamped it down. He had to stay focused. He growled for her ears only, "We'll revisit *that* later," as he stepped out of the elevator into a marble-floored suite with floor-to-ceiling views of the city.

Even though he cautioned Dakota about putting the cart before the horse, he was guilty of his own bias. Men like O'Malley and Lawrence lived by different rules, expecting to evade consequences. He'd seen it too many times during his time in Narcotics. Big money had a tendency to play fast and loose in ways that ordinary citizens didn't have the luxury.

Ellis resolved to be direct but professional with Patrick. Apply pressure if needed, but don't let emotions take the reins. He had to be ready for anything—or nothing. The decades-old lead might crumble to dust in their hands.

A sharp rap on the office door was answered by a crisp "Come in." Patrick O'Malley rose from behind a heavy oak desk, extending a manicured hand and polished smile. Ellis noted the smooth features, perfectly white teeth and nary a wrinkle betraying his age.

"How can I help you?" Patrick said, clasping his hands in front of him with an air of helpful concern. "It's not often federal agents show up to chat."

"Really? Considering how much money flows through

this firm, I'm surprised it's not an everyday occurrence," Dakota quipped.

Patrick chuckled. "We run a clean ship. We don't take risks with our clientele's assets and we don't have clientele that aren't thoroughly vetted. Our firm is one of the oldest in the capital and most trusted," he shared with pride.

"You used to work as Senator Lawrence's aide. What made you go from politics to finance?"

"To be frank, more money," Patrick admitted. "When I started as an aide, I was fresh out of college, a little naive and I idealized what it would be like to be a politician. In reality, it's less about making meaningful change and more about doing favors and it just didn't sit well with me."

"Careful, Mr. O'Malley, I might start changing my opinion about you," Dakota said with a mild smile. "When you left the senator, you came to work here?"

Patrick nodded. "With help from the senator. He wrote a very nice referral letter that got me in the door and then my qualifications got me the rest of the way. Been here ever since. Best decision of my life. This is definitely where I'm supposed to be. I probably would've made a mediocre politician but as it turns out, I'm a damn good financial adviser."

Enough chitchat. Ellis tossed the bait. "Do you recall a woman named Nayeli Swiftwater?"

"Nayeli...sounds vaguely familiar but I can't place it. Who is she?"

"Well, for one, she's dead," Ellis said, scrutinizing Patrick's reaction. But O'Malley's wide-eyed surprise seemed genuine.

"Dead? That's terrible. What happened?"

"She was killed in her Whitefish apartment seventeen years ago and her six-week-old infant was kidnapped," Dakota shared.

Patrick swallowed, looking horrified. "That's awful."

"It was," Dakota agreed. "We received information that you and Nayeli might've been dating while she was a house-keep at the Glacier View Hotel. Do you remember her now?"

Ellis regarded Patrick with keen interest. Even a cool liar could crack with the right leverage but Patrick looked more stricken than scared or guilty. "I... I don't remember her but that's just terrible."

A flicker of something passed over Patrick's gaze but it was gone in an instant. Ellis narrowed his gaze. "Are you sure, Mr. O'Malley, that you don't remember her?"

"I would tell you if I did. I'm trying to remember who she might be... It was so long ago, though. At the time, Senator Lawrence was on the campaign trail for his first shot at his current seat and we saw so many different people, they all started to blend at some point, but it feels terrible to admit that about someone who's dead. I mean, I would never want to imply that her life wasn't worth remembering."

"Of course, we understand," Ellis said. "But seeing as you were specifically remembered as a potential love inter-est... Would you mind submitting to a DNA test?"

"Why?" Patrick shook his head, lips sealed stubbornly even as a panicked sweat beaded his brow. His wide-eyed alarm seemed at odds with his claims of ignorance.

Ellis shared a tense look with Dakota. If Patrick knew nothing, why was stark fear rolling off him in waves? What-ever secret he harbored had him terrified right now. Enough to make an innocent man seem guilty.

"We'd like to test your DNA to see if you're a genetic match for Nayeli's daughter," Ellis explained. "And see if your DNA shows up from the samples taken at the crime scene."

"What? Am I a suspect?" Patrick gasped, truly horrified. "You can't think that I had anything to do with that poor girl's death."

"We'd like to rule you out," Dakota returned calmly.

"And if you have nothing to hide, the DNA will help exonerate you," Ellis said.

Ellis leaned forward, holding the man's frightened gaze. "If you're innocent, why are you so scared? Who are you protecting?"

"I'm not protecting anyone." Patrick wiped at his forehead. "Don't you need a warrant for that?"

"We can get one if you prefer but I thought you'd want to do this quickly and *quietly*," Ellis said.

Patrick flinched, his neck cording with strain. "I already told you everything I know," he insisted hollowly.

But the pallor of his skin, the pleading eyes of a cornered animal, told Ellis they were circling something dangerous. Patrick was in the crosshairs of powerful men who could make problems disappear.

They were running out of time to break through his fear. Ellis slid his chair closer, the threat implicit. "I don't think you have," he said grimly. "Now tell us about Nayeli."

He could almost hear Dakota's thudding pulse matching his own. They had stumbled into deep waters here. And he feared Patrick might not survive what came next if he refused to talk.

Patrick swore fervently, "I am not the father of that girl's baby. I swear to you, it's not possible."

"And why is that?" Dakota asked.

"Because I'm gay!"

And the plot thickens. Ellis shared a look with Dakota, shrugging, "Gay men can father babies. Were you openly gay seventeen years ago?" he asked.

Shame colored Patrick's cheek as he admitted, "No, I

wasn't. I didn't come out until I'd been with this firm for seven years. I was afraid of losing clients but everyone was quite accepting. Made me realize I'd lost a lot of years of potential happiness for no reason. But I swear to you, I wasn't sleeping with that girl."

Ellis believed Patrick wasn't Zoey's father but Ellis was willing to bet his eyeteeth the man was hiding something.

Something that scared him.

He leaned forward, pinning Patrick with a hard stare. "We're going to try this again—do you remember Nayeli Swiftwater?"

"Yes," he finally admitted in a horrified whisper, shaking his head. "But I swear I didn't know she was dead until you told me."

"If you weren't dating her…do you know who was?" Dakota asked.

Patrick lifted his gaze, fear in his eyes. "I can't—"

"Who was she dating?" Ellis cut in, not playing around.

"You have to understand, I was just following instructions," he pleaded, shaking his head. "I didn't like it but it seemed harmless enough. We would switch rooms so that when Nayeli came to see him, it looked like she was coming to see me. He was newly married and the scandal would've tanked his career and mine."

"Who was she actually seeing?" Ellis pressed, needing him to say the name, his nerves drawn taut. "Just tell us."

Patrick swore under his breath, realizing he was in a corner. "It was the senator. She was seeing Mitchell Lawrence."

We got him! Ellis wanted to crow but now things were about to move real fast and by the numbers.

They couldn't afford to miss a single step if they were planning to arrest a US senator.

Chapter 25

Euphoria coursed through Dakota's veins as they left Patrick's office. Finally, they had the break in the case they'd been chasing, and she was practically dancing on thin air.

"I told you he was dirty," Dakota crowed to Ellis as they climbed into the car. "Family values, my ass. If Patrick's lead pans out, it means the senator was sleeping with Nayeli months after marrying his wife. If the DNA comes back as positive paternity for Zoey, it gives the senator motive for killing Nayeli." She ticked off the reasons. "He was newly married and messing around with a young impressionable teen while peddling a family values ticket to the voters. If the news had gotten a hold of the fact that he'd knocked up the girl, his career would've been over. That's the oldest motive in the book—the inconvenience of a pregnant mistress."

"It's a damn good motive and a solid lead," Ellis agreed. "But we have to do this by the book or else that slimy bastard will find a way to wriggle out of our hold."

"The hell he will," Dakota growled, determined to bring the corrupt bastard down. She quickly called Shilah. "We got him," she said with excitement. "We need a DNA warrant for Senator Lawrence Mitchell, ASAP, and while you're at it, file the arrest paperwork for Zachariah Deakins."

"On what grounds for Deakins?" Shilah asked.

"For the kidnapping of Cheyenne Swiftwater," she answered boldly, earning a warning look from Ellis. True, they didn't have concrete proof yet that Deakins was guilty but there were too many threads that led back to those two being connected to be coincidence.

"You got it," Shilah said, clicking off.

Dakota drew a deep breath, blowing it slowly. This was the biggest case of her career and it was either going to be an epic win or a devastating failure. Poking the bear could get her bit in the ass but she couldn't back down when victory was so close.

But Ellis, of all people, was the quiet voice of reason as he said, "If the senator's DNA turns out to be a match for Zoey, it's a fantastic break in our case but I feel bad for Zoey. She deserves better than Mitchell Lawrence for a father."

"He has two other kids, too," Dakota shared, frowning. "Two sons. Just like that Zoey would inherit two half brothers that will probably want nothing to do with her. She'll be looked at as the enemy."

"They could create problems for her later on down the road," Ellis warned. "From their point of view, Zoey would be looked at as the downfall of their family."

They weren't supposed to make it personal but there was no way Dakota would let that happen. "We'll find a way to protect her."

Ellis nodded, silently agreeing to break that rule with her if need be.

"I know it'll take at least twenty-four hours to get the warrants but I wish we could just hit the road now. I have all this adrenaline and nowhere to put it," she said.

Ellis chuckled. "I know that feeling all too well. When

we get back to town, we could hit the gym, use up some of that energy so it doesn't drive you crazy."

Dakota knew it was a good option but she was riding a high and feeling reckless. "I know of a different way we could use up this energy," she said coyly.

"Dakota," Ellis warned, shooting her a quick look. "What are you doing?"

Something out of line. She unbuckled her seat belt and moved closer to Ellis, nuzzling his neck, inhaling his scent. "What does it look like I'm doing?" she purred against his skin, her tongue darting to taste him, tasting faintly of sweat and masculinity.

"Dakota, I'm driving," he said with a strained chuckle. "Knock it off and put your seat belt back on. This is dangerous."

"I thought you liked dangerous," she teased, going to unbuckle his belt. "I seem to recall you being addicted to dangerous."

Sweat started to pop along his forehead. "Yeah, well, I've since learned that maybe I was an idiot," he said, sucking in a tight breath as she popped his top button, reaching into his pants to grip his quickly thickening member. He tried to focus on the road but she was purposefully making it difficult. "Dakota," he half pleaded, half-sternly tried to get her to stop. "There are a million different reasons why this is a bad idea—and I can't believe I'm going to say this but... Get your hands out of my pants."

Was he serious? She paused, meeting his gaze questioningly. When he didn't back down, she realized he meant it. Swallowing what felt like a boulder in her throat, she gently withdrew her hand and quietly buttoned his pants, leaving him to deal with his belt.

Tears burned behind her eyelids as rejection burned a hole into her feminine pride.

"Actually, I think I should probably sleep in my own bed tonight," she said, her voice strangled.

There was no way in hell she could handle sleeping in his bed now—or ever.

Ellis wanted to swear, yell and pull the car over to have the conversation that needed to happen but he could tell Dakota had completely shut down and now he had to try and talk some sense into that stubborn head when she was likely to tell him to piss off.

He knew he'd hurt her feelings but did she really expect him to forget everything they'd already talked about just to get wild in the car?

The car was silent save for the hum of tires on asphalt. Ellis kept sneaking glances at Dakota, but she stared fixedly out the window. What a way to crap on an otherwise exhilarating win for the case. They ought to be celebrating the break, splurging on expensive takeout and taking a breather because they'd earned it.

But no—instead they were stuck in a bubble without enough space to breathe, the tension thick enough to knock over a buffalo.

Way to go, jackass.

He shouldn't have been so blunt rejecting her advances. And could he get a little recognition for how much strength it'd taken to make her stop? The memories of what Dakota could do with her mouth made him sweat, but as thrilling as it'd felt, he knew they were playing with fire. Nothing had changed between them—not really.

They'd already seen how this story ended the last time

they ignored their better judgment and ended up in bed together and they'd both agreed—never again.

So what gives? Now she wants to play around, ignoring the consequences? Wasn't that his role in their little dynamic? Being the reasonable one sucked.

After an interminably long, excruciating car ride, they arrived at his place and immediately Dakota exited the car, heading straight for his apartment. She waited for him to catch up, avoiding his gaze. He sighed, opening the front door and pushing it open for her. "Dakota…"

But she wasn't going to talk. She grabbed her things without a word, shouldering her bag with her keys in hand. "Thanks for letting me crash," she mumbled, heading for the door.

Ellis tried to catch her arm. "Hey, can we talk?"

She avoided his eyes. "I'm pretty tired. I should get home."

Frustration rose in his throat. Why was she being stubborn about this? "C'mon, Dakota, please. I didn't mean to hurt you. But you know this thing between us is complicated and we need to focus on the case."

At that, Dakota looked up sharply, her gaze bright. "Forget it, Ellis. I don't know what I was thinking in the car. We're partners, let's leave it at that."

Dakota's aloof tone felt like a slap in the face. But as she turned away, Ellis caught the sheen of tears in her eyes before she could hide them. His chest squeezed at the glimpse of vulnerability she quickly shielded behind cool indifference. Dakota would rather chew her own leg off than admit when she was hurt.

Ellis ran an agitated hand through his hair. "Why does everything have to be so black-and-white with you? Just talk to me, help me understand—"

"Understand what? That once again I'm the stupid one

acting on feelings you don't share?" Dakota choked out a bitter laugh. "Message received, trust me."

Before Ellis could respond, she slipped out the door, head held high despite the tears he knew she was fighting back.

That's not at all how he felt. How could such a smart woman be so clueless? He opened his mouth to clarify but Dakota wasn't in the mood to listen. The urge to go after her warred with giving Dakota space. He stepped toward the door, then forced himself back. She needed time to cool down and process. Didn't she?

Damn it, Dakota!

Should he chase after her? Or let her go? Was her place even safe? What if it was Lawrence sending people after Dakota to shut down the investigation? It wasn't that Dakota wasn't capable of handling herself, it was that he didn't like the idea of needlessly putting her in harm's way at all.

Raking his hands through his hair, Ellis swore under his breath. He should have handled that better instead of blurting the first frustrated thought. But the walls Dakota threw up infuriated him even as he understood their cause.

Ellis sank onto the couch they'd shared such a short time ago. The ghost of her still lingered as the scent of her perfume clung to the cushions. The idea of returning to his empty bed after she'd been in it for days made him angry all over.

He'd have to strip the sheets. There was no way he could sleep with the smell of her shampoo teasing his nose, torturing his senses. Rising, he stalked to his bedroom and started pulling the bedding, pushing thoughts of Dakota far from his mind so he could get through the night without chasing after her and forcibly putting her in the car, whether she liked it or not.

That was something the old Ellis would've done—the one with the heart full of rage and soul full of bitterness.

Hell, the old Ellis would've happily let her give him a blow job on the road, relishing in the carnal adventure, and screw the consequences but people had to evolve, right? In this moment, being an evolved man felt like a giant crap sandwich.

But that was just a remnant of who he used to be.

The kinder, more sensitive Ellis cautioned that he needed to let Dakota choose what she wanted to do and when she wanted to talk it out—if at all.

The ball was in Dakota's court now.

And he'd just have to be okay with that.

He lifted the balled-up sheets in his hands to his nose and deeply inhaled, groaning as her particular scent enveloped him like a sensual blanket. Why did she smell like heaven and hell at the same time?

He dropped the sheets to the floor.

Forget sleep, buddy, just take the couch again.

He knew a lost cause when he saw one.

Chapter 26

Dakota spent an uncomfortable night in her own bed, tossing and turning, alternately burning with rage and crumpling in on herself with embarrassment. By the time her alarm went off, she gratefully climbed out of bed and walked like a zombie to her coffeepot.

Shake it off, there are bigger issues than your messed-up relationship with Ellis Vaughn, she reminded herself sternly.

They were poised on the precipice of a major win in the case. *Cling to that, not how epically you fell on your face in the seduction department.*

Both she and Ellis had their issues but returning to the case as professionals wasn't one of them. Gulping down her coffee, burning her tongue in the process, she jumped into the shower and washed off yesterday. By the time she left her place to meet up with Ellis at the office, she was back on solid ground.

Ellis took one look at her and knew her mind was razor-focused with a healthy distance between her feelings for him, which was the best way to handle the post-seduction fail of yesterday.

If she lived to be a hundred, she never wanted to think of yesterday's car ride again.

Shilah was close to getting their warrant for both Western Horizon Solutions and the senator. All that remained was going to the compound and picking up Zachariah Deakins.

Sayeh rounded the corner before they hit the road, concern in her expression. "Are you sure you don't need backup? We can all go or we can call local PD to provide assistance."

But Dakota felt confident they could handle one fruit loop cult leader. "Even if Deakins decides to put up a fuss, I think between the two of us, we can handle him."

"What about the rest of his cult?" Sayeh said, worried. "One ant isn't dangerous but a whole colony coming at you will mess your shit up."

"They're a bunch of pacifists who don't like confrontation. We'll be fine," Dakota said, knowing Sayeh was reliving her own experience when her partner, Levi, almost died because they didn't call for backup. "The worst that might happen is someone throwing a cucumber at us as we handcuff their fearless leader. It'll be fine. Right, Ellis?"

Ellis jerked a short nod, agreeing, but his eyes were hard. She tried not to take it personal. Ellis went into a different zone when he was going to arrest someone. She'd seen it before. It was only because of what'd happened yesterday that she was even remotely twinged by it.

"You ready?" Ellis asked, grabbing the keys, taking the lead. She adjusted her vest, nodding.

They exited the building and climbed into the car, tingles of excitement overriding the lingering awkwardness between them, and she was fully prepared to pretend that yesterday didn't happen but Ellis had different plans.

"We need to talk about—"

"No we don't," she cut in more sharply than she intended. Her heart rate kicked up a notch at the thought of touching that hot stove between them. She forced a brittle smile even as her heart thundered in her chest. "Let's just focus on the case, okay? We need to stay on target. The stakes are too high to mess around with anything that might get in the way. We can't afford any screwups."

It was good, solid advice but Ellis wasn't happy about it. "Fine," he muttered, shaking his head, clearly irritated at her unilateral refusal.

But she'd prepared this time. Pulling her headphones from her bag, she hooked into her phone and closed her eyes to listen to her favorite true-crime podcast, eliminating the need to fill any silence between them.

Soon enough, they pulled into Stevensville and went straight to the compound. Immediately Dakota's intuition prickled at the energy difference on the compound.

There was a heavy tension, a seeming dark cloud that hovered over their heads that wasn't there before. Even Eden's Bounty was closed, which given how that was their bread and butter—or so they said—it seemed odd to have the booths empty and unmanned.

"Well, this is creepy," Dakota murmured. "Where is everybody and why does it feel like we interrupted a funeral?"

"I don't know. Let's go find out," Ellis said, his sharp gaze taking in everything.

They headed straight to the main building where Deakins's office was located, shocked at the general disarray. It looked like a bomb had gone off in the building. Loose paperwork fluttered along the hardwood floor like broken planes run aground and the sound of crying children was a jarring change from the usual laughter that rang across the campus.

"What happened here?" Dakota asked, getting a bad feeling. They weren't stopped by anyone, which felt distinctly different from the last time they were escorted everywhere. Stepping into Deakins's office, they were alarmed at how everything was trashed. File cabinet drawers were left open, the guts ripped open and emptied of anything of value, as well as Deakins's desk. "Someone left in a hurry," he murmured, taking in the scene.

Dakota grimly agreed, a sinking feeling in her gut. "How much you want to bet Deakins is gone?"

Ellis didn't have time to answer. The Grojans appeared in the doorway, their eyes red and gritty as if they hadn't slept since returning to the compound.

Tensing, Dakota readied for anything. The last time they had any interaction with the harried couple, they'd been openly hostile.

But this time, they seemed desperate.

Dakota didn't know which was worse—or more dangerous.

Ellis moved into a better position to protect Dakota if need be. He didn't trust the Grojans, but also the general vibe of the compound was unstable. "What happened here?" he asked.

Barbara-Jean's eyes were raw and swollen, her face pale and tightened by grief. Ned's hands trembled though his jaw was set—whether from rage or shame, Ellis couldn't tell. Their despair was palpable. Ned spoke first. "He's gone," he said, unable to meet Ellis's gaze. "Took every last cent and left us with nothing."

"What do you mean?"

Barbara-Jean said bitterly, "Zachariah… He left in the middle of the night, liquidated all of The Congregation's accounts and left us to rot. At first we didn't want to jump to conclusions—he was always doing something for the good of The Congregation and didn't always explain his actions. But when he didn't return after a few days, then a week…we checked the accounts and they were empty."

Ellis bit down on his frustration that Deakins had managed to escape. "I'm sorry. I know you believed in him."

"You don't understand what he's done to us," Barbara-Jean insisted, tears spilling from her eyes. "It was more than just believing in him. We put our lives in his hands, thinking he would protect us, but he was no better than the world we were trying to escape. He took everything we had…and we still lost Zoey."

Ned swallowed, looking as if his pride was in tatters and he didn't know which way to turn. "Please, can you help us? We don't know what to do."

It was an earnest plea. He'd have to be a stone-cold asshole to be immune to the devastation in the man's voice but Ellis knew this was their one chance at getting them to talk when they'd been buttoned up before.

"We'll do what we can but we need your help to bring this con man to justice," he said gravely. "Tell us everything about how you came to adopt Zoey."

In the stark meeting room, the morning light cast unflattering shadows across the Grojans' haggard faces. The lingering scent of stale coffee did nothing to warm the Spartan space. This had been Deakins's inner sanctum, Ellis realized. The nerve center of his power.

"If we tell you, do we get to see Zoey?" Barbara-Jean asked, the hope in her voice almost heartbreaking.

Dakota, less moved by the woman who'd been a royal pain in the ass, was noncommittal. "We can't make promises but if your information turns out to be truthful… We can try."

It was the best they could—or would—offer and the

Grojans knew it. Ned jerked a nod, looking to his wife, who was wiping at stray tears. "We'll tell you everything."

Dakota leaned over to murmur in his ear, "I'm going to step out and let Shilah know what's going on. Be right back. You good here?"

Ellis nodded and returned his attention to the Grojans, recording the conversation on his phone. "Go ahead, whenever you're ready."

"We just wanted a baby," Ned said gruffly, his mouth trembling. "We'd been to countless adoption agencies but the waiting list was years long and IVF wasn't an option any longer. We were desperate and when Zachariah Deakins showed up, right when we were at our lowest... We thought it was a sign from God. Then he brought us here to the compound and we fell in love with the ideology, the possibilities and the wholesome way of life that seemed lacking where we were coming from. Then, he said he had a baby available for adoption, a newborn baby girl, and he could facilitate the adoption if we were ready to commit to The Congregation."

"And by commit...?" Ellis asking leadingly, needing them to state the financial scheme for the record. "Please be specific."

"We had to liquidate our assets and turn them over to The Congregation. If we did that, we'd have our baby girl within the week," Ned said. "We prayed about it and decided by morning it was ordained by God to have this baby. We did as he asked, and Zachariah delivered Zoey into our arms a week later, just as he promised."

"You paid that monster for a stolen child?" Ellis said, trying to keep his voice devoid of the instant rage and disgust coursing through his veins, but when Ned flinched, he knew he had to try harder.

"We were fools," Ned admitted in a choked voice. "Blind, stupid fools."

"We were so happy," Barbara-Jean cried with a hysterical hiccup. "Why did this happen to us? I don't understand how he could do something so horrible to good people."

Ned wrapped his arm around his grieving wife in comfort, saying gruffly, "We were being selfish. We only cared about getting our happy ending, no matter the cost, and this is our punishment. We should've asked more questions, should've realized that no infant came that easily unless there was something shady going on."

Ellis shook his head, drawing a deep breath. These people weren't criminal masterminds, just a desperate couple willing to believe whatever they had to, to see a dream come true. Ellis's anger dissolved, leaving only pity in its wake. He tried to imagine the pain of wanting a child so badly that moral lines blurred. What lengths would any of them go to? "Our belief structures may be different but it seems unlikely that God put Deakins in your life as punishment for wanting a baby. Deakins conned a whole bunch of you from what I understand by preying on that desire. How many adoptions did Deakins make happen?"

"Fifteen," Barbara-Jean admitted in a shamed whisper, fear and longing mingling in her eyes. "We thought he was a miracle worker."

"And we were desperate enough to believe it," Ned said heavily. "Even when my gut said something wasn't right. But holding Zoey for the first time..." His voice cracked. "Nothing else mattered."

"He preyed on your hopes and dreams," Ellis said, shaking his head. "Tell me about where he said the baby came from."

"He explained about the substance-addicted mother, the

overdose," Barbara-Jean said. "How the baby needed a good Christian home. It seemed meant to be."

"What'd he tell you about the money?"

Their shame was palpable. "That the adoption fees were high. Worth it for a miracle. We paid every cent, no questions asked." Barbara-Jean's face crumpled. "I should've known we'd bought a stolen child. How will God forgive us?"

Ellis had to turn away, breathing hard. The enormity of Deakins's deception was staggering. How many lives were destroyed chasing his twisted vision?

"We realize now he trafficked those children," Ned said heavily. "Every family here paid Deakins for their sons and daughters, believing his lies." He met Ellis's gaze, eyes shining with tears. "We just wanted to be parents. To love her. I swear to you, we had nothing to do with the murder of Zoey's mother."

Maybe he was getting soft but he believed them.

"We know we can't atone for our mistakes," Barbara-Jean said, swiping tears away. "But please, if there's any way…"

Ellis held up a hand, emotions churning as Dakota quietly returned to the room. "I'll do what I can. But you may face charges," he said, not willing to sugarcoat the truth of their situation, harsh as it may be.

They nodded, faces pale but resolute. "As long as Zoey is all right, nothing else matters now," Ned said.

But the general energy of the compound was unstable. They needed some semblance of order returned for everyone's mental health. What would come next was likely to rattle everyone. They were going to have to do an audit of every child here at the compound to find their original parents. That news was likely to go down like a turd in a punchbowl but they'd deal with that after Deakins was in custody.

"We need you to help rally your community here," Ellis directed. "They need someone to look to now that Deakins is in the wind. Keep everyone calm. Can you do that?"

Ned wiped at his eyes, eager to find some purpose. "Yes, we'll do that. Anything to help."

He watched the Grojans hustle from the office, heading out to talk to their people. He turned to Dakota, shaking his head. "How far could any soul be pushed by desperation? Makes you wonder what really separates the guilty from the victims in all this."

"Well, as soon as we get Deakins and the senator into custody, I'll be sure to ask," Dakota said grimly. "Shilah has the warrant and a BOLO's been sent out for Deakins. We'll catch him."

They stepped out of the main building, preparing to head back to Billings, when a shot rang out and screams followed.

And then the agony of something burning hot like a sizzling poker taken straight from the fire rammed into his shoulder and sent him to the ground as screams erupted all around him.

Ah, hell… He'd just been shot.

Chapter 27

Everything slowed. The crack of gunfire. Ellis crumpling. Dakota's vision tunneled, the edges going dark.

Then rage exploded through her veins, white-hot, obliterating all else. She became a vessel of raw fury, honed by years of ruthless training.

With a feral scream, she launched herself at the shooter, channeling every ounce of strength into her tackle. They crashed to the ground and Dakota became a vicious, single-minded machine, determined to disarm the threat. The woman landed a few weak strikes in return before Dakota pinned her down, wrenching away the weapon with a snarl, "Stay down, you crazy bitch!"

The red haze receded as Dakota zip-tied the woman, extra tight. As she scrambled to Ellis, she hollered to Ned Grojan, "Call 911, now!" Her breaths came in ragged gulps, the copper tang of blood thick in her mouth.

"The righteous will—" the woman tried spouting but Dakota roared over the top of her as she tried to find something to stanch the bleeding.

"Shut it before I stuff a sock in your mouth!"

Ellis swore loudly as she applied pressure. "Talk to me, Ellis. What's the damage?"

"Right shoulder, through and through," Ellis ground out. "But it hurts like a son of a bitch."

She released a shaky breath. A through-and-through on the shoulder. Nonlethal. He was alive, but it could've been so much worse if the woman had been a better shot.

Within minutes, sirens split the air and ambulance and local police flooded the compound. The local cops hauled the weeping woman to her feet. "Gun's over there," Dakota directed, refusing to leave Ellis's side, giving room for EMS to stanch the bleeding.

"Always looking for the glory, aren't you?" she teased, though tears tingled behind her sinuses.

Their eyes locked through the chaos. Wordlessly, promises and confessions passed between them, Ellis's pain reflecting her own. She couldn't fathom losing Ellis. She kept replaying that awful moment over and over in her head until she thought she might break down and sob in front of everyone.

But Ellis seemed to know she was privately falling apart, and he grasped her hand with his good side. "This is nothing. A few stitches and I'm right as rain," he told her, trying to soothe her growing anxiety.

Dakota chuckled ruefully, rubbing the moisture from her eyes. "Only you would call a bullet wound 'nothing.'"

The EMS loaded Ellis into the ambulance and Dakota followed behind to the local hospital.

As the compound faded into the distance, Dakota faced the truth—her feelings for Ellis had never gone away and likely never would. He was burrowed into her soul like a burr tangled in a woolen blanket.

And she would do anything to protect what they had together. Anything to keep him with her.

The ghosts of the past could wait. Right now, she just needed Ellis to be okay. They would figure the rest out later.

Dakota paced the hospital lobby, emotions seesawing

between relief and dread. Even though the bullet didn't hit any major arteries or nerves, going under the knife, even to repair damage from a bullet, could go sidewise.

She used the time waiting to quickly update her team.

"How's Ellis?" Shilah asked, concerned.

"I don't know. He's still in surgery."

"He's going to come through. He's tough," Shilah assured her.

Dakota's shaken nerves appreciated Shilah's confidence. "I hope so," she murmured, drawing a deep breath to ask, "Any news on Deakins or Senator Lawrence?"

"An arrest warrant was issued for Senator Lawrence just a few minutes ago. Let me tell you, it was pulling teeth to get the judge to sign off. You need to stay with Ellis. Sayeh and Levi will serve the warrant with local backup. You just focus on Ellis."

Before Ellis was shot, the idea of letting someone else put that politician in handcuffs made her teeth hurt, but now all she cared about was hearing that he was going to come through.

"Thank you," Dakota said, "keep me in the loop."

"Will do."

Shilah clicked off, leaving Dakota with her anxiety, chewing on her fingernails as she awaited news from surgery. *It's just shoulder surgery*, she told herself when her nerves threatened to drown her good sense. *Almost routine. Except for the part where a bullet shredded his musculature.*

It seemed like an eternity before the doctor walked through the doors to deliver the news. "Agent Foster, I'm pleased to tell you your partner is going to make a full recovery." The fatigue etched on the doctor's face told Dakota the damage must've been extensive to repair. "Although the bullet missed the major nerves and arteries, it really did make a mess in there. He's stable, sleeping off the anesthesia. If you want to go home and get some rest, we'll let you know when he's awake."

Leave Ellis? No way. She shook her head vehemently. "I'd like to stay. I want to be there when he wakes up."

The doctor understood. "I had a feeling you'd say that. Follow me. You can wait in his room. There's no sense in sitting in the lobby when you can just as well sit by his bedside."

Dakota was thankful for the doctor's compassion and followed him to Ellis's private room.

She should feel calmer knowing the worst had passed. Instead, an anxious pit gnawed in her stomach. Ellis was going to be okay physically, but where did that leave them?

This brush with tragedy had shaken something loose inside Dakota. Seeing Ellis bleeding, faced with the potential of losing him, stripped away her stubborn defenses. There was no more denying what he meant to her. No more wasted time.

But doubt crept in as she stalled outside his door. Did he feel the same? Were they ready to confront the past? So much still felt unresolved. Sometimes love wasn't enough to get past some of the obstacles in your path. You can love a road, love the scenery, and yet love wasn't going to move the boulder blocking you from traveling down the road. If love were enough, she and her mom's relationship would be repaired by now, but it remained awkward and strained on both sides. Was that the future she and Ellis faced?

Quietly entering the room, Dakota studied Ellis's sleeping face. Dark lashes fanned against his cheek. Her fingers twitched, aching to touch him. To assure herself this wasn't a dream.

Settling into the bedside chair, she twined her fingers together tightly, fighting against the tears that sprang to her eyes as a wave of emotion crashed over her. Why'd she have to fall in love with a man like Ellis? Why was it only him that made her heart beat like a wild thing inside her chest? Why couldn't she have fallen for Tom, the engineer who'd been calm, stable, a little on the serious side and drove a sensible car? Probably because he kissed like a middle schooler afraid of sneaking a peck from his girlfriend between classes for fear of getting caught by a teacher. Also, he'd been too fussy about table manners, gently chiding her when she didn't immediately place her napkin in her lap at the restaurant.

Ellis lived life with a joy that seemed to fill the empty spots in her soul. He grinned in the face of danger, and laughed at situations that could likely get him killed.

Except with this case. He'd been subdued, reserved and more cautious because he'd been working with her. Ironic that the one time he started playing by the rules he was the one who got shot.

She brushed a lock of stubborn hair away from his brows, releasing a small exhale as the questions crowded her brain, demanding answers she didn't have.

Somehow, she fell asleep in that awkward chair, but the second Ellis started to stir, she was instantly awake and alert. Their eyes met, and the breath caught in Dakota's throat.

"Hey, you," Ellis said hoarsely, fighting against the pull of a drugged sleep. He started to sluggishly shift, then grimaced and stopped. "That hurts like a mother," he said.

She laughed softly. "Yeah, well, your little 'through-and-through' made a big mess, according to your surgeon. You should get him a fruit basket or something."

"You think Eden's Bounty will deliver?" Ellis joked weakly, ending on a short cough as his lungs readjusted after being under anesthesia. "What's the w-word?" The stutter in his words showed the lingering hold of the powerful drugs in his system.

"Don't worry about that. You focus on healing." Dakota hovered anxiously until the pain meds kicked in. He was hooked to a high-tech, state-of-the-art automatic drip that would start as soon as he woke. When he relaxed back against the pillow, she reached for his hand and held it tightly. "You scared the crap out of me," she said quietly.

Ellis's mouth quirked with loopy sass. "Going to take more than one zealot to finish me off."

Dakota tried to acknowledge the joke with a smile but she couldn't get her mouth to cooperate. Tears welled in her eyes. "Ellis… All I could think about was, 'What would I do if I lost you?' And I couldn't think straight. Pure panic turned me stupid and all I wanted to do was cry. We've both been so damn stubborn about everything and I don't have all the answers but I know I don't want to live without you."

Ellis focused bleary eyes on her and with complete tenderness said, "Dakota… I'm…s-s—" and then he was out.

Ellis drifted in a drugged sleep for an indeterminate amount of time but he sensed rather than saw Dakota by his side. When he finally truly woke up, he saw Dakota sacked out in an uncomfortable chair beside his bed, curled up like a cat, resting her head on her knees. The poor woman was going to need magic to unkink her spine from sleeping like that.

He blinked against the pain that sucker punched him and as his blood pressure spiked, a calming influx of medication kicked in, soothing the ragged pain within minutes. *That's handy*, he thought as he relaxed.

But his mind was no longer dulled by the anesthesia hangover and he wondered if he'd dreamt Dakota saying she didn't want to live without him.

Something about both of them being stubborn and something-something-something and then, did she say she wanted to buy a broom? That had to be the anesthesia. God, he loved that woman. What he didn't say was he'd gladly take a bullet if that meant shielding her from harm. It'd been pure luck that that deranged zealot had gotten him instead of Dakota and it could've ended a lot differently.

He couldn't stomach the thought of losing Dakota like that.

Or at all.

Was it possible to find a way back to each other? To push past all of the obstacles that seemed stacked in their way?

Was he willing to try? To brave the possibility and the heartache of a fresh breakup if it all fell to crap again?

And he knew his answer—almost immediately.

Being with Dakota was worth any potential heartache down the road.

She was the missing component in his life, the solid stability that kept him grounded when he was about ready to spin off into the distance.

He loved that she fell asleep halfway through a movie, hated brussels sprouts but insisted on trying them because they were full of "good vitamins" even knowing that every time she put one in her mouth, she spit it right back out. For all of her serious nature, there was a sweetness to Dakota that she only let a few people see—and that sweetness was something he craved unlike any other.

So, how did they move forward? What happened next?

Should he wait until this case was done or put his personal life first and let the case follow?

The pain meds started doing their job and his eyelids grew heavy. Time to sleep again.

But as his eyes drifted shut, knowing Dakota wouldn't leave his side was more powerful than any pain med to lull him into a healing sleep.

Chapter 28

Several days later, as Ellis was released from the hospital, Shilah called to let them know that both Deakins and the senator were finally in custody and Dakota was willing to bet Deakins was ready to squeal to save his own ass.

"Are you sure you're okay to do this?" Dakota asked as they drove to the local police station where the two were being held without bond. Deakins was apprehended at the airport trying to leave the country under an assumed name and the senator tried to use his lawyers to stonewall but eventually turned himself in to avoid the embarrassment of press.

"Even if my arm was hanging by a tendon, I wouldn't miss this," he said with a steely look. "I want to watch these two jackasses turn on each other and enjoy the carnage."

"So bloodthirsty," she teased. "But yeah, me, too."

They arrived at the station, their credentials allowing them immediate access. Deakins and the senator were held in different rooms for questioning. They chose Deakins first. Dakota was willing to bet a kidney the slimy con artist would flip the fastest and they needed his testimony to nail the senator.

Dakota and Ellis walked into the holding room, both taking great satisfaction in seeing him handcuffed to the metal table.

They seated themselves opposite Deakins as he regarded them with wary expectation. He was a smart man. He knew he was busted but he seemed content to wait and see what they knew first.

"Hello, Mr. Deakins," Dakota started, clicking the recorder, purposefully using "Mister" instead of his fake cult personification. "Seems you weren't entirely honest about a few things."

Deakins smiled but said nothing.

Ellis wasn't in the mood to play. "Let's cut to the chase. You're busted. We know you and Senator Lawrence are connected and you're responsible for the death of Nayeli Swiftwater and the subsequent kidnapping of Cheyenne Swiftwater, so why don't you help yourself and connect the dots for us."

"And why would I do that?" Deakins returned calmly.

"Because it all comes down to who's going to give up the most information. Right now, the senator is pinning it all on you. He's a US senator with a lot of clout and influence. Who do you think is going to get hit the hardest for this without conflicting testimony? You or him?" Ellis said. A silent thrill chased Dakota's spine as she watched Ellis play hardball. "If you don't want to end up taking all of the blame, you'd better start offering something of value."

Deakins's smug smile faltered, as if realizing he might actually be in trouble, but he stalled. "What happened to your arm?"

"One of your loony tunes followers shot me. You've got those poor people hopped up on a dream that doesn't exist and now they're in a tail-spin—and armed, apparently," Ellis answered bluntly, returning to the topic. "Did you kill Nayeli Swiftwater?"

"I didn't have anything to do with that," Deakins said. "And you have nothing proving that I did."

"Just the senator's testimony saying otherwise," Dakota lied coolly with a shrug. "Are you saying that's not true?"

Deakins's gaze narrowed. "He would never say that."

"Why not? Are you close? As I recall, you hardly know the man," Ellis said.

Deakins seamed his mouth shut as if realizing he was in a bad position, but his friend wasn't going to save him. At this point, it was every man for himself. He exhaled a long breath before admitting, "Mitch and I go way back. We met at a Montana State frat party freshman year. He was a prelaw and I was a political science major with a minor in theology."

"So you've always been interested in religion at some level," Ellis said.

"More of a fascination in belief structures and how easily people are led when faith is involved," he answered without a hint of shame.

"I imagine with your background it was easy to start your own group," Dakota said.

Deakins shrugged. "Broken people are eager for a way to rebuild themselves. Patch those broken pieces with 'faith' and they'll do anything."

"Even kill?" Ellis interjected.

"Yes. But again, I didn't have anything to do with Nayeli's death. That was all Mitch."

Excitement built under her collar. This was it. Deakins was about to roll on his partner—and Dakota was ready for it.

Ellis shared Dakota's excitement. This was the moment everything had the chance to blow up or fizzle to nothing.

They were holding both men on circumstantial evidence that loosely connected them to Nayeli's case but neither seemed to realize this yet.

They needed one of the men to roll on the other to make this case stick. "All right, so tell us what really happened the night Nayeli died," Ellis said.

Deakins shook his head. "You have to understand where it all started, not just that night," he said. "You have to understand it wasn't exactly planned out what happened. It just sort of evolved."

"Go on," Dakota said.

"Mitch liked my talent for...creative money management," Zachariah continued. "In the early days I helped fill his campaign coffers, no questions asked. We made a good team, but for obvious reasons, we kept our friendship private."

"Until the pregnancy complicated things," Ellis said.

"I warned him about messing with that girl," Deakins said. "She was too young and she idealized what was happening between them. It was a red flag from the start but Mitch was addicted to how that girl adored him, thought the moon rose and set in his eyes, definitely believing that he was going to leave his *new* wife and be with her."

Ellis caught Dakota's wince, feeling her pain for a girl she'd never known. Nayeli had been sheltered, naive and ripe pickings for a sophisticated predator like Mitchell Lawrence.

"Then she got pregnant and the senator felt threatened," Dakota surmised.

"Mitch offered to help the girl get a termination. Offered to pay for it and everything. She would've had the best, private care at the senator's expense but she refused and Mitch panicked, cutting off all ties to the girl. She promised she wouldn't come after him for child support but I didn't believe her and told him as much. Six weeks after the kid was born, she called him looking for money—just like I figured she would."

"She couldn't find affordable childcare," Ellis said, unable to hide the contempt in his voice. "She was a kid with a kid, trying to hold on to a dream."

Deakins shrugged as if that wasn't his problem but more of a headache. "I told Mitch to ignore her calls but he went against my advice and tried talking some sense into her in person."

"And when that failed?"

Deakins spread his hands, limited as they were by the handcuffs, with a fatalistic expression. "And you know what happened that night."

"The senator killed Nayeli," Dakota supplied.

"He panicked. Strangled the girl, then realizing what he'd done, called me. He couldn't stomach killing his own daughter so he left it to me. He told me to 'handle' the situation and left. But I'm not going to kill a baby, either. Besides, babies are big business. All I had to do was scope out the fertility clinics, look for the couple reeking of desperation and lure them in with the promise of a newborn. It was really too easy but before you pin the badge of villain on my chest, I gave that child a beautiful life with wonderful parents. I watched that little girl grow into a smart, kind and capable young adult. How is that a bad thing? Would you rather I snuffed out her life that night instead?"

"I would rather that she grew up with her *actual* mother who loved her more than life itself," Dakota returned with a cold stare. "Don't bother trying to rewrite your part in this story. Make no mistake. You are a villain."

"A matter of perspective, I suppose," Deakins said. "Life is about seeing when one door closes, another opens."

"When did the larger child trafficking operation begin?" Ellis asked tightly.

"After we realized how easily we could expand on the private adoption idea," Zachariah answered, holding back nothing. "Desperate people will throw money at you to get what they want most. We were giving them a gift, really. Tell me, did any of those children look unhappy? No. They were raised in loving homes, with traditional values, eating fresh food they helped grow. They had a better life than any of their biological mothers could provide."

"How did you get access to so many newborns?" Ellis asked, narrowing his gaze. "Do you have an unmarked grave full of dead biological mothers?"

"That's pretty macabre, Agent," Deakins said with an amused smirk. "But to answer your question, no. You'd be surprised how easy it is to source infants from third-world countries. They practically toss unwanted babies in the trash and walk away. Trust me, those children were better off with me than where I found them."

"That's not your right to decide," Dakota said. "You might have played at being a messiah but you're not God."

Revulsion roiled through Ellis. This man didn't care about the lives he had ruined, only the money he made exploiting them. He never wanted this case to end more than he did right now.

He looked to Dakota with a short nod. "I think we have what we need. Is there anything else you'd like to add?"

Deakins leaned forward. "I'll hand over every document, every bit of evidence linking Mitchell to our scheme, including the firm that does our books for the adoptions, if you can promise me I'll be sent to a minimum security prison. I want Club Fed, you hear me?"

Dakota snorted. "And why would we do that? You've already given us what we need."

"It'll take you months to ferret out our financials—we were very diligent in hiding our tracks—and if you don't move fast enough, Mitch's lawyers will eat you for lunch, sending this case straight to the toilet and your careers with it."

Ellis knew Deakins was right. The senator had far more influential contacts and their case had to be airtight. A DNA draw would prove paternity to Zoey but was that enough to push the case to trial for murder? Even with Deakins's testimony?

Ellis hesitated, then gave a curt nod. "We'll see what we can do."

Dakota shot him an incredulous look, but didn't contradict him in front of Deakins. They'd debate this later.

"In that case, let's talk paperwork," Deakins said, visibly relaxing. "I can have my lawyer draw up an immunity agreement in exchange for everything I've got on the operation."

"You'll remain in custody until it's all verified," Ellis countered.

Deakins waved a hand. "Of course, of course. But we have a deal?"

Saving his own ass, just as Ellis figured he would. Ellis stood, signaling the end of the interview. "We'll be in touch."

In the hall, Dakota rounded on Ellis. "You can't seriously be considering a deal with that man."

"I don't like it, either," Ellis admitted. "But we need leverage on the senator, fast, and he's got it."

Dakota crossed her arms. "There has to be another way.

That monster doesn't deserve immunity after profiting off innocent lives."

"You're right," Ellis said heavily. "But the justice system doesn't always serve the righteous. Sometimes you have to get dirty so the truly dangerous face punishment." It was a valuable lesson he'd learned in Narcotics. Compromise wasn't something Dakota was familiar with in her line of work but she was a fast learner.

"Look, I hate it, too. But it could be our only shot at victory. We have to do it."

After a tense silence, Dakota swore under her breath. "Fine. Draw up the damn deal if we have to. But that piece of garbage better deliver everything as promised."

Ellis let out a breath. They could loathe Deakins and still use him—distasteful as it was. The ends had to justify the means this time, for Zoey's and Nayeli's sakes.

With Deakins flipped, Senator Lawrence's house of cards would soon come crashing down. The ghosts were so close to resting in peace at last.

Chapter 29

Dakota's heart was heavy as they drove to the safe house. Telling Zoey the truth about her parents would change the girl's life forever but there was hope to be found in the closure—something she and her mother never received with the murder of Mikaya.

"You think she's ready to hear the truth?" Dakota asked quietly.

"She's a strong kid. She'll be able to handle the news." Ellis was confident but Dakota worried how it might scar the girl. Ellis seemed to read the private thoughts running through her brain and he reached over to squeeze her hand. "She won't be doing it alone. We'll help her get through this."

It was breaking the "Don't get personal" rule but neither cared. Zoey had managed to wriggle into their hearts and she wasn't going anywhere. Damn the rules.

The safe house was located on a sprawling ranch property, far from any major roads. As Dakota and Ellis pulled up the long gravel driveway, a quaint cabin came into view, smoke curling from the stone chimney.

They walked up the short sidewalk to the front door, used their key cards to open the door and walked inside. At the chirp of the front door opening, an agent appeared and they identified themselves. "We're here to talk to Zoey," Ellis said.

"She's in the living room, playing with the Xbox. For never playing video games before, the kid has beaten me more times than I can count."

Dakota chuckled as they went to the living room.

The cabin was cozy and a bit rustic, designed more for function than aesthetics. The main living area contained a stone fireplace surrounded by a couple of dated yet sturdy couches and armchairs. Braided rugs covered the hardwood floors.

It was comfortable yet secure lodging. The cabin's remoteness and solid construction ensured it could safely house endangered witnesses like Zoey until the trial concluded. A perfect temporary haven from the threats of the outside world.

Zoey heard them walk in and turned, controller in hand, smiling broadly at the unexpected visit. Then her gaze fell on Ellis's sling and she gasped. "Oh my goodness, are you okay?"

Ellis grinned, playing it off. "This? Just a flesh wound. Besides, scars make me look cool." They both picked a place to sit and prepared to give Zoey the news. Zoey sensed something big was coming and put her controller down. "Zoey, we have news to tell you about your mom's case," he said.

Zoey swallowed, preparing herself. "You caught who killed my mom?" she asked.

"Yes, we did, but there's a lot to this case that might be hard to hear," Dakota said gently. "Some of the truth is… difficult."

She summarized the sordid tale as best she could. Zoey listened silently, eyes downcast, absorbing everything with a maturity that stunned Dakota. Finished, she asked, "It's a lot to take in but do you have any questions?"

"So my dad is this senator guy? And he... He killed my biological mom?" Her voice wavered uncertainly.

Ellis leaned forward, compassion in his eyes. "Yes, but he's going to answer for his crimes. We're going to make sure of that."

Zoey blinked back tears. "Does he...have any other kids?"

"Yes," Dakota answered, hating this part. "He has two sons."

"So, I have two half brothers," she said.

Dakota nodded, but wanted Zoey to know that it might not be a happy reunion for them. "They might not want anything to do with you and I don't want you to take that on as your burden. However, your mom's sister, your aunt, very much wants to have you in her life. You have a grandmother, too. They're very excited to meet you."

Tremulous hope brightened Zoey's eyes. "Really?"

"Really. They're just waiting for the green light. It's all up to you. They'll go as fast or slow as you need. You're the last piece of their sister and daughter that they have, which makes you very precious to them."

Zoey absorbed that, looking small and lost. "What happens to me now?"

"You get to decide where you belong," Ellis said. "We can arrange visits with your mother's family, if you'd like."

Hope flickered in Zoey's eyes. "Really? I'd like that." She bit her lip. "And, I know it's a lot to ask, but..."

"You want to see the Grojans," Dakota finished gently, understanding. At Zoey's nod, she squeezed the girl's hand. "Now that we know they didn't have anything to do with the murder of your mother, of course. They love you so much, Zoey."

Ellis asked, "One thing that's been lost in the shuffle of all this happening... Why'd you run away in the first place, Zoey?"

Zoey drew a deep breath before answering. "I know it sounds selfish but I'd been struggling with the rules at The Congregation. Don't get me wrong, I loved my family and I had a good life, but I wanted to do more. I wanted to go to college and my parents were adamantly opposed to the idea of me leaving the compound. They said the world was an ugly place and I was safer with them. I was angry and felt suffocated. Then I found the adoption paperwork and I lost my temper and bailed. Looking back, I realize how childish it all was but I couldn't get my parents to hear what I was saying. I honestly didn't even have a plan aside from getting out to make my own life choices. Then I took that turn too fast and rolled the car, putting me here in this situation."

"It's not selfish or immature to have your own needs and wants, Zoey," Dakota said. "And everything happening like it did... Well, I think it was meant to happen that way."

"You think so?"

Dakota shared a look with Ellis considering everything that'd happened between them as well, answering, "Yeah, I do," and realized she was ready to see where the road might take them.

Ellis sat lost in thought as they drove back from the safe house. Dakota's words about things happening for a reason echoed in his mind. Could this be their second chance? After all the pain, did he dare reach for happiness again? His heart ached to bridge the distance still between them. But the old wounds they'd inflicted on each other made him cautious.

After all they'd endured, was a second chance possible? He'd been scared of the violence that potentially lurked inside him but getting shot had changed his perspective. Living in fear was robbing him of a future with the woman he couldn't stop loving.

That was the downside to having the kind of connection they shared—there were scars and hurts to navigate but he'd wasted too much time letting fear stand in his way of what he really wanted.

Glancing at her profile, Ellis swelled with gratitude that she was there beside him. He'd been given a gift—the gift of time to make things right. He refused to waste it. Time to take that chance or spend the rest of his life wondering "What if?"

Taking a bracing breath, he reached to caress her cheek. Dakota startled briefly before softening into his touch. The feel of her skin under his fingers was electric. Ellis pushed down the surge of hope rising within. He had to be sure Dakota felt the same way before he risked his heart again.

"It's not often our cases get a happy ending," she said. "But I'm so glad it was this one that did."

Ellis hesitated, struggling to keep his voice steady. "I've been thinking… What about our happy ending?"

"I didn't think we had one," she murmured, her gaze shining with vulnerability. "Do we?"

The question hung between them, weighted with past hurts and the promise of a fresh start. Ellis searched Dakota's face, looking for a sign that they shared the same hope.

Everything hinged on this moment. He had to place faith in the knowledge that he wasn't his father and that he'd worked hard to heal what his father had broken inside him. If she was willing to walk the road ahead together, no matter how long and winding, he was, too. He held his breath, scarcely daring to hope for the words that would make him whole again. He grasped her hand. "I was afraid of being unable to control my demons but I realize running from the one thing in my life that was ever beautiful and pure was a cowardly way to avoid facing my fear."

Dakota risked a look his way, her gaze cautiously optimistic. "Watching you get shot… It made me realize I don't want to live without you any longer. I'm willing to try if you are but I'm scared of your need to return to Narcotics. You're right—Narcotics will always need an investigator like you in the field because you do make a difference, but I don't know if I can stomach the toll it takes on you."

She was willing to brave the darkness that may lurk inside him but his driving ambition to return to Narcotics was the thing that scared her most. Getting shot must've knocked some sense into him. That hot need to return to the streets was gone. For the first time since transferring to Missing Persons, he saw how fulfilling the work was—and bringing families back together was a true way to make a difference out there in the world. A difference he could see with immediate effect.

He didn't need the adrenaline high of a chase to tell him that he was doing a good job. In Missing Persons, he had a chance to heal wounds within families that would reverberate for a lifetime. He couldn't say the same thing with Narcotics. It wasn't that he didn't believe in the importance of the work—no, it was still a vital component—but it wasn't his reason for getting up in the morning anymore.

Letting go of that need felt like he'd finally shucked off his father's phantom grip on his soul.

But he hadn't told Dakota that yet. Now was a good time to come clean. Ellis rubbed the sweaty palm of his uninjured hand on his pants as nerves took hold. This was his chance to show Dakota he'd changed—that she was more important than the thrill of the chase.

He took a shaky breath. "I've been thinking…" His voice cracked and he paused to steady himself. Dakota glanced over, surprise flickering in her eyes. He tried again. "I don't think Narcotics is where I belong anymore."

The words hung between them as Dakota processed their meaning. Ellis held himself tense, pulse racing. Everything hinged on this moment.

Finally Dakota risked a longer look his way. Her eyes shone with tentative relief and something that looked like fragile hope. "You don't?" she asked.

Ellis let out a breath he hadn't realized he was holding. "No. I think I was chasing something that had nothing to do with the job. Getting shot cured me of whatever it was." He gave a small, apologetic smile. "I know I've been stubborn about going back. But none of that matters now and I'm sorry it took getting shot to realize where I belong."

He reached over to brush a stray hair from her cheek, heart swelling when she leaned into his touch instead of pulling away. There were tears in her eyes when she met his gaze again. "Oh, Ellis," she whispered. "Are you sure? I know I've been vocal against your desire to return to Narcotics but it's not right of me to keep you from where you truly want to be. I want to be supportive even if it scares me."

The crack in her voice pierced him to the core. Ellis had vowed not to hurt her again—to be the man she deserved. As joy surged through him, he knew he was finally on the right road.

"That's just it, I don't want to return to Narcotics anymore. I want to stay with Missing Persons. The work matters and I'm embarrassed to say that it took me this long to see past my own bullshit to what was right in front of my face."

"You really mean that? You're not just saying that to make me happy?"

"As much as I would do anything to make you happy, no, I'm being honest about my own feelings. Going forward, I always want us to be honest with each other. Even when it's easier to bend the truth to prevent an argument."

Tears leaked from Dakota's eyes as she chided with fake frustration, "Damn you, Ellis. Why'd you have to tell me this while I'm driving? Now I'm crying and I can barely see the road."

"So, pull over," he said, grinning. "It's hard to kiss you like this, anyway."

The second the car rolled to a stop, Ellis couldn't hold back any longer. He leaned over the console in a rush, his mouth finding Dakota's in a fervent kiss. She made a small sound of surprise before melting into him, her fingers tangling in his hair.

Ellis poured everything he felt into that kiss—all the longing and heartache of their time apart, and the dizzying joy of this reconciliation. With the press of her lips, the stroke of her tongue, Dakota erased any shred of doubt. She was his future.

They came up for air both breathless. Ellis rested his forehead against hers, overcome with emotion. A thousand unspoken words passed between them in the space of a heartbeat.

There would still be uncertain days ahead, obstacles to overcome. But they would face it together. Dakota was his anchor, his guiding light. And he would walk by her side wherever she led.

Ellis brushed his thumb over her cheek, lost in her shining eyes. "No matter what comes, we'll figure it out," he murmured. "Always."

The past could not be changed, but they could shape what came next. Hand in hand, heart to heart, they would build something lasting from the ashes. Something beautiful.

Epilogue

A week later during the debrief session, Isaac Berrigan groused, "What is it about this task force that makes love bubbles pop around my team?" when Dakota revealed her past—and her planned future—with Ellis. "First Sayeh and Levi and now you and the FBI agent. Well, seeing as Agent Vaughn isn't one of my employees and was only a co-op agency thing, at least I don't have to fill out any paperwork." He eyed Dakota, then shifted to Shilah with an arched brow. "How about you? Planning on falling in love on a case?"

Shilah openly balked as if the thought made her instantly nauseous. "Me? Oh hell no, that's definitely not my style." Shilah shuddered dramatically. "I've sworn off dating, probably indefinitely. I'm already looking into a rental that allows lots of cats." She paused, a wry smile touching her lips. "Maybe just one cat, though. I'm not that lonely yet."

Sayeh snorted with laughter while Levi chuckled.

Isaac returned to business quickly, though his eyes shone with pride. "All right, that's two major wins for the task force. I gotta say, I didn't see the senator being dirty, but thankfully I didn't vote for the guy so at least there's that." He smiled, folding his arms across his chest. "However—love bubbles aside—I'm real proud of this team. I don't say this often but this team is probably one of the best I've ever had the privilege of working with. Let's keep up the momentum. Shilah, you're taking point on the next case."

"No pressure," Shilah joked.

With a rare smile, Isaac returned, "No pressure, just bring home another win."

Isaac ended the meeting and everyone filed out, the click of heels and shuffle of feet echoing down the hall. Dakota checked the time and hurried to gather her stuff. Shilah, who knew where Dakota was going next, gave a wink and a thumbs-up.

Outside, the sun was bright, glinting off the rows of cars. Dakota grabbed her purse and shut down her office, anticipation welling inside her. She pictured Ellis waiting, grinning from ear to ear, and quickened her pace.

Ellis waved with his good hand when she emerged, his smile wide. Dakota rushed to meet him, heartbeat quickening. She kissed him deeply, sinking into a deliriously happy place, the stress of the day fading away.

"You ready to do this?" she asked breathlessly.

"I should be asking you that question," he teased. "Because I've been wanting to do this since the day we met."

Dakota smiled up at him, thinking of the hints he'd been dropping all week, the ring she'd caught a glimpse of that he wouldn't let her see until he slipped it on her finger at the courthouse. "Oh, you did not," she shot back, calling him out with laughter in her voice.

They exchanged excited, joyful looks, both ready to start their new life together.

"Okay, maybe not the first day but definitely after you did that thing with your—"

"Ellis!" She gasped in fake outrage but he kissed the fake indication right out of her. He was her other half and always would be. She would happily marry him, today, tomorrow and every day for the rest of their lives, if only to ensure she was never without him again.

They'd lost two years to their stubborn natures and she vowed to never let her ego, pride and rigid need to be right ever get in the way of her heart ever again.

With Ellis she'd learned that it was better to bend with the wind rather than letting it break you. She'd even made the first step to truly work on repairing her relationship with her mother. No more avoiding the past—no matter how painful the healing.

She wanted a family—a real family—and that was hard to do when you were hanging on to a bitter past.

That's what she liked to imagine Mikaya would offer by way of big-sister advice.

Or maybe she just would've smacked her in the arm and said, "Stop being stupid. He's a good man. Marry him before I do," and then told her what the color scheme for the wedding should be because Mikaya looked best in winter shades—and Mikaya had been notoriously bossy.

Either way, Dakota knew Mikaya would approve of the man she was ready to call her husband.

And that felt like sunshine on her happy heart.

This was what a new beginning was supposed to feel like.

And she was ready for whatever the future might bring with Ellis by her side.

* * * * *

Be sure to look for the next novel by Kimberly Van Meter, coming soon from Harlequin Books!

HARLEQUIN
Reader Service

Enjoyed your book?

Try the perfect subscription for Romance readers and get more great books like this delivered right to your door.

See why over 10+ million readers have tried Harlequin Reader Service.

Start with a Free Welcome Collection with free books and a gift—valued over $20.

Choose any series in print or ebook.
See website for details and order today:

TryReaderService.com/subscriptions